OUT OF THE SEA

OUT OF THE SEA

DON SMITH

CUTTING EDGE

ISBN-13: 978-1-962896-98-6

Published by
Cutting Edge Books
PO Box 8212
Calabasas, CA 91372
www.cuttingedgebooks.com

OUT OF THE SEA

CHAPTER ONE

"Sometime about ten o'clock," I told Paco Gómez, my first mate, "you should be able to see the light from Dragonera Island lighthouse. Wake me up when you do. I'm going to turn in."

I climbed down into the cabin of the ex-H.M.M.L. Chucha. The little ship, similar in size to an American PT boat, but not built for the same speed, was rolling rather heavily in a swell from the east. As I passed the barometer I tapped the glass. The needle fell slightly. There was no wind, but every indication pointed to a *levante* blowing up the following day. I arranged the cushions so that I could lie diagonally in the corner of the couch. I had found from much experience that this was the best position in which to rest, whether the ship was pitching, rolling, or both.

But sleep was elusive. It was a long way from my first trip up the Spanish coast with a load of contraband. And as always during the final hours before reaching the rendezvous and transferring the cargo to the fishing trawler that would be waiting, my mind worked overtime, conjuring up all the dangers, real and imaginary, that we were about to encounter.

And I worried whether Francisco Gonzales, the man who was to meet me at the contact point and pay for the cargo, would be there on time. Or would I have to spend hours rolling about these perilous waters waiting for him? And the east wind would bring heavy seas with it tomorrow.

Just before Paco gently shook my shoulder I fell into a heavy slumber. I got up with the resolution that someday I'd go to bed and sleep for a week.

On the open bridge the night air revived me. Through the binoculars I could make out the blink, blink, blink of a light-house over the port bow. From long experience I knew it to be the beacon on Dragonera, that tiny island off the southwest tip of Mallorca. More to pass the time than anything else I pressed my stop watch and timed the flashes. I asked the mate how long since he had first seen it. He said about five minutes. I found the light again and could just make it out now without glasses. I reckoned that we were about twenty-five miles away.

Another hour and we were closing into the rendezvous position, ten miles off the light. I took the engines out of gear and turned the ship into the swell. For the past hour we had been running without lights. Now I switched on the white masthead lamp and scanned the horizon. Slowly, interminably the minutes ticked by.

The first half hour seemed a year as we rolled softly to the swell, the exhaust from our idling engines chuckling in the night. The second half hour was a century.

Sharp-eyed Paco saw it first. But it was still some time before I could make out the dim light off to port. Gradually it strengthened as it approached us. It was either a revenue cutter or Francisco's fishing boat. I put the engines back into gear and turned toward it, easing the throttles forward.

While the light was still some distance off, I flicked the switch and made the recognition signal with our lamp. If it was Francisco, he would give the correct answer. If not, there was still plenty of sea room between us to make a getaway.

With my hand on the throttles, I waited. Finally the distant light blinked. I counted the flashes. It was the correct signal. It was repeated and then the light went out.

Now I could hear the sound of the fishing boat's engine above our own. I followed it as it swung to the left, then around and astern. Suddenly, so suddenly I wondered why I hadn't seen it sooner, a dark hull broke through the gloom, and there, not a hundred feet off, was a ship.

"*Oye, Chucha!*" A soft voice came over the water. It was Francisco, all right, and the sound of his voice was good to hear. The worries of the past few hours disappeared. I wanted a drink. I wanted to buy Francisco a drink.

"*Oye! Estabas durmiendo?*"

"Ahoy, Francisco," I answered. "No, we're not asleep, but by God, you're late."

"*Ah, Capitán Hart. Muy bien, muy bien.*"

By this time the fishing boat was just off our stern and I could hear its engine throttle back. The high pitched-back bow crawled forward until it was opposite ours. A black coil snaked out of the air and landed across the engineer's shoulders. He hauled it in and made fast. Slowly the two ships came together. The mate made fast aft. A figure leaped across the rail.

"*Amigo mío, mucho tiempo sin verte. Cómo estás?*" Francisco asked. Before I could reply he had his arm about me and was pounding me on the back, saying, "*Bien, bien, bien.*"

I asked him if everything was O.K.

"O.K., O.K.," he mimicked, slapping his chest. "*Mucho dinero, mucho dólares.*"

Warning Paco to keep a sharp lookout, I told the rest of the crew to get cracking and transfer the cargo. I led Francisco down into the cabin and poured out two large neat whiskies. He held his up to the light, then knocked it back. I knew that he didn't care for it, but to offer him cognac, especially Spanish, which he vastly preferred, would have been an insult. Whisky was what we drank; therefore he must do the same.

Knowing Francisco, I cut him short and said that we could talk on deck after we settled our business. I felt uncomfortable below. I wanted to be out in the night, listening. I had no desire to find a coast-guard boat coming alongside at this stage of the game.

I told him we had a hundred and fifty cases of cigarettes, twenty sacks of coffee, thirty of sugar, fifty cases of saccharine, and fifteen sacks of white flour. I gave him the itemized list together with the amounts he owed. He glanced through it.

"No whisky?"

I laughed. "Let's see your *dinero* first."

He pulled out a large cloth-wrapped bundle from inside his coat, undid it, and dumped a mountain of thousand-peseta notes on the table. They were pinned together in packets of ten thousand. I ran through the packets, checked them against the total, and returned the few notes over.

Out on deck nothing could be heard but the low rumble of the idling engines. From time to time I flicked my lighter and glanced at my wrist watch while Francisco droned on happily with his one-sided conversation. So long as he didn't ask questions, I didn't care; most of my mind was out there searching the black night for danger.

Half an hour after the fishing boat had come alongside, the cargo had been shifted. I handed Francisco the parcel containing six bottles of whisky, *the regalo* he had come to expect. He in turn produced a heavy packet of *sobre-sada,* that wonderful Mallorcan sausage; he said his wife had made it for me herself.

I climbed up the bridge and called to the men to let go the lines. I opened the throttles slowly, and as soon as the bows of the fishing boat had dropped astern, I put the helm hard over. The deep chuckle changed into a mighty roar as I pushed the throttles up against the stops. I switched on the binnacle light, and when the ship's head came up to south-southwest, I straightened her up and let her rip.

Whether it was the sudden cessation of the strain of the past half hour or the sheer glory of charging into the black night, I didn't know. But as I looked back at the long pale ribbon of phosphorus as our propellers churned up the sea, I felt like singing.

I told Paco and Jim Corby, the deck hand, to turn in, and asked the engineer to bring me up a drink. After we had been running at full speed for fifteen minutes, I asked the engineer to take over. It was good to just fold up on the cabin couch and pass out with nervous exhaustion.

The early sun was beginning to take the chill out of the air as we ran into Tangier Bay two days later. We found a vacant spot in the crowded roadstead, midway out the mole, and dropped the anchor in four fathoms. I had the mate bring me some hot water, but before I had finished shaving a heavy bump informed me that Ricardo Lewis, my agent, was alongside. His boatman was the most careless *marinero* in the port, and I had often threatened Ricardo with a bill for paintwork removed.

Ricardo Lewis, followed by a tall rangy Englishman, crowded into the tiny cabin. I held the razor out of danger while he pounded me on the back and shook my arm.

"It's good to see you," he said with his wide toothy grin. "Have a good trip? Did you see Francisco? Run into any revenue cutters?"

"Whoa," I laughed. "One at a time. Hello, Johnny." I nodded to the Englishman. "What will you fellows have to drink—coffee or something stronger?"

"Both," Ricardo answered. "I've been up since seven waiting for you."

I called to Paco to bring down some more coffee and to get out a bottle of rum. I handed Ricardo a package of letters Francisco Gonzales had asked me to deliver to him. I went on with my shaving.

"What are you doing in port, taking a holiday?" I looked over at Johnny Summers, who had stretched out on the bunk. He broke open a packet of cigarettes and offered me one.

"No," he said. "We're putting in new rings. About time, too. The last trip I made I must have been losing a hundred and fifty revs on my starboard engine."

"Well, when you're through you can go to work on this baby."

I had got to know Summers pretty well during the war years in England. The fact that I had become a free trader in the western Mediterranean was due, in no small part, to the long discussions we'd had over a pint of the best in some small pub as to what we would do with ourselves after the war. And when 1944 swung into 1945, those discussions became more real and definite in tone. Johnny had spent a great deal of time sailing in the Mediterranean and knew it well. And he had pointed out that countries like Spain and France and Italy would be on the verge of starvation after the war. His idea was to purchase a former naval craft—they'd be a dime a dozen, he thought—turn it into a cargo vessel, and do some trading. He'd buy supplies in the States and have them shipped to Gibraltar or Tangier, pick them up, and sell them to the highest bidder.

"It's going to take three or four years," he had said, "for the world to get squared away after this mess. So instead of being one of the millions struggling to relay their anchors in civilian life, we could have ourselves some fun, make some money, and help feed the starving Europeans."

I had often recalled his benevolent observation about the starving Europeans, and once years later when I saw him loading a cargo of cigarettes in Tangier, I asked him if he had found a country where the natives used tobacco for bread.

"It's the icing on the cake," he had commented with a laugh as he kicked a case of Camels into the hold.

At first he could never understand why I hadn't transferred to the U.S. Air Force during the war. He argued that with my RAF experience I'd be sure to get a good job and certainly twice the pay.

"And get myself posted back to the States as an instructor," I had replied one day after brushing him off countless times.

"What's the matter with going back to the States? For an American, you certainly fight shy of your homeland. You wanted for murder or something back there?"

"If I went back I might possibly be."

"Tell me more."

I recall that day vividly, even now. We had had a pretty thick night and were lying out on the beach in front of his house trying to dry out in the pale Cornish sun. It was the first and last time I had let my hair down.

I remember digging around for my wallet and extracting a worn envelope. Inside was a cable and a very faded letter. I tossed the cable over to Johnny.

"Who is Joan?" he asked, looking up.

"The gal I was going to marry."

"Well," he observed after a long pause. "At least she told you that she had married the other fellow."

"About time, too. They had a kid about three months later."

"When did all this happen?"

"A few months after I joined up. Here's the other half."

I handed him the letter. He had trouble opening the single page. It was starting to split at the folds. He spread it out on the sand before him. After a moment he looked up.

"Sure you want me to read this?"

"Might as well. Then maybe you can tell me what's wrong with the Hart men. My father gave me that letter just before he drank himself to death. I guess I was about nineteen at the time and going to college. He said he'd intended to wait till I was twenty-one, but he was afraid his old ticker wouldn't last that long. Anyway, he explained that he had found that letter one night fifteen years before when he had returned from the sea. It seems my mother fell for some smart guy with a shore job. But the poor bastard she ran off with must have been pretty frightened of the old man. He tried to beat a freight train on their way to New York, and that was the end of that. I knew that my mother had died under somewhat mysterious circumstances when I was a kid, but I had been spared the gory details. I sometimes wish the old man hadn't told me."

"What did your father do? What work, I mean?"

"Fisherman. He had his own schooner, and in his day he was considered one of the hottest skippers on the Banks. There was always a lot of money around, and I suppose, since he had only one child, his expenses weren't too great. But way back he trimmed my sheets; no turtle-neck sweater for me. I was packed off to Princeton with a white collar on. A year or so later he died. I guess he didn't believe in saving money. By the time I'd paid the bills, I knew my school days were over. I wasn't sorry."

"You cared a lot for this girl?" Johnny had picked up the cable again.

"Hard to say. When I received that, I thought the bottom had dropped out. But now that I look back, we used to fight like hell a lot of the time."

"Perhaps if you hadn't been carrying this letter around in your pocket it might have worked out differently."

"Yes—yes, I hadn't thought of that. Maybe I should tear them up." I folded them carefully and put the envelope back into my wallet.

The spring of 1945 had found both Johnny and me still alive, and our Mediterranean project down on paper. I had wangled a short tour of duty at Gibraltar, and after a month of the Rock I realized that our idea was pretty sound. The only thing that Johnny didn't know, or hadn't told me, was that it had been going on for the past hundred years. But down there some people called it smuggling.

Then, not long before VE Day, Johnny got posted to the Far East as a torpedo-boat squadron commander. He made me promise when we said good-by that I wouldn't wait for him. He pointed out that since he was regular navy, it might be years before he got back and got his discharge.

He had been right. By the time he turned up in Tangier in his own M.L., I knew every cape from Gibraltar to Genoa. I offered him a partnership when I heard he had received his discharge, but he declined, claiming he had become such a crotchety old skipper that we'd probably remain friends longer if we had our own ships.

I'd been working for Ricardo Lewis now for the past four years. He was getting on toward fifty and was a typical Tangerian. He was a British subject, but just how he'd become one I never knew. I presumed that his father had been one of those empire-building Englishmen who had paused long enough in Tangier a half century ago to plant a bit of old England in the colorful port. His mother, I knew, was Spanish. Ricardo was jealously proud of his nationality, and unlike a number of his fellow townsmen, had served his country well. During the occupation of Tangier by the Spaniards during the last war, he had steadfastly refused to work for them, and as a result he'd found it difficult to scrape together enough for his large family to eat. He was well thought of in Gibraltar, and I had a strong hunch that he had been one of their willing agents during hostilities.

He was one of the ugliest men I've ever seen. His face looked as though it had been carved out of an old riding boot. His nose, much too large for the rest of his features, was the streaky purple of the sky after an intense sunset. His teeth must have been made by some traveling Moorish dentist up from the desert. He was reasonably tall, and despite a rigorous diet of whisky and promiscuity, kept himself in good condition.

When he smiled the ugliness disappeared. It was like drawing up to a fire on a cold night. You could feel the warmth in his twinkling blue eyes enveloping you.

"How is my señorita?" I inquired when he'd shoved the letters in his pocket.

"Juanita said that she'd be at El Morocco tonight if you came in. Why don't you marry the girl and settle down?"

"And get me a family like yours? Can't afford it."

"You'd save money, the way you go bitching around."

"Speaking of money, here it is."

I got out a pencil and paper and started to figure. I checked off the inventory of the goods we had delivered, figured out my charges, and deducted them from the amount Francisco had paid me. I told Ricardo how much I owed him. He agreed without even looking at the paper, and I gathered he had figured out his share the moment we sailed, if not before.

Making sure no one was looking through the porthole, I unscrewed a panel and unlocked the safe concealed behind it. I took out several wads of currency, pealed off five *mil* notes, and put them in my pocket. I tossed the rest over to Ricardo, and asked him to deduct what I owed him and deposit the remainder in my account with Moses Pariente's bank.

"When do you want to make another trip?" he asked.

"Take it easy, chum, I've only just landed. Tonight I'm going to get very drunk. Tomorrow I shall have a hangover. The next day I'll rest, and then perhaps we can talk business. But don't forget it's almost November. A bit late in the season for cruising around the western Med."

Ricardo left with Summers after exacting a promise that I'd stop by his office that night and have a drink with him. I called in the crew, advanced the engineer and deck hand a thousand pesetas each, and told them they could go ashore. I told Paco to stow all gear below decks, lock all hatches, and close all portholes. I had had experience with those *bandito* fishermen in Tangier Bay; they sneak alongside at night in their rowboats, and it's amazing what they can steal with their long bamboo poles armed with a hook on the end.

Juanita was sitting at a table in the corner of the bar with some of her friends. As soon as she saw me she stood up and walked over. We sat at the bar. I took her hand and kissed the palm. It smelled vaguely of the sensuous perfume she used.

"Glad to see me?" I asked. She put her head down on my shoulder and squeezed my arm hard.

"Oh, Brian, darling, you were supposed to be in yesterday. I was so worried."

"The hell I was. I haven't got an airplane. That bastard Lewis is a two-headed idiot when it comes to figuring out sea miles."

I told the barman to mix two Martinis with Gordon's gin, eight to one.

"*Sí, sí, señor.*" He smiled.

It was a sort of game we played. He never used anything but Gordon's gin and never mixed them for me less than eight to one.

"What have you been doing besides being unfaithful?"

"I don't like you when you speak like that," she said.

I glanced down into her shining black eyes. For all I knew, she may have slept with other men in the past, but those eyes told me that since she had fallen for me there had been no one else. I followed the line of her slender nose down to her mouth. Her rather full lower lip pouted seductively, accentuating its moist color. She was wearing a black velvet suit that would have been more at home in Maxim's in Paris than El Morocco. The jacket was draped across her shoulders and underneath she wore a black lace blouse that displayed to full advantage her beautiful figure. Her rather large breasts stood out firmly with their own muscles; no telltale crease between them revealed a high-slung brassiere. The clinging velvet accentuated the slender hips and black nylon had been discovered for her legs. A tiny white cap of ermine sat well back on her blue-black hair.

I brushed her ear with my lips and turned back to the Martini. I wondered if I could wait long enough to get through dinner before making love to her.

She seemed to sense the debate I was having with myself.

"Where will we eat?" she asked.

"Hungry?"

"No, but you must be after a week of Paco's cooking. Besides, we have all of tonight and tomorrow."

"And tomorrow and tomorrow and tomorrow."

Four Martinis later we sent the boy out for a taxi. I told the driver to take us to the Villa de France. Despite the garish light as we drove through the Grand Socco, I slipped my arm around her and pulled her close to me. I wanted her so badly I could hardly control myself. She took my face between her hands and slowly pressed her lips against mine.

The taxi jerked to a halt. I stumbled out, paid the driver, and followed the girl through the patio, scrubbing my lips with a handkerchief. We went into the bar.

Miguel, the barman, smiled, shook hands, and reached for the gin bottle all with one motion. As he poured the Martinis I told him to get two more on the way. I asked him to ice two bottles of Moet and Chandon '28 if he had any left. I picked up his little block of paper and pencil and wrote: "Turbot with cheese sauce, *à la maison. Tornedo* with mushrooms, ditto. Green salad with garlic, ditto. Rum omelet, ditto."

I showed it to Juanita. She took the pencil and crossed out the garlic.

"You've been at sea too long," she laughed. "Paco is such an awful cook, he must have everything strong with garlic so you won't know how bad it is."

We went out and chose a table on the terrace overlooking the bay. Some *dama de noche* was far enough away so that its scent was faint and exciting.

We said little during dinner. With the rum omelet I told the Moor to bring the check and wrap up the second bottle of champagne in several newspapers to keep it cold, because I was taking it with me.

At Juanita's suggestion we walked home. The very closeness of her as we crossed over into the casbah made me walk slower. It was a moment to savor, to unleash one's thoughts and let them race onward.

Her Arab was asleep across the doorway. I shoved his round cap down over his nose and he leaped up. His face beamed when he recognized us and I patted him on the back. While unlocking the door he kept muttering praises to Allah.

"Sherrif is very glad that you are back safely," Juanita said.

"So am I. And someday I'm going to steal that boy of yours."

"You'll have to take me as well."

"Can you cook?"

She laughed and pinched my arm.

Sherrif led the way through a series of narrow passages and up several stairs to a large room at the front of the house. I opened the shutters and instinctively looked up at the sky. High cirrus clouds obscured the half-moon. Looks like a front coming up; I checked my thoughts and laughed. And what the hell do I care if it snows? I'm not going anywhere tonight.

Juanita was giving the boy some rapid instructions in Spanish.

"Would you like some coffee?" she asked me as I turned back into the room.

"In about eight hours. Right now tell him to bring a couple of glasses and go to bed."

She came over and closed the shutters. Hungrily I crushed her to me. I moved my hand down her back, around her slender waist, and up under her breast. I could feel her body quivering as she clung to me.

Sherrif came in and set the glasses on a table. He went out and closed the door. Lifting my hand, she pressed it against her lips, murmuring, "Darling, darling, I have missed you so much. Why must you always be leaving me?"

"But it's so exciting when I return."

"Ah, but I love you more than just that."

"And I'm falling in love with you, too. A few more months and I'll quit this life and take you far away from here and we'll live in the hot clean sunshine, and we'll make love all day and all night until you get tired of me."

"Never. But when I grow old and fat and ugly you'll leave me."

"Darling, when that day arrives you'll be putting flowers on my grave. You're still a child."

"Child," she pouted, and broke away. "Just wait. I'll show you how old I am."

When she had left the room I opened the champagne, poured out a glass, and lit a cigarette. Taking the drink, I went into a small bathroom off the hallway. I undressed, bathed, and put on a silk dressing gown I found hanging behind the door. It rather amused me to find that it was one of my own. I smelled the sleeve.

"God, but you're a mistrustful bastard," I told the mirror. Absently thinking that it was about time I got a hair-cut, I inspected the face before me. As usual, the dark circles under each eye revealed a need of rest. I leaned forward and down toward the glass; few mirrors in Morocco were slung high enough for my six-foot-plus height. I ran my hands through my thick black hair. It rather surprised me that it was still thick and black, but I thought ruefully that another five years on the coast and it would be as grey as Sherrif's pants. Self-consciously I relaxed the hard set of my jaw. The tiny white lines running down from my lips disappeared in a wide grin. Must laugh more often or I'll be getting a face to frighten little children.

She was sitting on a small bench slowly sipping her champagne. She wore a soft white negligee. She had unloosed her blue-black hair and it fell forward over her shoulders. I lifted her up to me, and the top of her head just touched my chin. I carried her over to the couch and, still holding her, sat down. She bent over and reached toward the lamp. I caught her hand and kissed it.

"Have you forgotten already what I look like?" she asked.

"No, but such loveliness is not for darkness."

She laughed gaily and, standing up, undid the strings of her gown, letting it slip to the floor. In the soft light I drank in the bewitching figure, the smooth dusky flesh, the strong firm breasts standing wide apart, the slender waist and sleek narrow flanks.

"Do you still think I'm a child?"

"Child, woman, beguiling witch. You're everything a man could desire."

Kneeling down beside me she caught my lower lip between her teeth and bit hard. Under her breast I could feel her heart pounding. Or was it mine?

"Please, yes. Oh, please," she was whispering.... .

Sometime later I awakened, my brain fully alert. But when I felt the wide steady bed I relaxed and realized that its very steadiness had awakened me, so accustomed had I become to the constant movement of the ship's bunk.

I watched the softly sleeping head beside me. One could measure now the long lashes as they lay still against the pale skin.

"What are you thinking of?"

The lips, no less seductive in repose, had hardly moved.

"I thought you were asleep," I said, turning toward her.

She opened her great eyes and smiled at me.

"I sleep when you're not here. All day and all night. It makes the time go quicker until you return."

"You'll be getting fat."

"*Qué va!* That's not what makes a woman fat."

"Tell me more."

"No, I'll show you."

"Where did you learn to make love?"

"Not where you think."

I laughed and slid my arm under her head. She pushed me away, swung around, and sat beside me.

"Why are you always so doubting?" she asked. "So distrustful? I have never loved anyone but you. Because I let you make love to me when we first met so long ago, you have always thought that my body was cheap, that there had been many men before you."

"But darling …" I reached up and held her. She pushed my hand away.

"No. You think that because some of your American women go to bed with anyone they want whenever they want, we Spanish are the same. And I think that someone has broken your heart and now you don't trust anyone, not even yourself."

"Could be."

"And you believe that because we don't go to bed and lie there like a stone, we have been trained in some bordello. My darling, you have a lot to learn about Latin women. Oh, if I could only make you understand!"

Two great tears welled up and dropped like heavy diamonds. I reached up and pulled her down to me.

"I think that you would like me more if I was cold and shy and never let you see me except in the dark," she murmured.

"Would you like that?"

"No, I would shrivel up and die."

"So would I. But you were going to show me how a Spanish woman puts on weight."

Suddenly, vivaciously, she laughed. "But you will get no sleep," she said.

I could feel her muscles grow taut as she leaned over me, her hair caressing my body.

"Wait, Juanita, wait," I murmured as I pulled her face up to mine. "This is for you, too. We've got to feel it together."

She covered my mouth with hers, whispering through the crushed lips, "Oh, darling, if only I please you!"

Taking her head between my hands, I looked into the deep smoldering fire behind her eyes.

"If *only* you pleased me, darling, for you it would be better. But you excite me too much. I can't wait."

"But thus it is better. Then we can make love again."

Suddenly her fingers dug into my shoulders as she pulled me toward her. I could feel the long, slender body curling against mine, curve fitting hollow, hollow fitting curve.

"*Prisa, prisa,*" she was saying. "*Tampoco puedo esperar.*"

CHAPTER TWO

J UST before noon I got up and called for Sherrif. I gave
him some money and told him to go out and buy a case of
Mumms, two bottles of Johnny Walker, and a bottle of VSOP
cognac. On his way I asked him to pick up some peaches in the
market. I warned him that if he was more than half an hour he
would never see Mecca again.

The maid came in with a tray of coffee, rolls, and butter. I
took it from her, went over, and sat on the bed. Juanita opened
her eyes with a long sigh and stretched voluptuously.

"I'm so very, very happy," she said. "You must never leave
me."

I set the tray down and took her in my arms.

Sherrif returned in well under the half hour. I asked him to
bring up a bottle of champagne, the cognac, peaches, and ice, and
two large glasses. Outside the *levante* had blown itself out and the
day was dull and cold. I closed the shutters to keep out the acrid
stench of the casbah as well as the chill. It amazed me again to see
how much less alluring this district was by daylight. And again I
wondered why wealthy Americans went to great expense buying
and fixing up homes in the area. At least they hadn't been taken
in by Charles Boyer's intimation that every house was a bordello.

Into each glass I poured one finger of cognac, dropped in
half a ripe peach and some ice, and filled the glass with champagne. I walked over to the bed and handed the drink to Juanita.

"*A mañana y mañana,*" I said.

"To tomorrow and tomorrow," she replied, raising her glass.

Later that afternoon Juanita asked me when I was going back to sea. I replied that if the weather was fine I would probably be off the next day or the one following that.

"But you told me that after this trip you would stop. Why do you change your mind?"

"Ever hear of something called folding money?"

She wrinkled her brow.

"Well, it's an internationally known commodity of which we haven't enough," I went on. "Maybe in a month or so, provided you aren't too expensive, Moses Pariente will tell me that I have a hundred thousand dollars in his bank."

"But that is an enormous amount!"

"Have you ever been to the States? No, of course you haven't. Well, darling, where I come from, for every dollar's worth you want today you have to spend two dollars."

"You mean it's something like Spanish currency?"

"Not quite," I laughed. "But any moment now."

"But why do you want to return to America?"

"That, my sweet, could be called the sixty-four-dollar question. And before I try to answer it I'd better pour us a drink."

"If you use those funny phrases I won't know what you're talking about. Why should anyone want to pay sixty-four-dollars for a question?"

"Darling, you're wonderful." I walked over and kissed the back of her neck. "Don't ever change. Don't ever buy a radio."

I sat down on the couch beside her and slipped my arm around her shoulders. She turned her face up toward mine.

"No, that's no good." I got up and walked back to my chair. "If I'm going to tell you the story of Mrs. Hart's little boy, I have to keep my mind on it."

Again that warm silvery laughter.

"O.K., to hell with it. I can think of other things I'd rather talk about."

Juanita was suddenly serious. "No, please," she protested. "You never talk about yourself. I don't know anything about you, really, yet you are my whole life."

"Well, I was born in a part of the United States called New England in a state called Maine. That mean anything?"

"But of course. You know, we do have schools in Spain."

"You surprise me. Anyway, I was brought up within sound and smell of salt water. I could handle a boat before I started to school, and a ship before I left. But when I tried to make a living by it, it was a different story. However, I scraped along until the war came along and bailed me out."

"But Ricardo Lewis told me that you were in the United States Air Force during the war. Why didn't you join the Navy?"

"Ricardo talks too much. What else did he tell you?"

"I'm sorry. Please go on."

"I didn't join the Navy because in 1939 there was no war in the States. I was running from Boston to Halifax in those days— I had a half interest in a coaster. One trip I picked up a lifeboat a hundred or so miles off the coast. They'd been torpedoed ten days before. It was during the first months of the war, and such things as water and rations hadn't been very well organized. Among the survivors there were three women. I put them ashore the next day, but only two were breathing. It wasn't pretty. The experience decided me; I'll admit I'd been toying with the idea. You see, my mother's family was English; half my relations still live in England. Even after her death we kept in pretty close contact. There was always an uncle or aunt turning up to visit. Used to make my father sore as hell, or so he said. He called them 'old country snobs,' claimed they only came to see what a mess he was making of bringing me up. I think he was wrong. I saw a lot of them during the war and they had a great affection for the old Yankee sailor, as they described him. But to get back to my story—after we unloaded in Halifax I sold my interest to my partner and went to England. I tried to join their navy, but they hadn't had their Dunkirk yet, so they told me to return in a month or so. I'd done a lot of flying from time to time and had a license, so I went around to their air force. They weren't so particular, and there I was. The next five years were good years, and I had a lot of fun."

"But after the war was over, didn't you wish to return home?"

"Well, I thought about it. But you see, I really didn't have anyone back there to return to. And I think you always go back to people, not places. Besides, I had no job waiting for me. I remember how often we used to sit around the mess during the last days of the war, discussing what we were going to do when we got our discharge. I seemed to be the only one who didn't have to think about it. I knew what I wanted."

"What?"

"One hundred thousand dollars and an interesting life."

"But why is money so important?"

"Actually, it isn't. I just like to have it around. I don't suppose I could ever explain it to you, but it's a hang-over I've had since the early 1930's. I got my first good job then and I was all set. I was going to be the biggest shipping man that ever walked a Wall Street quarterdeck. I even designed my own house flag. Well, I got fired six months later. The depression had set in and there were a lot of lean, hungry years.

"I'm not going back to that. You see, I decided a long time ago that someday I'd get back into my father's old business. Only I wanted to start up where he left off, not where he started. I want to own the ships and pay someone else to stand the dirty watches. Then I might live a longer and happier life than he did. And that will take the best part of a hundred thousand dollars. If you or anyone else can show me how, with my limited capabilities, I can make that kind of money as easily as I think I'm making it here, I would appreciate it."

"But even when you have that much, you won't stop," Juanita broke in. "You'll simply say you need more. I don't believe it's the money. The life has got into your blood. You'll be just like my father."

"If you'd said that a couple of years ago, I might have had to agree with you. Now, no. Definitely no."

"But why have you changed? And if you're so definite now, why don't you stop?"

For a long moment I remained silent. I found it difficult to answer that question myself. For the past few months I had given the future more thought than ever before. I had written several letters home and found out from former associates of my father's that I could buy into his old business provided I had the capital. And I was pretty sure that I had enough now. Also what had once been, high adventure to me here had developed into a pretty routine way of life. In fact, going home and tackling a new project appeared much more exciting right now than taking the old Chucha up to Mallorca and back with another load of contraband. Which pretty well laid the fear that most of us had, that once we left the coast and went home we'd soon find ourselves smothering in a morass of monotony.

But it was only the top of my mind that was carrying on this argument. The one big question that remained unanswered and would remain unanswered until I faced up to it was sitting just across from me. Did I love her enough to take her with me? Accept the risk and marry her?

Marriage.

Why in hell couldn't we go home and live the way we were now? No strings, no promises to be broken. And if it didn't work—well, it had been a lot of fun while it lasted.

Yes? A voice from that solid part way back in my brain made itself heard. I can just see you and your sultry Spanish mistress setting up housekeeping in New England. What's so wrong, so frightening about the thought of marrying her? The kid loves you, you know that. She'll do her share to make it work. It's up to you to get rid of that warped, embittered attitude you're carrying around, that feeling that as soon as you start tying domestic knots somebody will put you behind the eight ball.

I switched that record off and stood up.

Juanita leaned toward me, her black eyes searching my face.

"Take me with you and let us go now, today. Please. This life is dangerous, too dangerous. Please, please …"

"Baby, you're frightening me. Let's have a drink."

I went over and spent a long time mixing a couple of champagne cocktails. "Incidentally," I said finally, over my shoulder, "I'm glad you mentioned your father a moment ago. I've been wanting to speak about him, but I didn't want you to pin my ears back the way you usually do."

I walked over and handed her the drink. "You know it's about time you and Francisco buried the hatchet."

As I caught the imploring look in her eyes, I felt four kinds of a heel for switching the subject so suddenly. But I had had enough self-analysis for a while; I was beginning to feel cornered. And what better evasive action, I decided rather defensively, than to throw her father at her? In her present mood she might soften toward him, something that I had been praying for for months.

I had known Juanita quite a while before she told me that Francisco Gonzales, our man in Mallorca, was her father. And I thought that even now I was probably the only person in Tangier who knew it. She had made me promise never to tell anyone. I was never absolutely sure what started the family feud. There were only the two of them; the mother had died when Juanita was born. But for the past year or more Juanita had refused to communicate with her father or even speak of him. And whenever I tried to mention him, she threw such a tempestuous tantrum that I soon decided it wasn't worth it.

In spite of everything, I felt that they loved each other deeply and wrote off Juanita's continued peculiar behavior as just another of those Spanish characteristics that cropped up from time to time to baffle me.

As far as I could make out—I'd heard Juanita's side only once, Francisco's often—when the girl returned home from the convent where she'd been sent away to school, she found that her father had sensibly moved a woman into the house to look after his domestic needs. But knowing Francisco as well as the customs of the island, I presumed she was taking pretty good care of his other requirements at the same time. Where he had made his mistake, and I had told him so, was in not taking it easy for a while until Juanita had forgotten some of the hell-fire and brimstone teachings she had been filled with at the convent. Anyway, they had a stand-up-and-knock-down fight with the result that the housekeeper was not only moved out of Francisco's bedroom, but out of the house as well.

After a period of quiet remorse, during which he hit the bottle a little more than usual—and usual to Francisco was considerable to most others—he began to forget to come home at night, sometimes several nights. Even this wasn't too bad, Juanita had explained to me, until one night he and some of his men broke up a bordello that belonged to the mayor. So the *guardia civil* were turned out and they tossed him in jail. And I could imagine the amusement that gave the islanders.

When he finally got home, Juanita had left. She went to Barcelona and stayed with some friends until she got a job dancing in a cabaret in Tangier. Just why she picked Tangier she would never explain to me. But I suspected that she felt that down here, through such men as Ricardo Lewis and skippers like myself, she'd be able to keep an anonymous eye on her father. How good a dancer she was I never knew. The first and only time I saw her perform I was so fascinated by her young love-liness that time itself seemed to stop. I had gone to sea the next day. By the time I returned the show had closed, and before she could find another opening I had convinced her that taking care of me was a full-time job.

Francisco knew that I was looking after Juanita. For some reason this seemed to please the old boy, and I think it was the only thing that kept him from coming to Tangier and having it out with the girl. He had tried sending her money by me, and when I told him the next trip that she had used the notes to light her cigarette with, I thought he'd blow a fuse. I usually informed him that the girl had sent her love to him, but when time passed and I could never produce anything more tangible, I know he realized that I was just trying to make it easier for him.

I glanced across at her now. I could see tears nearing the surface. And as I went over and sat down beside her, I thought that perhaps this time she would break down. Usually she was dry-eyed with anger when I tried to talk to her about him.

"Your father looked pretty well the last time I saw him. Hasn't been drinking so much, and from what the boys tell me, he's living a fairly quiet life."

"Probably got some awful creature living with him again," she sobbed.

"What the hell do you expect?" I said, standing up. "You won't go and take care of him. You don't even write to him. The poor old guy is lonely, that's all. If he's got someone to look after him, I'm all for it. Here." I took out my pen and laid it on the table. "I'm going down to the port for an hour or so. Get some paper and write him a letter. And if it's not done when I get back, I'll go on running contraband until I'm older than he is."

CHAPTER THREE

W HILE dawn daubed its first touch of color in the east three days later, we slipped out of Tangier Bay. The weather had settled down and I was looking forward to a quiet trip to Mallorca. We were running the usual cargo of coffee, cigarettes, and sugar, and the only difference between this and previous trips up the coast was that we had a new engineer on board. My old one had decided he'd made enough money to last him for a while, and had gone ashore to spend it. The present man was an American called Harry Strathers, who had been recommended to me by Ricardo Lewis. He claimed that he knew all there was to know about Diesel engines, so I had signed him on for one trip, explaining that if he proved efficient I would give him a permanent berth.

Our rendezvous had been arranged for the same spot ten miles south of Dragonera Island. This area was a favorite one, as it was not too far from the little port of Andraitx in Mallorca, where Francisco Gonzales landed most of his contraband.

The third evening out of Tangier we picked up the strong beacon marking the island.

I switched on the navigator's compass fixed to the wing of the bridge. I found that we were bearing roughly 210 degrees from the lighthouse. I told Paco to swing the ship to starboard, and when the distant light was abeam to straighten out and hold that course. The Chucha was now heading into the swell and she rode much easier.

Down in the galley I dug out a half-full pot of coffee left over from supper and put it on the stove to heat. I awakened Harry Strathers, the new engineer, and Jim Corby, the deck hand, and told them to get the covers off the hatches and start piling the cargo on deck, I warned them against stacking anything higher than the rail.

The coffee went down well and I forgot the amount of sleep I had missed since we cleared Tangier. Back on the bridge I found that the beacon, stronger now, was bearing 005 degrees. I took the wheel and brought the little ship around to port in a wide turn. Gradually the bearing became 360 degrees and I pointed the bows straight for the light. I asked Paco to take over again and steer for the lighthouse. I cautioned him to check his compass from time to time and make sure he didn't fall off the bearing.

In the light of the binnacle lamp the weather-bronzed face of the mate looked almost black. Two days' stubble gave him a piratical touch, and I couldn't help smiling when I thought of the great soft heart that lay beneath that fearsome exterior. I had found Paco on my first trip up the coast right after the war. One day when I was anchored in Palma Bay he had come aboard seeking a job. He'd been on the wrong side during the Spanish Civil War and was finding it difficult getting steady work. The authorities had finally returned his seaman's papers, but Spanish memories are long and their war had been bitter.

Born in the Balearic Islands, Paco, like so many of his countrymen, had traveled to Cuba as a boy and learned his profession of sponge fishing there. I could never be quite sure whether he'd adopted me or I'd adopted him. But after the first few months I found my shadow had become flesh and bone. In the beginning I rather resented his entry into my jealously guarded privacy. But gradually I succumbed to his persistent consideration for me and my affairs until I ceased thinking of him as a separate human being. He had become a sort of second right arm; a latent force waiting to translate my thoughts into action.

He could speak English quite well, and although I don't think he had been a professional *contrabandista* before he started to work for me, there wasn't much about smuggling that he didn't know. He was tall for a Mallorcan, and despite a prodigious appetite for rice and potatoes, rather thin. He was just over forty-five and hard as nails.

There was little I wouldn't do for Paco G6mez.

The other two members of the crew were hard at work aft. A mountain of cases and sacks began to form in the faint glow of the waning moon. I glanced at the patent speed indicator, checked my watch, and estimated that we had shortened the distance between us and the land by ten miles. I looked back at the moon. It was beginning to turn a dull rose color; another half hour and it should be below the horizon.

Impatiently I waited until we had run in another five miles. I went aft, checked the log, and hauled in the spinner. Back on the bridge I closed both throttles. The ship bellied down into the sea as we lost speed. I told Paco to just keep her moving ahead. In the cabin I had another look at the chart together with my instructions. There was no mistake. I was to be ten miles off Dragonera Island bearing 180 degrees at eleven-thirty the night of October thirtieth. I picked up the binoculars and went forward and sat on the anchor winch. From here the sound of our motors was almost inaudible. Harry Strathers came forward and said that they had brought up all the cargo they had space for. I told him to leave the rest and stick around and listen for Francisco.

"He's got a Bollinder," I explained, "and you can hear him miles away on a night like this."

"What's a Bollinder?" he inquired.

I had forgotten that Harry was on his first trip.

"It's a heavy Diesel engine," I informed him. "Slow running. Most of the Spanish fishing boats use them. They have plenty of power, but I wouldn't have one in a ship like this because of the vibration. But then, I'm not a fisherman. Those lads swear by them. And once you've heard one, you'll never mistake it. It goes thump, thump, thump. The coast guards use a different type engine. Sounds more like our Gleniffers."

I turned back to the night and lit a cigarette. The half-moon was a definite rose now and just about to set. A warm breeze came off the land, bringing the heavy scent of pine and baked earth.

"Geez, I'd sure like to visit these islands."

"Quiet." I was beginning to get nervous. It was after eleven-thirty and I could see in the soft light the black dampness of the deck. "Sorry," I murmured. "But we've got to make contact tonight. Tomorrow there's going to be wind. I don't want to be caught hanging around outside."

Harry remained silent. I looked at my watch. It was eleven-forty. The last few minutes had appeared so long I thought that surely my watch had stopped. I walked back to the wheelhouse and. checked the ship's clock. It said eleven-forty. I told Paco to take the engines out of gear and turn the ship into the swell. His tranquil features reflected in the binnacle lamp were reassuring.

"Nice night," I said, and I smiled.

"*Por ahora.*" These damn Spanish sailors would never commit themselves when it came to weather. I returned to the bows.

"But how do you expect to make contact on a dark night like this?" Harry, irrepressible, went on. "It's a mighty big sea."

"You'd be surprised how simple it is. We've sailed up a straight line on a definite course toward the southern tip of Dragonera Island. It's just like driving along a road. Francisco Gonzales sails down from the opposite direction in his fish trawler. When we reach ten miles off the point, we stop and wait. On a night like this we carry a small white light at the masthead. And you can see it three, four miles away. If the visibility is bad, we put up a stronger light and circle around. You'll pick up either the light or the sound of his engines."

"And how do you know that the ship you see or hear isn't a Spanish revenue cutter?"

"That's a chance we take. As far as Francisco's concerned, he's simply on his way to the fishing grounds. If they stop him, they find nothing but his nets. We have to be more careful. They actually have no right to stop and search a foreign ship beyond the three-mile limit. But recently they've been stopping ships as far as twelve miles out. It's a case of might is right off this coast.

"But it's not so one-sided as it would appear," I went on after a lengthy pause. "In the first place, we know that the fastest revenue cutter in these islands does about fourteen knots, no more. These seventy-five- foot ex-navy ships like the Chucha can do up to eighteen if we push them. So even if a revenue cutter managed to sneak up close, we could still outdistance her. Anyway, after a time you get to know the different sounds engines make at sea, particularly at night. So far, the ships I've met have all had Bollinders, and you can identify them."

"Why don't the customs smarten up and install the same type of engine in one of their cutters?"

"They could, but then their top speed would be cut to about ten knots."

"O.K. So they can't catch us. But what happens if they get close enough to open fire?"

I leaned down and hit the deck. "To date they haven't. And let's hope we aren't the first ship they practice on. If we should be, you'd better pray for poor marksmanship, poor visibility, or both."

Harry was silent. I imagined that he was trying to think up further questions. Suddenly he leaned far out to port, hanging onto the forestay. .

"You hear something?" I asked.

"Yeah. At least, I thought I did."

Turning my head slowly from right to left, I made out the heavy beat of an engine to port. Then I picked up the same sound to starboard. Hell, I thought, I've reached the wishful hearing stage. Time to quit.

But Harry's hearing was sharper than mine. Pointing to the left, he said that there was a ship out there. And sure enough, I finally spotted a light well down on the horizon. Returning to the bridge, I pointed it out to Paco and told him to make for it. Soon we could hear distinctly the thump, thump, thump of the fishing trawler's exhaust. I called down to Jim and told him to get the fenders over the port side and to stand by with the lines. The light was sharper now. I pressed the light switch and blinked our masthead light. A few minutes later the oncoming light flashed. I signaled once, then three times, then five. With the binoculars I watched the other light. It flashed twice, then four times, then twice. It was Francisco.

I pulled the throttles back as far as they would go.

"Just keep her rolling," I told Paco. "When he comes alongside, turn slowly down the swell and save the paint-work. If I give a shout, turn out everything and open up."

The mate knew the routine as well as I did. But as usual, my imagination was beginning to work overtime, and instead of Francisco's fishing boat, I began to see the dark gray hull of a revenue cutter bearing down on us.

By now it was really black. When you looked up at the stars they were silvery bright, but the reflected light was nil. Francisco had switched off his light, and out of the night came only the sound of his engine.

Five minutes later the squat yellow hull of the trawler was fast alongside.

Instead of the usual banter, Francisco was all seriousness when he leaped aboard.

"Me cargo en Dios," he said, his Spanish fairly rattling. "We must hurry. There's a revenue cutter in Andraitx, and I think some *hijo de la gran puta* has tipped him off that you are coming in tonight. I lend you some men to help."

Several dark figures had followed him across the rail, and already the cases were disappearing into the dark hold of the fishing boat.

I picked up the binoculars and swept the sea to the north. In the blackness, nothing; not even a horizon. But then, if a cutter was coming out to investigate us it would surely be running without lights.

"How long to start your engine?" I asked Francisco.

"Un momento."

"Bien. We'll stop our engines and listen."

I shut down and gave Francisco the list of the cargo. He in turn handed me a pile of bank notes, and I said that I'd count them later. If the amount wasn't correct we could settle the next trip. And for once the Mallorcan was silent as he leaned against the wind dodger listening to the soft slap of the sea and the low grunts of the men aft.

"You saw the cutter in Andraitx?" I asked him.

"Sí, sí."

"Which one was it?"

"Old Sixteen."

"She still got the same engines?"

"But of course, señor. Where in this country would she find new ones?"

"Fine. If we hear her I'll start up first and try to head her off. Don't you start your engine until you're sure she's heard mine. Which direction are you going tonight?"

"Southeast, toward Ibiza. The fishing fleet is down that way."

"I'll try to take our friend west, then. By the way, I brought you up a letter. From Juanita."

He seized the envelope and held it close to his face, trying to make out the writing in the gloom.

"Do you want a light?"

"No, no, *amigo mío.*" He tucked the envelope carefully in an inside pocket. Suddenly he threw his arm around me and pulled me close to him. "You think maybe she comes back to see me?"

I couldn't see his eyes, but there was a catch in his voice.

"Yes. Perhaps I can arrange to bring her with me the next trip."

"*Olé!* I start right away to arrange the fiesta. After you unload you bring the Chucha into port. I will fix everything with the *carabineros.* We celebrate one week, maybe two weeks. You and Juanita come and live with me and *nos divertiremos eternamente!*"

I could feel the enthusiasm bubbling up within him.

"Why not?" he ran on. "I have plenty of money, big house, six boats. O.K., I give you the money and the boats and you run the business up here. I sit in the sun and look after your *niños.*"

"But what if Juanita won't marry me?"

"Maybe you should ask her, eh?" He chuckled as he squeezed my arm. "*A quién le importa eso?* I didn't marry her mother, but the padre comes to see me two, three times a week."

"Sure, trying to convert you, you old sinner."

"Yes? Well, this *conversión,* or whatever you call it, is costing me a lot of good cognac."

"You write to her right away, anyway. Mail it or send it down with the next ship. I know she's anxious to hear from you. And now it's about time we got the hell out of here."

I dropped down to the deck and asked Paco how the unloading was getting on. He said they'd be finished in another ten minutes. I told him that we might have to make a run for it and to be ready to let go the lines in a hurry.

The last few sacks were going over the rail when Francisco called down. His voice now was icy calm. "There's a ship coming down from the north," he said.

I yelled to the crew to let go the lines and leaped up to the bridge. As Francisco passed me on the way down, I gripped his arm and told him to be sure to remember what I had said to him. I pressed the starting buttons, and one after the other the engines roared into life.

"*Vayas con Dios*," a voice called across the water as I put the helm over.

"*Ya nos veremos*," I shouted back into the night.

I switched on the binnacle lamp and all navigation lights and kept the ship swinging until we headed just west of north. Then as we reached our maximum speed I made a wide circle westward. I realized that it was purely a gamble; over the thunder of our own engines there was no possibility of hearing the other ship. The only thing I was sure of was that unless they were all asleep they'd certainly hear the tremendous noise we were making or see our lights.

Ten minutes later I closed the throttles and listened.

Astern and to the north I could hear the sound of a heavy engine at full speed.

"Well, that saves Francisco's hide," I said to Paco as I opened up again. "They're coming after us."

❧ ❧ ❧

At noon next day we swung around Cabo de Palos and altered course westward. We'd dumped our pursuer sometime during the night, for when dawn came the gray rim of the sea astern was unbroken. I took two or three fixes on Los Hormines and the cape to make sure we rounded the corner outside the international three-mile limit, plus the additional three miles the Spanish revenue cutters considered their territory. This six-mile limit had been argued in every bar and a number of courts in the western Mediterranean. But it was one thing to stand up for one's nautical rights in Dan's Bar in Tangier with a drink in your hand and another while looking down the throats of a pair of Bofors debating the point with some trigger-happy *español* on the high seas.

As I had feared, a *levante* had come up with the morning, but after we rounded Cabo de Palos it simply heaved us on our way. Off Cabo de Gata we altered course for the last time westward and headed for the Straits of Gibraltar. The wind continued with the night and I was glad that we weren't punching into it. Even so, the combers glistening white in the moonlight began to take on dangerous proportions. I cautioned Harry, who was at the wheel, to ease her up a bit and make doubly sure he didn't let her broach to. I didn't know how much experience he'd had with these short, vicious seas, so I remained on watch with him.

"Gee, but it's a great life," he said. "And for the kind of money we're making, why doesn't everybody get into the racket?"

"You'll learn, lad. You'll learn. Last night we were lucky and got away with it. But one of these days our luck might not be so good. And when that happens, you'll wish you'd stayed on that Idaho farm you were telling me about."

"But it seems to me old Francisco is taking all the risk. We dump the cargo and beat it. He turns and heads for shore, and I should think any cutter could catch that lumbering fishing trawler."

"True, he's taking a bigger risk than we do. And for that he's making more money than we make. But when we load him he doesn't head back into port. That *would* be dangerous. He continues on out to the fishing grounds. There he meets five or six of his men with their own boats actually fishing. He divides his cargo among all the ships. They go on trawling until dawn or whatever hour is customary, then make their separate ways back to land. Ninety-nine per cent of the time no one is caught. After all these boats go out fishing every night in the week. And I'd say they bring in contraband less than one night in ten. The odds are all in their favor."

"So they get into port safely. But how in hell do they get the stuff—sixty-kilo sacks of coffee, for example—across the quay to wherever it's to be hidden?" he asked.

"That's when the pay-off starts," I explained. "And believe me, it takes a big cut out of the profits. But once you've arranged the price and they know you'll pay up, they bend over backward to help you. Remember these *carabineros* receive something like fifteen bucks a month to live on. Why, in the old days when I used to run cargos right into port myself, many times it was the *carabineros* who came out and gave me a hand to unload. You try bringing up a wife and a bunch of kids on six hundred pesetas a month, even in this country, and you won't be so damn honorable.

"Actually, though," I continued, "most of the contraband is dumped off on various beaches and coves. These locals know where they can bring even their big fishing boats right alongside the rocks. There's a gang of men waiting, and the sacks and cases are loaded onto donkeys, taken inland to the nearest road, piled into a truck, and disappear. That's the cheapest method of landing. And I'll tell you why. The coast is divided into sections of say ten miles each. Each section is guarded by so many *carabineros;* a *sargento,* for example, and five men. O.K. You have only six men to take care of. You tell them what night you're going to land and where, and they either stay in bed or are down watching another section of the coast miles away."

"But I don't see where all this contraband goes. As I understand it, there aren't many foreigners here, and the average working-class family can't afford black-market cigarettes and coffee and all the rest of the stuff that pours into Mallorca."

"Less than ten per cent of the stuff stays here. All the rest of it goes on to Barcelona or Valencia or some other part of the mainland."

"Then why don't we take it direct to the fishing boats off Barcelona? It would save a lot of handling."

"A good question," I rejoined. "The best answer is that the mainland coast is closely guarded, and especially the ports. It's mighty tough to land a cargo without being caught. So it's a question of bribery. But the mainland isn't like the Balearic Islands. You finally make a deal with the *carabineros* in a spot, say, like Arenys de Mar. It's a little fishing port in a good location; just a few miles north of Barcelona on the main highway. You bring in your first cargo and everybody's happy. You might even bring in two or three more. Then one morning as you're making fast to the quay, you see some green uniforms strolling toward you. Damn it, you say to yourself, those bastards should be on the other side of the town. You look at them more closely. Instead of Pepe or Luis or Juan, these are fellows you don't recognize. They drop down to the deck, bid you good morning polite as hell, and tell you they're just going to have a quick look around.

"The next thing you know, you've lost your boat and the cargo, and you're faced with a stiff fine. You storm around the cafés looking for Pepe or Luis or Juan, only to find that they've been posted to Tarragona.

"In Mallorca it's different. The *carabineros* are more like the policemen at home. They're members of the community. They have their little houses and their families, and as long as they behave themselves—publicly, that is—they stay in the one *pueblo* all their lives."

I took over the wheel, and suggested that Harry go below and make some coffee. The wind had gone down with the moon, and although the seas were still heavy, there was less spray coming into the open bridge.

The hot coffee took the nip out of the air. I had just about decided the engineer could cope by himself, when he spoke.

"You were saying?"

"Saying, hell. I was about to get some sleep. If I tell you any more, when you get in from this trip you'll be a specialist on smuggling."

He laughed. "But I've always wondered why the Balearic Islands were the contraband center for Spain."

"Don't misunderstand me. A lot of shipments are landed directly into Spain proper. But the majority go via Mallorca, and for my money it's much safer."

"Just how big is this business? When I was hanging around Tangier I used to see freighters come in from the States and unload thousands of tons of stuff—cigarettes, coffee, sugar, to say nothing of radios and cars and nylons. Tangier couldn't use half the stuff they unloaded there."

"The only difference between these shipments and the Marshall Plan is that these goods are paid for, strictly cash. But my God, it's becoming big! Just stop and think that seventy-five per cent of the black market in Spain, France, Italy, and points east is supplied through the Straits of Gibraltar. And have you any idea of the size of these markets? In Spain, for example, I don't think there's a cup of pure coffee sold legally. Yet Spain drinks almost as much coffee per capita as America, and they not only like coffee, but they like it sweet. The sugar ration, when you can get it, is enough for about ten cups a month. Yet you can walk into any store and buy all the candy and cake and ice cream you want. And any baker will sell you, at a price, all the white bread you want. Yet Spain hasn't sold white flour legally since 1936. In France it used to be the same. But now it's mostly cigarettes, radios, nylons—things like that. The same with Italy.

"And those are only a few of the things that are shipped in. I recall one trip I made, I carried on board everything from sewing-machine needles to Scotch whisky, with women's rubber girdles, color film, ball-point pens, radio tubes, white flour, penicillin, spectacle frames, and automobile tires in between. I felt like a floating Macy's. God! Never again. I had to deal with so many different men with so many different prices that by the time I returned to Tangier I think I lost money on the trip. Now I stick to the essentials and to hell with the carriage trade."

"Do you finance these trips yourself?"

"Not any more. In the old days, just after the war, anyone who had a boat that could be sailed, motored, or rowed up the coast used to go to Tangier, buy as much contraband as he could pay for, and bring it up to Spain, France, or Italy and sell to the highest bidder. But the trade got so big that the amateurs fell by the wayside or were pushed out, and the professionals took over. Now it's controlled by a few big shots in Barcelona, Palma, Marseilles, and Naples.

"We work for Francisco Gonzales, the man you saw last night. His boss probably lives in Madrid; maybe he's a close friend of Franco. I don't know him and I don't want to know him. Francisco's agent in Tangier is Ricardo Lewis, whom you know. He handles all the buying and shipping from the States. We collect a straight sum per case or sack of whatever it is, depending on the value of the commodity. If we fail to make contact or lose the cargo or get caught and are fined, Francisco or the syndicate he represents pays the shot."

"How did you ever get into the game?" Harry asked.

"I'll answer that by asking you what *you're* doing, hanging onto that wheel out here in the western Med with a *levante* on your tail. No, I won't ask you. I'll tell you. You were in the U.S. Navy during the war, you told me."

"Yeah. P.T. boats. Out in the Pacific most of the time."

"So after your victory hangover you went back to your old shore job. No I don't suppose you ever had a job. They probably took you right out of college. O.K., you looked for a job. The first one was easy. You were a hero with a chestful of ribbons. They gave you a desk with a view; a brick wall across the street. Along about three o'clock every afternoon you got to thinking of the hard living and hard drinking, the free and easy life you'd known with Uncle Sam paying all the bills. Your work suffered. You kidded yourself that maybe if you had a different job you'd do better. So you looked around for a desk with a better view. The Martini ration before lunch was now up to four. Pretty soon your new boss called you in and reminded you nicely but firmly that the war was over and that you'd better get your finger out. You happened to be just in the mood to sound off, and that was the end of that job.

"You started to drift. You really don't know anything about anything except the sea and marine engines. So you drifted back to her. The next thing you know, you're a budding *contrabandista* running out of Tangier."

"Geez, you could write the story of my life," he laughed.

"Well, in many respects I guess I felt the same way. Only I didn't waste time proving something that I already knew. I had this ship and this work lined up before I got out of uniform."

As the first finger of dawn lay along the horizon astern, we picked up the beacon from Gibraltar and corrected our course accordingly. Now we were wallowing ahead through a heavy swell. As we neared the Straits the swell became an uncomfortable chop. We passed close in to the Rock, headed across the bay, and kept well under Point Carnero. Beyond the point we found the going much smoother as we entered the countercurrent running back into the Atlantic. Opposite Tarifa we left the north shore and swung across the Straits to Tangier.

CHAPTER FOUR

S OMETIME around noon the next day Juanita and I were wondering if the weather was warm enough for a picnic down the coast when Sherrif came in with a message from Ricardo Lewis. He wanted to see me and suggested that I meet him that evening in his office. I sent down word that I'd be there at eight o'clock.

About seven I left Juanita, explaining that I should be back by eleven and asking her to have her cook prepare a supper for us. I was rather pleased, as things turned out, that I'd ordered that meal.

Dropping down through the casbah, I crossed the Petit Socco and continued on out the dock. The clean night air was a bracing tonic as I walked along the quay. Opposite *quatrocientos* I whistled for Paco. He was sitting on the foredeck of the Chucha, and after waving, he drew up the dinghy and rowed across.

"How are things?" I asked him, getting into the boat.

"*Bien, bien.* Two men came out to the Chucha yesterday to see you. I don't know who they were. They said they'd return."

"Nobody goes on board when I'm not there."

"No, *Capitán.*"

The rest of the crew were sleeping off a night in the town. I asked Paco to keep them on board, and said I'd be out first thing in the morning. From past experience I knew that he cared little about going ashore. He rowed me to the dock. I said good night and turned away.

A taxi driving in along the quay slowed down as it came abreast. I waved it on. It stopped and the driver got out. I thought I recognized him.

"You Captain Hart?"

"Yes."

"Señor Lewis asked me to come and get you. He says to bring you out to Pepe's café. He is waiting there for you."

I climbed in. We passed up through the town and headed out toward the mountain. I had been to Pepe's *bistro* once or twice before, but only at night. I knew the general direction, but I'd hate to have to find the spot alone. Somewhere along the highway to Cape Spartel, we turned down a side road toward the sea. The engine missed a few times, then died. The car rolled to a stop. The driver spent some time fiddling with various knobs and buttons and pressed the starter. The engine turned over but didn't fire.

"You got any gas?" I asked.

"*Sí, sí señor. No sé que pasó.*"

He got out and lifted the hood. I opened the door, got out, and felt for a cigarette.

The next second my head exploded with a tremendous red flash.

Slowly, slowly I came out of it. My neck felt as though a street-car had run over it. The little pinwheels behind my eyes gradually changed to bigger ones, slowing up. Then there was only one wheel and it ground to a stop. My mind began to knit together and work. My first coherent thought was: Don't move. It's going to hurt. And don't open your eyes till the fog clears a bit more.

To start with, I thought I'd been run over by another car. Then I recalled that I had stepped out of the taxi on the right side; a car would have had to drive up the ditch to hit me.

Don't kid yourself, a corner of my brain finally said. You've been well and truly slugged.

Further considerations of the situation were interrupted by a man who came in and switched on a bright, single bulb overhead. He bent over and asked me if I was awake yet.

I could see no future in stalling. I groaned and rolled over. He disappeared, and in a few minutes returned with a glass of brandy. I was sitting up. He handed me the drink and I knocked it back. It was a brandy too sweet for my taste, but the alcohol changed the sharp thumping in my head to a slightly less painful ache. I held my neck and slowly twisted it.

"You bastards have broken my neck," I said.

"No, señor. You struck the side of the car when you fell."

"Thanks for the information. Now explain just what in hell is going on."

"*Momentito, señor.*"

I crawled to my feet and looked around. I was in someone's back room. There were no windows. A table and some chairs stood in the center. I sat down and rested my head in my arms. The stench of a nearby lavatory was strong.

Four men came in and started speaking together in Spanish. I looked up but didn't recognize any of them. One, a short, rather paunchy individual, appeared to be the ringleader. He pulled out a chair opposite me and sat down. He asked the first man to bring more brandy. Nothing was said until the bottle arrived and I poured myself a full glass.

"Feel better?" the man across from me asked.

"Thanks to you, I feel terrible. Just what do you want and why?"

"Captain Hart, we wish to know to whom you sold your cargo on your last trip to Mallorca."

Bingo. My senses suddenly tied themselves together. The haze vanished, and with it my semiconscious ideas of robbery, kidnaping, mistaken identity. These were some of Carlos Aguzado's henchmen. I had been warned that Aguzado was out to get me because I'd been hauling contraband into Andraitx. That particular part of the island was, according to Aguzado, his own private territory. What a damn fool I'd been to let them pick me up so easily! Despite the pain, I couldn't suppress a rueful grin.

"I'm glad you're feeling happier," my man said.

"Whatever your name is, I'm smiling at my own stupidity. I can only blame it on a certain mental sluggishness brought about by too much of a favorite drink for which you require champagne, cognac—"

"I don't understand," he broke in.

"I'm sure you don't. But let's get on with it. I have no intention of telling you who I do business with in Mallorca. Surely you must realize that."

"Señor, we are willing to pay you well. We will buy your ship at a fair price. On top of that, we will give you two hundred thousand pesetas. With this you can return to America and forget about Tangier. I have the papers right here, and the name of an Englishman to whom you can transfer the registration of your ship."

"And while I'm on my way to America, a certain friend of mine in Mallorca will have his throat cut."

"Oh, no, señor. We will simply warn him."

"Look," I broke in. "You know me, or rather you know of me. You must, or we wouldn't be enjoying this rather peculiar fiesta. So please; don't add insult to injury by thinking that I'm stupid. I know that the moment you find out who my friends are in Mallorca, certain cables will be sent and certain accidents will happen. If you want to know who I work for, go to Palma and ask."

The little man smiled and pulled out a long Manila envelope from which he extracted a pile of *mil* notes. Each tenth one was folded carefully across the other nine. He counted out twenty packets, then five more, and shoved them across the table.

"I will go as high as two hundred and fifty thousand. Now please give me the name."

My thoughts turned to gay little Francisco Gonzales. He was going to roar with laughter when I told him that he was worth a quarter of a million pesetas. I could hear him telling me what a damn fool I'd been not to take the money and split it with him.

"Please, señor. It's getting late."

I picked up the bottle of brandy and held it up to the light. It was still two-thirds full. I poured another glass.

"I hope there's more where this came from," I said. "Because if we sit here all tonight and tomorrow night, I'll never tell you his name."

The man cursed in Spanish, stood up, and with a sweep of his arm sent the bottle crashing to the tile floor. Some of the *mil* notes followed. Slowly I set the glass down. And now, I thought, the fun is over. I glanced around the room. We were five to one. Three of the five were fairly small, but the two standing behind me were husky types, their faces bronzed with the sea air. The single door was shut and looked fairly substantial. There had never been a sound from outside, so I gathered that it was a thick-walled room or else we were well away from anybody. I rather imagined that they had taken all that into consideration. I looked at my watch. It was three A.M. Poor Juanita.

My thoughts were suddenly interrupted. The two men behind me grabbed my arms and lifted me out of the chair. The little man came around the table and stood in front of me.

"I ask you once more. And I warn you that you won't leave this room alive if you don't speak."

When I started to smile, he swung. I attempted to protect my face, but both arms were held tight behind me. The blow caught me on the side of the jaw. But it didn't hurt so much as my neck, as I instinctively jerked away. I saw him rub his knuckles.

He went around and sat down, motioning one of the others to go to work. It didn't take me long to figure that there was no future in it. I relaxed suddenly. The two sailors practically had to hold me up. When the third man came at me again, I leaped up and kicked back with my heel.

I caught one of the sailors on the shinbone and he let out a bellow. I heaved the other one off and took a mighty swing at the man in front of me. I felt his nose bone crunch like dry spaghetti as I connected. I followed him down to the floor and someone went over my back. I grabbed a chair on the way up and caught the second sailor on the side of the head. The flimsy wood came to bits in my hand. I threw it at the other sailor and leaped across the table. As I suspected, the door was locked. Before I could twist the key, three of them came for me. I picked out the biggest and kicked him in the groin. He doubled up. I felt my right arm go numb as someone caught me on the shoulder with a billy. I could hear loud pounding on the other side of the door. I let out a yell and swung blindly with my left. Just as I felt my knuckles connect with bone, the billy came down again. I could still make sense, but my muscles wouldn't react. I fell to my knees. I tried to hold myself up with my arms, but they were made of rubber.

The door behind me was really taking a beating. I could hear the wood begin to splinter and I was left alone. The ringleader called out something and ran across the room. He lifted out a tile from the floor and pulled a handle. A small door opened. Two of them came back and helped out the man I had kicked. The door swung shut. I sprawled out on the floor.

The next thing I knew, Ricardo Lewis was bending over me.

"You still alive?"

"They gave me quite a going over," I mumbled. "Let's get out of here."

The room was full of men. Even Sherrif was there, wringing his hands in the background.

"Where did they go?" Ricardo asked.

I pointed to the handle beneath the tile. He told some of his men to go after them.

He helped me along a passageway and into a bar. It was a shambles. Broken bottles littered the floor. There wasn't a table standing on its four legs. The bar itself had been tipped in against the wall. Along it lay a couple of bodies.

"Dead?" I asked.

"Hell, no. Just sleeping," Ricardo said.

We went out into the road and he helped me into his Buick. I noticed several other cars drawn up behind. I slumped back in the seat and closed my eyes.

"How did you know where I was?" I asked finally.

"About two o'clock Juanita came to my house and asked for you. She said you had come to see me about seven o'clock. I got worried and sent the boys out. They discovered that you'd been seen in a taxi driven by one of Aguzado's men. I guessed the rest."

"But how—"

"Never mind the details. I'll explain tomorrow. Where do you want to go? You'd better come home with me."

"No, thanks. Your old woman would have a fit if she saw me like this. Drive me out to the dock. I'll be all right on the ship."

Paco was watching from the deck. Apparently Ricardo had sent out to see if I was on board after Juanita had awakened him. A few minutes later he was alongside in the dinghy. He held it steady while Ricardo helped me down. I told Sherrif to explain to his mistress that I would see her in the morning, but not to tell her too much of what had happened.

Ricardo wanted to send a couple of his men on board for the night, but I said that it wouldn't be necessary, that Aguzado's thugs were probably still on the run.

On the way out to the Chucha I related the night's adventure to Paco. He had little to say, but I could see the fine lines about his mouth tighten. On board I unlocked the safe, took out a .45, and gave it to him with a box of cartridges. I slipped a .38 under my pillow. I told Paco to get some liniment and give me a rubdown.

Before he had finished working on my back I had passed out.

The next afternoon I got up, and with the mate's assistance got dressed. My body felt as though I'd stepped on a land mine. Ricardo came aboard just before sundown, bringing with him one of his partners. We gathered in the saloon over a bottle of whisky. Ricardo seemed pleased with himself.

"What's up?" I asked him.

"Well, we have taken care of one of your friends of last night. It won't be long before we have them all accounted for."

"The little Joe What's-his-name who ran the show?" I said hopefully.

"No. That's a chap called Despojo. I imagine he has left town for a while. But he'll be back. You remember, however, last night when you were trying to identify them for us, you said something about looking for a man with a smashed nose? Well, Mateo here did some detective work this morning and found that old Doc Rodríguez had patched up a fellow's nose before breakfast today. The doc said that it had been a hell of a job. It took him an hour to dig out all the bone splinters."

My aches seemed less sore.

"Mateo got the man's name and tracked him down to Sebastiano's bar—that place on the corner of the Rue Aduano. He finds the guy sitting inside cauterizing himself with cognac.

He didn't know it, but Mateo's brother-in-law owns a half interest in the bar.

"After he has several drinks, Mateo figures he's pretty ripe, so he gets one of the waiters to hand him a micky. They carried him out back to sleep it off. We picked him up and brought him down to the cellar below the shop. He woke up an hour ago and one of the boys tickled him a bit and got the dope on last night's affair."

"Go on."

"It's more or less what we thought. Aguzado has been raising hell because we're cutting into his territory in Andraitx. Apparently every damn cellar in the port is full of cigarettes and the price has dropped to five pesetas a package delivered. Unfortunately, someone let slip that you brought up the last cargo, so Aguzado sent word down here to either bribe you or frighten you into telling them who our local men are in Andraitx. It's really damn funny, because I know that Francisco Gonzales and Aguzado are pretty good friends. I'd like to be around if and when Carlos finds out it's Francisco!"

"What interests me more at the moment," I broke in, "is the name of the little organizer of last night's party. You say it's a man called Despojo? What else does he call himself and what does he do?"

"Pablo Despojo. He's an outside man for Aguzado. He doesn't stay in Tangier very long at a time, but you're likely to run into him anywhere along the coast."

I took out an old envelope, tore off the back, and carefully printed out the name. I folded the paper and tucked it into my wallet.

"And now what?" I asked. "Are we declaring open warfare? I must say I don't like the idea of having my skull cracked every time I come to Tangier."

"Don't worry about it. We'll beat up a couple of the goons who were in last night's show. Then I'll go around and see Aguzado's agent here and we'll settle it. After all, they don't want a war any more than we do. But we'll have to be a bit careful from now on. I don't think they'll try any more rough stuff, but if they can find out when we're making the next shipment, they'll tip off the *aduana* up there as sure as hell."

"Even so," I remarked, opening my jacket and tapping the butt of the .38 I'd tucked into a shoulder holster, "the next time it's not going to be so one-sided."

Ricardo laughed.

"It's those damn women," he said. "They take your mind off your work."

"You should talk. How many children you got now?"

"Nine. That's why I don't get drunk any more. Every time I go home tight, I get me another mouth to feed."

I passed the bottle around.

"How would you like to run down to Casablanca?" he said. "You can pick your weather and be back in a couple of days."

"What's cooking in Casa?"

"Well, I figure there isn't much use in making another run to Mallorca for a while. As I told you, the market up there is flooded. Besides, maybe it's a good idea to let Aguzado think he's frightened us off for a time. Make it easier for Francisco."

"I think you've got something there."

"I got a deal in Casablanca that sounds pretty good. I don't know whether you know it or not, but a lot of gold has found its way from France to French Morocco. They tell me the banks down there are bulging with it. We used to bring it up to Tangier by road, but they soon got on to that. The last time I drove back, the customs damn near took the gold out of my teeth. Anyway, they want this gold in Tangier. From here they can stack it away in Montevideo or New York or wherever they like."

"And so we bring it out by ship."

"Yeah."

"Sounds easy. Why hasn't someone done it before?"

"Ever been to Casa?"

"No."

"Well, when you see the port," he explained, "you'll realize why it's not so simple. You can't walk a foot along the quay without tripping over a gendarme. And you can't make a landing along the beach except one or two days a month; there's always a big surf running. And the little port to the north of Casablanca is also closely watched."

"I just like to know these things."

"Sure. Well, the setup is this: You go down to Casa, and go in to buy-fuel oil and stores. If anybody asks you, you're on your way to the Canary Islands. You go ashore and just hang around for a couple of days. Then make sure no one is tailing you and go telephone a friend of mine in Fez. I'll give you his name and telephone number. Just ask him if he still wants to go to the Canaries with you. He'll say yes, and that he'll be on board the next day or the day following at such and such an hour. And he'll say, 'I hope we have a smooth passage.' Remember that, so you'll know you're talking to the right man. Whatever day and hour he tells you, you add four hours on, and be at a point I'll tell you outside the harbor."

"You mean three miles outside the harbor."

"More," Ricardo said.

"But why go into Casablanca at all? Why not leave here just in time to make the rendezvous?"

"Because of the difficulties at that end. They can't tell from day to day whether they're going to be able to get the gold together in time, and if they do, whether they can get it through the port and out to sea. They can't afford to have you stooging up and down outside Casablanca. Too much French navy hanging around. You got to remember this isn't a cargo of cigarettes or coffee that you can dump over the side if the going gets rough. This is real folding money."

"How real?"

"Well, I told them it wasn't worth it for less than half a million dollars."

"That's a lot of kilos."

"Yeah. You'd better make sure your engines don't break down or we'll both have to leave the country."

The bottle was empty and I was beginning to feel hungry. I told Ricardo that I'd think about it and let him know. I decided I was fit enough to collect the dinner I'd missed last night from Juanita, and got Paco to row us all ashore. Ricardo's driver was waiting with the car at *quatrocientos*. I asked him to let me off in the Petit Socco.

When we pulled up at the entrance to the casbah one of the men followed me out of the car. Ricardo leaned out and said, "Manuel is going to take care of you for a few days. You better be careful where you go."

"O.K.," I laughed, "I'll keep away from your girl friend."

I went up the alleyway, followed by Manuel.

Sherrif let me in. I asked him to feed Manuel and find him a bed if he intended spending the night. Sherrif led the way up through the maze of corridors and stairs. He said that the señorita was very unhappy because Ricardo would not let her come out to the ship to see me.

At the top of a short stairway I asked him to wait. I put my arm around his shoulder.

"Look, Sherrif. You're a good boy. Someday when I leave this part of the world I'll take you with me."

He beamed. "Master," he said with his fascinating accent, "with Allah's will, I follow you wherever you go."

"Well, we'll ask Allah. Right now, though, you have a tough job on your hands. You know what happened last night?"

The grin left his face. His body seemed to shrink as he drew his head down between his shoulders. I looked down and saw a big knife in his right fist. Slowly he ran a thumb along the blade. God, I thought. I'm glad he's a friend of mine.

"Someday, Allah willing, I'll cut their throats."

"Thanks, Sherrif. But I'll take care of them. You've got to look after the señorita. I'm afraid that these men might make trouble for her. You see, they want some information from me. If they know that I like the señorita, they might kidnap her and hold her until I tell them what they want to know. You understand?"

"Yes, Master."

"So from now on you must never let her out of your sight. No matter where she goes in the town, you go with her. When she's home, you lock everything up and don't let in anyone that the señorita or you don't know. Savvy?"

He mumbled something in Arabic and slid the knife back into the folds of his pantaloons. I felt that it would only be over his dead body that harm came to his mistress.

CHAPTER FIVE

W E RAN through a heavy ground swell all the way from Larache to Casablanca. I tried keeping well off the coast, but the Chucha rolled just the same. I figured that we would have to go halfway to America to get out of it. We sighted the coast again off Fedala. Off to port we saw a couple of Breton fishing vessels. I asked Paco if he knew how to cook lobster. He smiled and reminded me that he came from Mallorca, known as the home of the lobster.

I motored up alongside one of the ketches and eased the engines out of gear. The fishermen gathered along the rail and waved to us.

I called across and asked them if they wanted any cigarettes. Their chorus of *ouis* was so loud I gathered that they must have been on short rations for quite a while. I told Paco to get a basket, put a few cartons in it, and pass it across with the boathook. The Frenchmen took them out, and after fishing four beautiful lobsters out of their well, dropped them in the basket. The mate hauled them aboard. Inviting the fishermen to come and visit us if they came to Casablanca, I swung the Chucha away and headed south for the port.

We rounded the outside quay of Casablanca harbor late that afternoon. Slowing up opposite the pilot's shed, I asked them where we could moor. They told us we could either go alongside in the inner harbor or hook onto a buoy in the outer basin. I chose the latter berth as being less conspicuous.

The customs and police were soon on board. I showed them the ship's papers and told them I was in to buy oil and stores. They were satisfied, and after a drink they left. I told Paco to get the dinghy over the side, that I was going ashore and sample some French cooking.

It took me less than an hour to realize that Casablanca bore no living resemblance to Hollywood's version; so I bought Juanita some French perfume at Parisian prices, and returned to the ship and slept.

During the night I watched the barometer more than usual. It was dropping slightly, but the sunset was good. The following day I went ashore at ten, walked slowly up to the Hotel Miramar, and had a brandy in the bar. As far as I could see, no one was even interested in my existence. Two or three early topers were sitting in a corner. I asked the barman where the head was. He directed me out into the corridor, down two doors on the left. When I reached the corridor, I kept on walking until I came to a telephone booth. I asked the operator to get me Fez, and gave her the number there. She said it would take about ten minutes to make the connection. I told her I'd wait.

Finally I heard a faraway voice on the line. It was speaking in French.

"This is Brian Hart," I said in English. "You still interested in booking passage for the Canaries?"

"Oh, yes, Captain." The voice was louder now. "I'll join you day after tomorrow at five in the afternoon."

"Day after tomorrow is Wednesday. And you'll be on board at five P.M. Is that right?"

"That is right, Captain. And I hope we have a smooth passage."

"O.K. See you then."

I hung up, waited until no one was in the hall, and returned to the bar. The threesome was still arguing in the corner.

I ordered another brandy. It was a damn nuisance to have to lay over another day. Then I made a rapid calculation of 2 per cent of $500,000 and decided that it was worth it.

The barometer was down to 29.7 when we let go our lines and stood out into the black night. There was no wind, but the sun had set behind a wreath of mares' tails and low scud. I told Paco to make doubly sure everything was battened down. Outside the swell was still there. When it came, I prayed that it would blow up from the southwest.

I headed northwest, using the Fedala light as a marker. It was just after eight P.M. and the rendezvous was for nine. At eight-forty-five I took a bearing on Fedala light and a cross bearing on the Roches Noires light at Casablanca. I was eight miles off the coast and a mile south of the rendezvous point. I swung the Chucha to starboard and went slowly northward.

This was going to be something unusual. I had no idea of the type of ship I was to meet or who would be in her. All I had been told was that a ship would be somewhere in that position at nine o'clock bearing a green light over a red light at the masthead. She would show no other lights. When I saw it, I was to flash my masthead light twice, pause, then once more.

I asked Paco to take the wheel and threw the engines out of gear. I warned the rest of the crew to keep a sharp lookout. The wind was coming up now, from the northwest. The barometer was down to 29.5.

It began to rain. I was too anxious to go below to get a so'wester, but stood in the shelter of the bridge. The old saw about "rain before wind, get your tops'ls in," ran through my mind. Vividly I cursed the unknown joe in Fez. If he had only made it yesterday, we'd be rounding Cape Spartel now, with Tangier an hour away.

Harry in the stern gave a shout. I looked back and spotted a red light with a pale green light above it. The visibility was getting low, and I figured we had been damn lucky to pick him up. Perhaps our luck would hold. I told Paco to swing the ship while I flashed the signals. A few minutes later the red and green light went out and was replaced by a white one. It returned my signal. Paco kept the Chucha turning until she was nosing into the swell.

I followed the white light as it dodged toward us. I don't quite know what I expected to come out of the black night; I was certainly not prepared to see a dark cloud of canvas tower above me. Fascinated, I watched the ship make up along our lee side. With a rattle of blocks her mainsail came down and was gathered in. Then under an experienced hand she glided up amid-ships and sheered off, and there she lay alongside. A line shot out. Jim took it and made it fast forward. I recognized our visitor; she was a Breton fishing ketch. I couldn't help wondering if she had any lobster to trade.

A flashlight flared in my face. A voice demanded in English if I was Captain Hart. It was the voice of the telephone. I enlightened him and asked him aboard. The light went out and I gave a hand to a long lean individual who hopped across.

Unlike my Mallorcan friend Francisco Gonzales, this fellow was all business. He asked if he could see my passport. I went below and got it out of the safe. He declined to come with me. Using his flashlight, he looked at the photograph and again I blinked in the glare as he turned the light on me.

"Satisfied?" I asked, a little shortly.

"Yes." He succeeded in getting a bit of pleasantness into his voice. "I'm sorry, but you must understand we cannot take chances."

"O.K., but let's get on with it. I don't like the look of the weather."

My visitor called across to his ship. A sailor leaped aboard. He deposited a small sack on the deck. He returned and brought another. I picked up the first sack. For its size it was very heavy. I turned to the man beside me.

"Got a list of what's here?"

He reached into his wallet and extracted a typewritten sheet of paper. I ducked into the hatchway and flicked my lighter. The paper listed so many hundreds of napoleons, so many sovereigns, and so many U.S. twenty-dollar gold pieces.

"Am I supposed to count it?" I inquired.

"As you like."

"Well, I don't, particularly. In the first place, I don't like the idea of us being alongside like this any longer than absolutely necessary. Secondly, she's going to start blowing strong any minute now and we'll have to break contact. Besides, I'm not paying for this cargo; that's up to you and the boys in Tangier."

"I think that you'll find it's all there." I sensed that my friend was at last smiling.

By this time there were several sacks on the deck. He counted them, bade me *bon voyage,* and was over the side almost before I could say good-by. Black water came between us, and, sheeting home his foresail, the fisherman fell away to leeward and out of sight. I told Paco to leave his navigation lights off for a few minutes, open up, and set course for Cape Spartel.

I got a wrench out of the engine room and, going aft, unscrewed the plug from one of the spare forty-gallon drums of Diesel oil lashed on deck. I carried the sacks back, opened them one by one, and dropped the coins into the oil. The napoleons and sovereigns were easy. But the twenty-dollar gold pieces were a tight fit. After I had dropped the last coin in I screwed back to the plug and chucked the bags over the side. I returned to the bridge and put on our running lights.

The glass had steadied at 29.4.

I advised Paco to turn in. The wind was coming in hard now from the northwest. There was so much fine spray coming aboard it was difficult to know whether the rain had stopped or not. I kept the ship moving at fifteen knots until she started to pound. For three waves she would ride up and over, but the fourth and fifth she banged into and white water roared back as far as the wheelhouse. Unfortunately our course was four points off the wind and she was pounding and twisting with a vicious corkscrew motion. I shut her down to five knots but kept on course. The pounding eased considerably.

By three o'clock a full gale was blowing. I turned out the binnacle lamp and steered by the white breakers roaring down on us. The wind had driven the low scud before it, and a dying moon shone damply through the high cirrus. I closed the throttles until we just had steerage way. I kept dodging to starboard whenever I had the chance, until once I left her too long and a tremendous sea caught us on the port bow and almost swung us into the trough. She wouldn't come back with the helm so I opened the starboard engine wide and brought her up. I gave two blasts on the horn.

Paco crawled onto the bridge with the other two boys behind him. I told Harry to pump up his service tanks and check his engines, Jim to add an extra lashing to the oil drums aft, and Paco to make some coffee, strong.

An hour later I gave up any idea of trying to make our course and just kept the ship plunging into the heavy seas a point off the wind. She seemed to like taking them better this way than straight into them. Every so often a cross sea would catch us and it was only by full use of the lee engine that I was able to straighten her out.

I let Paco take the wheel for a time while I checked the chart. I figured that we were only about thirty miles off Casablanca, and wondered if it would be safe to turn around and run for it. It would take a pretty smart customs official to find that gold. But if he did, not only would I lose my ship, but I would probably find myself rotting in some Moroccan jail.

I checked such wishful thinking with the knowledge that we would never be able to turn the ship about in those seas anyway. Certainly not until daylight.

I went aft and, sheltered by the wheelhouse, watched the little ship take it. A huge white comber would come out of the night with the noise of a freight train. Before it struck, the wind would blow off the top and bang it into the superstructure. Then just when I thought the wave itself was going to crash down upon us the ship would miraculously nose up and into it, splitting it. A mountain of white froth would come hissing past on either side high above the rails. Then with a sickening plunge we'd go over and down the other side, as the stern reached for the stars.

As I watched the mighty seas my imagination began to work. What would happen if one engine died? Both? I thought I detected a different mutter from the exhaust. I went back and relieved Paco at the wheel. There you were too busy to think.

With the dawn the gale eased up a bit, but without its flattening pressure, the waves increased in height and began to break dangerously. One finally caught us just as we were lifting up to it and several tons of green water crashed down on the foredeck. The vegetable locker went over the side and the starboard anchor tore loose from its lashings and swung dangerously across the foredeck. Before I had time to call the men, Paco was beside me. From down below, he said, they thought the deck had caved in. We put a rope around him and he crawled forward and made the anchor fast. At one moment he disappeared from sight as we nosed into another wave. But as we lifted up, I could see the dark figure with one arm around the forestay and both feet against the winch.

When he returned to the bridge he was a bit gray about the gills. He showed me his torn hands.

Just after ten A.M. the port engine stopped. It died slowly, without protest, and as I watched the needle of the rev counter sag back to zero I called to Harry, who had been standing by in the wheelhouse, that I thought it was dirty oil; to go down and check his filters before he looked any farther.

I opened up the starboard engine and laid her off a point to starboard. I was afraid to keep her headed dead into the seas; if she fell off to port her helm would never bring her up. We'd fall off into the trough and be rolled over. I held the wheel for a time and found that when the waves were kept on the port bow she corkscrewed over them without shipping too much water, I called Paco, explained how to handle the ship, and watched him for a few moments to make sure he understood.

Fastening a rope's end about my waist, I crawled forward and unshackled the starboard anchor. I lifted the chain off the winch and brought the end aft. Jim took hold and we pulled out about five fathoms. I got out the best mooring rope we had and took several turns around the dinghy. I crossed another rope under the seats up and around the mooring line so that the loops would not slip off either end. We hauled up on deck our heaviest warp and made one end fast to the rope around the dinghy; the other end we attached to the anchor chain. Making sure the warp was passed outside all stanchions and obstructions on the starboard side, I went forward and looped the chain back over the winch and through the bits.

Down in the engine room, I found that Harry had taken down the filter, washed it in gasoline, and replaced it. He said that it had been very dirty. He pressed the electric starter. The engine turned over but wouldn't fire. He yelled something about air in the fuel line. He disconnected the fuel pipeline from the rear injector and again pressed the starter. I watched the open line. No sign of oil spitting out.

He disconnected another injector. Still no sign of fuel.

"The pump must be fouled up," he shouted above the din of the good engine.

"How long will it take to dismantle?" I asked, my mouth to his ear.

"Fifteen minutes in this sea."

When I asked him about the other engine, he shrugged his shoulders. He explained that he had been using the same tank to feed both.

"No telling how long she'll last," he shouted. "But she's bound to foul up sooner or later. This Diesel fuel is as heavy as pitch."

Telling him to get to work on the pump and be as quick as he could, I returned to the deck.

It was a dirty morning. Low clouds had come with the dawn and were chasing themselves across the sky. The barometer had started to rise, but the wind was steady from the northwest. I kept thinking it had swung to westward, and just when I had kidded myself that the worst was over, a heavy gust would shriek in from the old direction.

In the wheelhouse I looked at the chart and reckoned that we weren't more than forty miles northwest of Casablanca. During the past twelve hours we couldn't have averaged more than two knots. If I turned and ran for it, provided the good engine held out, I could find shelter within three or four hours. And I thought longingly of rounding that outside mole and the calm waters behind it; of pouring out a tall glass of whisky; of telling Paco not to disturb me, that I was going to sleep for twelve hours.

My mind returned to the tankful of gold on the afterdeck. Instinctively I looked back to see if it was still there. I almost wished it weren't.

"Stop kidding yourself," I muttered. "That starboard engine wouldn't hold out for three hours."

"What do you say?" Paco broke in.

"I was thinking that that good engine is going to pack in any moment now, so I'm going to put out the dinghy as a sea anchor and let Harry clean the filters and pumps. Then he can switch over to another tank and we'll probably make it."

The mate said something about bringing sails along next time. I told him to throttle back and let the ship drift back with the seas.

I called Harry up from the engine room to give Jim and me a hand. The three of us unshackled the dinghy from the crane and heaved it over the side. She bobbed about a bit, then rolled over as a white cap caught her. She came up on the other side of the wave, full of water but floating right side up. Being practically underwater, she drifted more slowly than we did, and as the space between us widened we fed out the warp.

Slowly the dinghy disappeared ahead in the froth. When the warp was all out, we fed the chain after it.

I went in and took the wheel. When I saw the black chain stretching out dead ahead, I knocked the starboard engine out of gear and waited. A long curving roller caught us and threw us around to starboard. I reached for the gear handle, but before I could get any power the chain pulled taut and gradually her bows swung back and we were ready for the next wave.

I watched her for a while. Each time the Chucha would fall off, the weight of the waterlogged dingy up ahead would bring her back, and we rode much drier and easier than we had with the engines. It was only a case of how long before the dinghy broke up under the terrific strain, or the ropes wore through. I passed word down to Harry to waste no time cleaning his engines.

Leaving Paco at the wheel—he assured me that riding to a sea anchor was old stuff to him—I went down and curled up in the cabin. I wanted a drink, badly. But I felt that sleep was more important at this stage. The gale could blow for three days, and a drink would only post-pone fatigue, not eliminate it.

We lay to the sea anchor till late afternoon. The engineer had cleaned out both filters and pumps and had his engines ticking over. But I told the men to have some hot food and take it easy so long as the anchor held out; I suspected we were in for a dirty night. During daylight I could see the chain stretching out over the bow from time to time and I didn't worry. But in the darkness the first knowledge that our dinghy had come apart would be when we were broadside to.

About an hour before sunset I again took over from the mate. I explained that I thought that it was about time we said good-by to our small boat, that it would be too dangerous to ride to it during the night. I asked him to go forward, tie himself to something solid, and ease out the chain until he came to the first shackle. He was then to knock this out and let the chain go over the side. I'd rather lose the fifteen fathoms of chain than take a chance of overrunning the warp with the engines and getting a rope in the propellers. With the weight of the chain on the end, the rope would disappear well below us. In these seas there was no question of trying to salvage the dinghy. We'd never get it aboard.

When Paco gave me the signal I put both engines in gear and let the ship fall off slightly to starboard. She seemed to take the seas better, so I eased her over even more until we were making north-northwest. I don't know whether the day's experience had given me more confidence in what the ship could stand or whether the seas had eased, but I finally got her up to north by west and crashing forward at something like four knots. For the first time that day I began to look forward to making Tangier.

The sun dropped behind a curtain of black clouds. The wind was definitely lighter, and I suggested to Paco that he pray to his particular saint for rain. He said that he'd been doing that all day,

"What for, rain?"

"No, just praying."

I looked at his sun-blackened features, his penetrating blue eyes. I knew that he'd learned to be a sailor the hard way. He had spent years sponge-fishing in the West Indies, and often during the night watches he had entertained me with tales of hurricanes he had sat out in those waters.

"You been afraid?" I asked him.

"You buy a schooner and I'll go with you anywhere. I don't like motorboats."

"I think you've got something there. But if we have much more of this, I'm going to buy me a *finca*. You can come and milk the cows."

Rather impatiently I waited for full night to come. If the wind kept easing I was pretty sure we'd get rain, and with it less seas and a break in the weather. If it commenced blowing again, it would continue all night and possibly the next day as well.

After supper I turned in. I wrote the night off as another bad one and told the crew to prepare themselves to stand by for any emergency.

The next thing I knew, Jim was shaking my shoulder. He said it was midnight, my trick at the wheel. I put on my shoes and jacket. And as I stood up I paused. I could hear the patter of water on the deck overhead. It couldn't be sea water; it was too steady and there wasn't the howl of the wind bringing it aboard.

Rain.

CHAPTER SIX

RICARDO must have had a spotter sitting on Cape Spartel watching for us, for he was out in the bay in his launch waiting when we rounded the quay at Tangier.

"What's the matter?" I yelled across to him. "You worried?"

"Geez, you're twenty-four hours late."

"You're telling me? Don't you ever check up on the weather?"

"It hasn't been bad," he retorted.

"Next time open the window and look out."

As soon as the port doctor had come alongside and cleared us, Ricardo climbed aboard. We rigged up a hose and pumped the oil out of the drum aft into one of the tanks. I told Harry to go to work with a hammer and cold chisel and cut the top off the drum.

As I lead Ricardo below I warned him that there would be some extra running expenses this trip.

"What for?"

"A new dinghy, some rope, chain, and an oil drum."

He laughed and said he guessed he would be able to afford it.

That evening we emptied the drum. Ricardo had brought out four of his men, and from the way their pockets sagged, they weren't going to rely on their fists if any highjackers came along. Fishing boats that came anywhere close to us were carefully watched.

When we had the last coin wiped off and stowed away in the sacks that Ricardo had brought with him, I asked if he was taking it ashore legally or the hard way. He explained that from now on this was legal gold; the customs had an officer waiting on the quay and it would be deposited in their vaults.

"Won't they want to know where it came from?" I demanded.

"That's all been arranged. This gold came from South America."

"In this ship? They're not stupid."

"It could come in a rowboat for all they care. All they want to know is that it came by sea. They slap on their twelve-per-cent duty and everybody's happy."

"That's a big cut," I ventured.

"Sure. But I have to earn a living in this town. I might get away with smuggling it in once or twice, but no more. The customs here take a straight twelve per cent of everything that comes in or leaves the port. We simply add that to our charges."

When he had transferred the gold to his launch he asked me if he could give me a ride ashore.

"Thanks just the same, but from now on that stuff is your baby. I won't even ride ashore with it. When you're through with the launch, send it back for me."

"Oh, by the way, I've got some bad news for you. Our friend Francisco Gonzales got himself shot up in Palma."

"What?"

"Yeah. One of our men arrived this afternoon and told us they found Francisco out on the wharf a couple of nights ago with a bullet through his head. He had a gun in his hand."

"Don't kid me. Francisco kill himself? He's not the type."

"I'm only telling you what I heard. They say he'd been rolling around the town drunk as hell not long before he was found dead."

The launch started to drift away. Ricardo eased in the gear and it sputtered toward the shore. I was so stunned by the news that I could think of nothing further to say. I stood staring at the swirling black water where the boat had been.

So that's the way they want to play it.

I went down into the cabin and opened the safe. I took out a battered ledger and laid it on the table. I poured out half a glass of whisky, topping it with water. I sat down, flipped through the pages until I came to the last entry, and below it wrote, "November 23-28, Casablanca." Under the column of figures I put "$10,000." I added this to the grand total. It came to something over $135,000. Using the back page of the book, I worked out a third of this figure, the amount paid out as the crew's share. This left something not far under $100,000. Not bad; but not as good as I had hoped to have before I quit. There was, of course, the value of the ship to be added, but there was also a good piece of it missing. The champagne, the dinners and night clubs with Juanita.

I called the crew down to the cabin and told them about Francisco. Paco was the only one who appreciated the significance of it. The other two remembered him as a mysterious and practically unknown character who came out of the night to meet us. I doubt whether they would have recognized him by daylight. No one spoke.

I glanced away from the hard glint in Paco's eyes and said, "I'm going up to Mallorca for a few days, but first we'll square off for the last voyage. We grossed ten thousand dollars on the trip—about twice what we usually make. I haven't worked out the expenses yet and haven't time now. I'll do that when I return. Anyway, I imagine they'll run about four hundred dollars. If there's any difference, I'll apply it against our next run. That leaves ninety-six hundred, of which your fellows receive one-third among you. I make that ten-sixty-six per man. Everybody happy?"

Harry and Jim nodded. Paco's mind was about five hundred miles up the coast. I made a mental note to have a talk with him before I left. Gonzales and he had been old friends.

"I'll have this deposited in your accounts when I go ashore," I concluded.

I made a point of never keeping more than expense money on board once we'd returned to port. One never knew when the ship might be seized. I had opened bank accounts for each member of the crew when he signed on and simply asked Ricardo Lewis to deposit their share at the end of each trip. I figured that if the men had to go up and draw out their money every time they wanted some, there would be more left when the game was over.

"What are you doing with all this dough?" I asked Harry. I liked to keep posted on how the crew lived ashore. They could spend their earnings as they pleased, but I knew Tangier. With that kind of cash, there were many temptations, and I'd had too many bitter experiences with drunken sailors.

"I'm stashing it away. I'm still frightened of that desk job we were discussing the other night. By the way, can this bank we use, Moses Pariente's, transfer cash to the States?"

"Sure, he has correspondents all over the world."

"What a name for a bank!"

"As safe as they come. Why the grandfather, or maybe it was the great-grandfather, staked Nelson just before the battle of Trafalgar. Apparently the British fleet took three weeks to beat their way through from the Med, and when they arrived here they were starving."

"Ever collect?"

"I understand it took forty or fifty years, but Queen Victoria finally came through."

"I guess he can take care of me, then."

Jim had been with me for the past couple of years and was completely dependable. But I knew little of his past life other than that somewhere in the States he had a wife. Apparently it hadn't worked out, and a good share of his earnings went to keeping his mistake in the manner to which she pretended she was accustomed.

As for Paco, he had a wife and eight children in Mallorca. Just how he had got around to siring so many was a mystery. As far as I could figure out, the amount of time he'd spent at home during the past twenty years wouldn't add up to three months.

By this time Ricardo's launch had returned and I could hear the boatmen talking on deck. I threw a few clothes in a bag, locked the safe, and went up. I asked Paco to look after things and told him I'd return the following morning.

Ricardo was in his shop when I got up to the town. There was the usual crowd of sailors, would-be sailors, and lesser hangers-on milling about the place. I told him that I wanted to speak with him and led the way into his office. I tossed my passport on his desk and sat down.

"Have one of your boys get me a visa for Spain tomorrow," I said.

"What the hell, you going to take a holiday at last?"

"Yes. Between you and me, I've got some things I want to look into in Palma."

"Don't be a damn fool and stick your neck out. Here, have a drink and forget about it."

He reached behind him and took a bottle off a dirty bookshelf. He set out two small glasses. I picked mine up and wiped it out with my handkerchief. He filled it with whisky. I knocked it back.

"You go nosing around Mallorca," he said, "and you'll find yourself standing on bottom with a lot of lead wired to your feet. For all we know, Francisco *may* have ..."

"Don't be a damn fool. You don't believe it yourself, so why kid me?"

"So what? They find out he's been cutting into Aguzado's territory. They take him out, get him drunk, and knock him off. Just what the hell do you think you can do about it? What can I do about it? Anybody? Aguzado never leaves Spain, so we can't catch him outside. And in Spain he's so well protected you'd never be able to do anything to him and get away with it. I tell you, it's not worth it."

"You know who Francisco Gonzales was?"

"Sure, he was a hell of a good guy to be working with up there. Kept his mouth shut, kept us out of trouble, and paid on the nail."

"He was also Juanita's father."

"Madre de Dios!"

This time I filled the glasses.

"And you know what's going to happen?" I continued. "When Juanita hears about her father, she's going to put two and two together and it's going to make five. She's going to think I squealed the other night. And she's going to keep on thinking that, no matter what anyone tells her. I've got to *prove* to her that she's wrong."

Ricardo picked up the passport, pulled open the top drawer of the desk, dropped it in, and locked the drawer.

"I'll have your visa tomorrow afternoon. In the meantime, go get drunk and sleep it off. Maybe I can figure something out."

"Thanks, Ricardo." I stood up. "You might also find out when the next Iberia plane leaves for Madrid. From there I can pick up a plane to Palma."

❊ ❊ ❊

We drove out toward Cape Spartel. Just before reaching the light-house, we turned left and followed a narrow road that ran south along the coast. We passed several wide stretches of sandy beach, finally pulling up back of a little cove. I drove the car well off the road, took out the picnic baskets, and locked the car.

Juanita scrambled down the rocks. When she reached the narrow beach, she kicked off her slippers and ran barefoot into the surf.

"Ouch!" she screamed. "It's cold!"

I selected a spot under a high cliff. It was sheltered from the wind and trapped the hot sun. I unpacked the champagne and dropped it in a quiet pool of water.

"You going to swim?" I called out.

"Well …"

"Don't be a softy. Last one in doesn't drink."

She ran up to me and, digging in her enormous handbag, brought forth a bathing suit.

"What's that for, to keep you warm?" I laughed.

I glanced up and down the deserted coast.

"This is North Africa, not the Costa Brava," I said.

I dove into a long breaking comber. The cold was paralyzing. I swam out until my legs felt like two chunks of ice, then turned and headed back to the beach. She was just behind me, her long black hair streaming out in the surf. She turned when I did and beat me to the shore. She stood waiting for me.

"God," I murmured. "Have you ever seen anything more beautiful?" Her body was sheathed in a mantle of diamonds as the strong sun danced and played about her wet skin. I knelt and touched my forehead to the sand.

"What are you doing?" she demanded gaily.

"I am giving praise to Allah, the All-Knowing, for giving you to me."

She ran over, knelt down in front of me, and looked searchingly into my eyes.

"And every morning I thank God that He has brought you to me."

We walked back to our shelter, stretched out naked on the hot sand, and let the sun bake the chill out of our bodies. Time seemed to pause as we lay beside each other, not speaking, not thinking, our eyes closed to the glare. But the physical senses would not relax. I turned toward her. The salt on her skin tasted like bitter wine as I covered her body with kisses.

I followed the long slender throat down till it disappeared in the snowy valley between the breasts that, even though she lay on her back, proudly bore their shape. I watched the golden nipples come to life.

"You are very, very beautiful, Juanita *mía*."

"It is only because you love me."

"No. Because I love you, you are *preciosa* to me. But to all the world you are beautiful."

"No. No. I am too big here, and too flat here, too long here ..."

"And you have too much fire."

She laughed. "And my legs, they're too long and thin."

"All right. I will ask Allah to give you breasts like acorns, a stomach thick and short, and legs like a Moorish peasant woman."

"Would you still love me?"

"If Allah left the fire."

"But you have loved many more beautiful women. And when you go back to America you will forget me. Why do you laugh?"

"I was thinking of the havoc you're going to cause when America sees you. I'm going to get a golden collar and chain so no one can take you away from me."

"But I am your woman. I would never leave you."

Slowly she pressed me backward, got to her knees, and stared down at me.

"But you too are beautiful. You could have any woman you wanted."

"Thanks. It hasn't worked out that way."

Her fingertips were shot with fire as she ran them over my body.

"You are so thin; too thin. I will feed you. I must cover these ribs, these thick muscles…"

Gradually the roar of the surf receded, was replaced by the pounding of our blood. The heat of the sun was as nothing to the fire that swam up through her body.

"Oh, my darling, darling," she whispered. "Is it wrong that I want you, want you so badly?"

I reached up and held her swelling breasts as slowly, tantalizingly we made love until that tremendously complete moment engulfed us and the very sands seemed to shift. I drew her body, relaxing, down to my body, her face to my face. I could feel her warm tears as they ran down my cheek.

An hour before sunset the heat left the day and it began to get cold. We dressed, packed our bags, and climbed back up to the car. My skin prickled with the salt and the sun. I felt deliciously weary and happy.

But as we drove back to Tangier in the half-light, my mind kept swinging back to Francisco, to Palma and the whole complicated messy situation that I couldn't avoid much longer. She sat tightly beside me.

We turned up past the Emsalla Gardens, boarded up for the winter. I asked her what she would like to do.

"Suddenly you are very sad," she said. "Let's go and drink and eat and be gay."

"O.K. Where will it be?"

She thought for a moment. "Not the Villa. The food there is perfect, but it's not gay. Besides, it's too cold to sit outside. I know—we'll go to Lipsos."

"And where might that be?"

"Oh, you have never been there?"

"No."

"I am so happy! I can take you there for the first time. It is a Spanish restaurant and now they have some very good dancers from Seville."

"Swell. You direct me."

"First we will go to Dan's Bar and have a drink, because I think you will like that very much. Then we will send the car away and we'll get a taxi, because Lipsos is in the casbah. And after you are very drunk on wine and flamencos and very happy, I'll make you walk home with me, because by then the cold air will be good for you and we can make love all night."

She was bubbling over with enthusiasm.

Late that night, as I held her tightly in my arms, I told her that her father was dead.

Ricardo drove me out to the airport. It was not until we were walking around the enclosure waiting for the Iberia plane to gas up that he asked me how Juanita had taken it.

"Pretty grim."

"You want to talk about it?" he asked after a pause.

"Nothing to talk about. She blames me."

"My God, how can she do that? Doesn't she realize that you were like a son to the old guy? Besides, you were down in Casablanca."

"Oh, hell, she doesn't think I pulled the trigger. You see, it goes back to a session we had some weeks ago. She wanted me to quit. She said she knew something was going to happen. Well, I ended up by saying that I would—after another trip or so. Then I got beat up. And she knew why. Sherrif was there, you remember, and he told her. But what do I do about it? Nothing, she claims. I bugger off to Casablanca because all I can think of is money, money, more money. I don't even warn her father."

"I telephoned him that very morning," Ricardo broke in. "I told Francisco what was going on and told him to keep his eyes open."

"Sure, I know. I told her that. But about midnight last night it didn't sound as convincing as it does now. So there it is. If I'd quit, she says, when she begged me to, none of this would have happened. Give me an answer to that one and even I'll feel better."

"The hell it wouldn't. We'd have Summers or one of the other skippers delivering to Francisco the moment you stopped."

"I pointed that out, too. In reply she pulled out a letter she had recently received from her father in which he said that I had promised to bring her to Mallorca and that the three of us were going on some damn fool life-long fiesta. As I told you the other day, she hasn't spoken to him for over a year. And I can see where that doesn't make her feel any better now, either. What frightens me is that not once did she break down. I know that girl, and I'm afraid that when she cracks, she's going to crack wide open."

"Did you tell her he was supposed to have committed suicide?"

"Good God, no. Why upset her more with that stupid rumor?"

Finally the call came over the loud-speaker for *los pasaje-ros* to take their seats.

"And you know what she threw at me just before I left her? She said that it was mighty coincidental that her father had been killed only a few days after they had tried to beat his name out of me. And I thought the girl loved me. I've certainly got a lot to learn about Spanish women."

"Well, isn't that what you expected?" Ricardo said. "That's exactly what you said she'd do."

"I know, but I kind of hoped she wouldn't."

"What are you going to do about it?" Ricardo asked, as we shook hands.

"No use hanging around here biting my nails off. I'm going to Palma and find the son-of-a-bitch that killed Francisco and get a confession written in his own blood."

"Take care of yourself," he warned me.

CHAPTER SEVEN

I HADN'T had time to cable my old friend Tomás Cazoleta that I was coming; even *urgente* cables take two days to reach Palma. So when the Douglas finally decanted us in Mallorca, I rode into the city in the company's *camión,* picked up a taxi outside the Formentor Bar, and drove out to the Hotel Victoria.

Roberto, the manager, was hovering about the desk, and when he saw me he rushed over and greeted me with his inimitable Mallorcan enthusiasm. He said that they were full up but that he would find me a bed even if he had to give up his own.

"And the señora?" I inquired. Roberto had a very, very beautiful wife.

He roared with laughter.

"Ah, señor, how well you know our ancient customs! Of course, everything I have is yours."

"No, no," I protested. "I'm asking how she is."

Still chuckling, he told me to go and have a drink while he arranged things.

I bypassed the bar and went into a telephone booth. I called Tomás, found him in, and told him I was in town and wanted to see him. He said he had an engagement that night for dinner but would be around right afterward. I then called the consul, told him I had just arrived, and asked whether he had any mail for me. I didn't expect any, but I wanted as many people as possible to know that I was in town. If there were going to be any night rides, I certainly wanted them to be public ones.

I waited for Tomás in the hotel. I wanted to find out from him what was going on before I ran into certain individuals and had to answer questions.

It was too cold to sit in the patio, so I took him up to the room. I poured out a couple of brandies, slipped off my shoes, and sprawled on the bed.

"What do you know about Francisco Gonzales?" I asked after we had exhausted the interminable questions about the state of health of our families and friends.

"So that's why you came up."

"Yeah. In Tangier they say he knocked himself off. I don't believe it."

"Well, the police here do. They had a hell of a job getting a priest to bury him."

"Who did it?"

"My guess is that it was one of Carlos Aguzado's men."

"Aguzado?"

"No. He doesn't touch anything like that himself."

"What makes you think it was one of his men?"

"Well, Aguzado found out the other day that Francisco had been running contraband into Andraitx, his own back yard, so to speak."

"Who told him?"

"No one. It was just a damn unfortunate chain of circumstances. The other morning a fishing boat was coming in after picking up a load of contraband outside. A couple of miles off the coast his engine conked out. It was beginning to get light and he got his wind up. He was about to dump his cargo over the side when he spotted another trawler heading for the port. He got them to give him a tow. When he got in, he landed his cargo safely enough, but the damn fool dumped a sack of coffee onto the other ship. Told the skipper it was to pay for the tow.

"Well, you can imagine how that sort of thing would get around the water front. Everybody knew that it was one of Francisco's boats that broke down. And of course someone tells Aguzado. And Aguzado knows damn well that sack of coffee didn't come up with the fish trawl.

"So he gets to thinking about it. He meets Francisco the next day in the port and accuses him of running contraband into Andraitx. Francisco acts surprised and says he can't help it if one of his skippers runs a little cargo in from time to time. Hell, he says, there isn't a fishing boat on the island that doesn't.

"But this doesn't satisfy Aguzado. He knows damn well the small amounts the fishermen run on their own hook haven't flooded his market. So that night or the next somebody breaks into a couple of Francisco's houses. In the cellar of one, they find enough cigarettes to supply the island for six months. As a matter of fact, Francisco was waiting for a schooner to take them over and dump them in Barcelona.

"A couple of days later they find old Francisco down here on the wharf with a hole in his head."

I got up off the bed and refilled the glasses. I turned Tomás' story over in my mind. Knowing Tomás, I knew it was the truth or very close to it. He and I had worked together in the early days when I used to sail right into Palma Harbor with a load of contraband and drop the hook in the shadow of the Hotel Mediterráneo. As soon as night fell he would come out in his rowboat and run it ashore to the strains of the dance band from the hotel. He was the fairest man I ever dealt with. If he couldn't pay you one trip, you knew you'd get your money the next. In fact, often when I was broke he'd advance me money against future deliveries. But when smuggling became big business, he dropped out. He had made some money in real estate and said he wasn't going to risk it competing with the big boys.

Another thing that attracted me to Tomás was the fact that long ago he had worked in the United States for some years. This experience had not only armed him with an incredible vocabulary of American slang, but it had taught him to think more like a foreigner than a native. And he was able to explain and interpret the peculiar characteristics of the Spanish mind, which often baffled me.

"O.K.," I said finally. "You don't know who did it. So let me put it this way: Who do you *think* did it?"

I recalled that Francisco had also been a close friend of his. In fact, it was Tomás who first brought Francisco and me together.

He took the cigar out of his mouth, looked at the ash for a moment, decided that it wouldn't hold any longer, and knocked it off into the ash tray.

"Well," he leaned back and stared at the ceiling, "it's one of three men: Pablo Despojo, Juan Magdellán, or Manuel Carma."

"Despojo, eh? I remember that son-of-a-bitch. Is he in town?"

"He was. Why, do you know him?"

I rubbed the back of my neck and laughed. It was still mighty tender. "I know him. But that's another story. I'll tell you about it sometime. Go on."

"Despojo was here. I saw him the day of Francisco's funeral. Juan and Manuel *went* to the funeral."

"Without using too many four-letter words, describe them to me."

"Pablo Despojo you seem to know," Tomás said. "He is one of Aguzado's right-hand men. But he's not so important in the business as Juan. Juan is Aguzado's brother-in-law, and if Carlos ever decided to retire, Juan would take over control. Manuel is the man who looks after the fishing fleet and crews. He's a smart engineer, but he has little or nothing to do with the *negocios*. For my money, Manuel should be at the bottom of the list."

"What makes you think it was one of those three?" I asked. "Why wouldn't Aguzado pay some goon to do the job?"

"He's too smart. He knows that if he got someone outside to do it, he'd be paying for the rest of his life. For the same reason, it wasn't one of the lesser boys in the organization."

"Well, that makes it easier."

I dug down in my wallet and brought out a bit of paper. Printed on it was one name, Pablo Despojo. Beneath it I wrote Juan Magdellán and Manuel Carma.

"Now let's reconstruct the scene of the crime."

"You make it sound like a detective story," Tomás said with a short laugh.

"When was Francisco last seen alive?"

"Pepe, the barman down at the Bodega, said he had to throw Francisco out about eleven o'clock. He had been there drinking all evening and most of the afternoon. He seemed to be unhappy about something."

"Unhappy about his stock being discovered."

"Maybe. Anyway, when he started to abuse the cash-paying customers, Pepe called the boss and together they got him out and into a taxi. They told the driver to take him home. The police checked on the driver. He told them that Francisco had stopped the car at the end of the Borne, paid him ten pesetas, and walked away. That's the last anyone saw of him."

"That would be about eleven-thirty. Damn few people out in the Borne at that hour. He could have walked down to the wharf without anybody seeing him."

"He could have," Tomás said.

"But you don't think so."

"No. In the first place, according to Pepe, he could hardly walk when he left the Bodega. In the second place, you know Francisco. When he has a skinful he makes so much noise he *couldn't* go that distance without someone hearing him. For instance, he would have had some ripe comments to make to the *guardia* at the entrance to the decks."

"So Francisco disappears at eleven-thirty. When was he found?"

"Two *guardias* picked him up about four A.M. They were making their usual patrol along the wharf. They found him lying right out in the roadway that runs along the top of the dock."

"How then did he get there? Could he have been taken out in a car?" I asked.

"No. The *guardia* at the gate would have noticed a car."

"Could someone have carried him?"

"Hardly. You see, everybody knows there's a man stationed at the gates. I don't think anyone would have taken the risk."

"Might have rowed him out in a boat," I suggested.

"You've got something there. I never thought of it. They could have put him aboard from any one of a dozen beaches in the bay and not been seen, then rowed him across to the dock."

"Let's figure it happened this way, then: Francisco was stumbling around the end of the Borne around eleven-thirty. He runs into Despojo, Magdellán, or Carma, maybe even Aguzado himself. He accuses them of breaking into his house. They have a fight. One of them pulls a gun and lets him have it. They dump him into a car, drive along until they find a quiet beach, get a rowboat to take him across to the quay. They wait until no one is around, hoist him up and dump him on top of the dock, wipe the gun butt clean, open his hand, and put it in it."

"It's a good story. But there's one thing wrong with it," Tomás replied. "If anyone shot off a gun around midnight in that part of the city, fifty people would hear it. There's the Café Torredor on the corner, and there's always a crowd in the bar at that hour."

"Sure, and they're making so much noise they don't hear anything."

"And above the café is Señora Dolores' establishment. Probably just as crowded, but as a rule the boys don't go up there to make noise."

"Señora Dolores?" I asked. "She's a new one since my days here."

"Yeah, she came over from Valencia last summer. I'll take you up one night. She's just imported a couple of babes from Marseilles who're worth looking at."

"Thanks, but I prefer the local product."

"She's got those too. But as I was saying, Francisco wasn't shot in that neighborhood. But he could have run into one of our friends, who somehow enticed him into a car, drove him outside the city, knocked him off, and rowed him out to the quay."

"I know how easy it is to get into the wrong car," I observed feelingly. I looked at my watch. It was well after two.

"To hell with it," I said. "We've done enough for one night. Let's go to bed."

I asked Tomás to try to find out just where the three men he had mentioned had spent the night of Francisco's death.

He laughed.

"You think I'm the *comandante de policía?*"

"Francisco had a lot of friends."

He said he'd make some inquiries in the morning. I asked him to meet me at the Bodega around two the next day.

The only information Tomás had been able to pick up when I saw him the following afternoon was that both Aguzado and his brother-in-law had been out of the city the night Francisco was killed.

"They alibi each other?" I said with a smile.

Tomás laughed. "No. But Aguzado's driver said he took them both to Andraitx. Came back the next morning."

"Have you checked on that?"

"I've sent a man down there to find out. That's easy enough. I can't get a line on the other two. The only thing that I picked up is that Despojo has a girl friend who works at Señora Dolores'."

"That's it!" I hit the bar with my fist. "Despojo is calling on his girl friend, sees Francisco out the window, nips out of her bed, knocks him off, and is back beside her before she rolls over."

"Geez, you got a mind."

"Tonight it will be business with pleasure. We'll go to Señora Dolores'."

And we did. We entered the establishment through the main patio. Tomás said that you could go up through the bar, but I didn't want all the hams there to see us. A dim light shone from an iron lantern hanging in the center of the patio. We climbed the outside staircase, paused on the first balcony, and banged on a heavy door. It opened with a bright flash of light and a girl told us to come in. We waited while she closed the door, then followed her down a wide hallway. We entered a large room, and as we did so somebody started pounding on a piano. A tall, thin woman came out of the shadows and greeted Tomás. She had enough gold around her wrists and neck to put the country back on the gold standard. It was the real McCoy, too. You could tell by the dull clunk of the bracelets when she shook hands.

Tomás introduced me. Then, while he continued to speak to the señora, I sauntered across the room and looked around. Three or four women were sprawled about, and each in turn gave me the big smile. One got up and ran her hands down her ribs, either to smooth down her dress or to show off her jacked-up chest. She rocked over on her six-inch heels and asked for a cigarette. I shook one out and lit it for her. I glanced at her face over the flame of the lighter. She was on the downgrade and going fast. I put the lighter back into my pocket and handed her the package of cigarettes. I walked back to Tomás.

"What gives?" I asked.

"The señora has a girl here who is a good dancer. You want to see a flamenco?"

"Why not? But let's have a private showing. Those old bags are terrible."

"O.K. You go have a drink and I'll see what I can arrange."

"They got a bar up here?"

"Through that door. I'll join you in a few minutes."

I entered a small room across the end of which stretched a bar. Perched on one of the three stools was the barman, his head on his hands, asleep.

"O.K., Tony, time to get up," I said as I dragged out a stool.

He jerked awake with a smile. I ordered a cognac and soda water.

Tomás came in. He explained that the señora had sent out for a guitarist.

I winked at him and said in Spanish, "I thought Despojo was going to meet us here tonight."

Tomás said, "Oh."

"Maybe he doesn't know where it is. Did you tell him?"

"No, I haven't seen him for a few days."

The barman, who had been pouring out another drink, said, "Oh, Señor Despojo knows this place well."

"I guess he couldn't make it, then," I said. I turned back to Tomás and continued to practice my Spanish. At last he caught on. In the middle of a conversation about women in general he turned to the barman and asked if Despojo's girl was in tonight.

"Oh, yes," he said. "She's the new dancer."

We accompanied the señora up a flight of stairs. Here soft carpets covered the tiles and the furnishings were as rich as those below had been tawdry.

"The carriage-trade department," I said to Tomás as we turned into one of the rooms. Around the walls were two or three couches. They looked like imported jobs, but when I sat down in one the hard springs revealed their local manufacture. An elderly individual was sitting on the edge of a chair fingering a guitar. Standing beside him, her hands on her hips, her toe beating time, was one of the most beautiful girls I have ever seen.

The señora told Tomás to ring the bell if we wanted anything. She went out. He walked over and spoke to the girl in the Mallorcan dialect. And from the way she laughed and the sly comments the musician interposed from time to time, the conversation must have been pretty sultry.

Finally the man strung his notes together and strummed a haunting flamenco. The girl stepped forward, beating out the rapid tempo with her hands. When it had warmed up to her liking, she started to sing. Her voice was low and husky for a Spaniard. The ballad, as far as I could make out, concerned the loss of her sombrero. At the end of each verse she would hold the last note, her arms stretched out toward us until you thought she must collapse.

Then with a bright laugh she would catch hold of the ends of her mantilla and whirl away in the mad dance of the flamenco. As suddenly as it had begun she would finish a pirouette with a ballerina's grace on one knee, her head bent down, black hair covering her face.

As she arose she began again, softly, to tell us how much she had loved her sombrero.

I leaned over toward Tomás.

OUT OF THE SEA

"Why haven't you told me about her? I've never seen anything like it, and I've seen a lot of flamencos."

"She's just one of our local girls." He gave a pronounced shrug.

"Don't kid me, you rat. If you had known she was here you'd have bought the joint to get her. Besides, she's no Mallorcan—she's from Seville."

Whether it was because we were talking or whether it was the end anyway, the dance came to a whirling finish. I stood up clapping and calling out, *"Olé!"* Tomás, sitting back, was laughing.

"Where do you think you are, in the Villá Rosa in Madrid?"

"By God! And that's where that girl ought to be," I retorted.

I went over and left my finger on the bell button for a few seconds. I requested the musician to play an old favorite of mine, a *sevillana*. I asked the girl what her name was.

"Rosita Ruano." That haunting, husky voice.

"A lovely name for a lovely girl."

She glanced up at me, her black eyes laughing, her sparkling teeth ever more white than the living paleness of her skin.

The barman finally appeared at the door. I asked him to bring up two bottles of Codorniu Seco. I offered her a cigarette. She refused, saying that she didn't smoke. I asked her where she got the husky voice. This didn't amuse her; apparently to be good, Spanish singers must have sharp sopranos. I hastened to assure her that where I came from a voice like hers was worth a fortune.

"Then I'll sing you another song."

She walked over and spoke to the guitarist. He started several melodies. She checked him, hummed for a while. Finally they got together and she sang to us about some man who had made love to her one night and departed with the dawn, and how she had spent the rest of her life waiting for his return. As before she ended each verse with a dance, but this time it was mostly heel and hand work, the clack of her shoes and the clap of her hands startling the echoes.

She collapsed on the couch beside me.

"Oof, *mucho calor.*"

"This will cool you off." I handed her a glass of champagne. "You speak English?"

"*No, Señor.*"

"I'm going to the can," I said to Tomás in English. "Try to find out if this is really that rat's girl friend. I can't believe the bastard can be so lucky."

I went out into the hall and down the stairs. A maid was sitting by the front door. I told her that I wished to speak to the señora. When Dolores arrived she asked me how I liked Rosita. Thinking of the bill, I restrained my enthusiasm and said I thought she was a fair dancer but that her voice was too low. I felt like a heel, but I knew this hard-faced woman would add another hundred pesetas for every superlative I used.

Getting right down to it, I asked her if I could have the girl for the night.

"And stay here?"

"Sure."

She glanced at her watch. She said that it would be two hundred pesetas.

"You want it now?"

"If you like."

I took out two century notes and handed them over. I asked how much more I owed for the dancing. She said that Tomás had taken care of that. I told her I'd straighten out for the wine in the morning. I gathered that she knew Tomás well enough to extend me that much credit.

Upstairs I found him and the girl hard at it in the Mallorcan patois. The guitarist was slumped over his instrument half asleep. I gave him fifty pesetas and told him he could go home.

Rosita followed him out. Tomás explained that he had sent her down for another bottle.

"She's the girl, all right," he said as soon as the door had closed. "Seems Despojo discovered her one night out in San Antonio. You remember that district just outside of Palma where they specialize in flamencos? It's the old story. She's Andalusian and her father was a fisherman and got drowned and she has to help support her mother and a raft of kids. I don't believe a word of it."

"But what the hell is she doing in this high-priced bordello if Despojo is keeping her?"

"Apparently he's pretty tight with the dough. He only comes around once in a while. Besides, I don't think she likes him very much. I imagine she hopes to make enough on the side to become independent. Then she can tell him to go blow."

"Well, he won't be around tonight."

"Why?"

"I just bought her for the next eight hours."

"You beat me to it." Tomás laughed and got up. "I thought you came here on business."

"Yeah. But I believe in doing business the hard way."

"Geez, they must grow a lot of corn where you come from."

Rosita returned with another bottle.

"Only one?" I inquired.

"You've had enough."

"Well, I'll give you three quarters. Let's go somewhere and open it."

She turned to Tomás and said good-by. Dolores must have tipped her off as to who her guest for the night was.

"Don't hurry me, babe," he muttered in English, looking for his hat. "See you tomorrow. That is, if you get up in time," he flung over his shoulder at me.

"Not sore, are you?"

At the door he turned and gave me a wink. Rosita took my hand and led me up to the third floor.

CHAPTER EIGHT

A S THE CITY climbed out of bed and noisily stretched itself,
I woke up and looked at the black hair of the girl asleep
beside me in the wide bed. As I watched, her eyelids fluttered
open, and she smiled.

I sat up and looked for a drink. My tongue was on fire. I
asked Rosita how one went about getting some coffee sent up.
She wrapped a negligee around herself and went out into the hall.
I found the bathroom and ran a bath. When she came back, I
asked her if the tap water was drinkable.

"*Pobrecito,* you drink too much champagne. Now you are
thirsty and have a headache."

"It was worth it."

She took a bottle of water out of a cabinet and gave me two
small pills. I swallowed the pills and half the water. As I lit a cigarette I glanced across at her. Her naturalness fascinated me as she
stepped out of her negligee and drew on her stockings. She had
the lithe figure of the dancer; the firmly muscled legs and thighs,
the flat hard stomach. The small breasts and the nipples, still tiny,
still pink, were those of a very young girl. She was very exciting.
So why, at that particular moment, was I thinking of Juanita?

She misunderstood the quizzical expression on my face.

"In one minute you will feel better," she said, dancing over
and throwing wide the shutters.

"And not only feel better, but if you don't put something on
I'll feel strong enough to make love to you."

"I would like that," she laughed.

Whether it was the pills, the bath, or the coffee, by the time I was dressed the headache had disappeared and the fire was nearly out.

Rosita was sitting in the sun manicuring her nails. I pulled up a chair opposite her and lit a cigarette.

"You happy here?" I asked.

She looked up at me. "Last night I was very happy."

"Yo también, lo sabes," I replied. "But is every night like last night?"

She smiled and slowly shook her head.

"Why don't you leave?"

"I have to live."

"You can make a good living dancing."

"I've tried. In Mallorca there are many dancers."

"Why don't you marry one of your better clients and let him take care of you?"

"And have six children and get fat before I'm thirty?" She wrinkled her nose.

"All right. Suppose I get you a good job in a good cabaret. Would you settle down and work?"

She reached over and took my hand.

"If you will come and see me I'll go and work anywhere."

"Hold it, *preciosa,*" I put in. "I've got a girl friend."

Slowly she withdrew her hand. Tears welled up in her eyes. But I knew that come tomorrow, she'd probably forget what I even looked like.

"What about this fellow Despojo?" I went on. "Isn't he your boy friend?"

"He's been very good to me."

"How? By getting you a job here?" I was rather bitter. "Why doesn't the son-of-a-bitch take care of you?"

Her laugh sparkled across the balcony.

"Don't you like Señor Despojo?"

"I don't know him. But I like you."

You're getting nowhere fast, I thought.

"Look," I said. "If I get you a job in Barcelona, would you leave him?"

"Oh, yes." She gave me the impression of meaning it.

"But would he let you leave him?"

"I think he's getting tired of me," she said, looking down at her nails. "The last time he was here he didn't even want to make love to me. We sat here and had a drink, then he got up and went out."

"Did that break your heart?"

She looked at me and smiled.

"Why do you ask so many questions?"

"Skip it." Hell, who was I jealous of? "How long ago was that?"

"Oh, about a week ago."

My hand shook a bit as I pulled out a cigarette and lit it. It was difficult to keep the casual tone in my voice.

"Let's see, that would be last Tuesday." Francisco had been killed that night.

"Oh, I forget. Why do you ask?"

"I just want to be damn sure that I don't come next Tuesday. He might be here and that would make me jealous."

"But how can you be jealous? You told me that you already have a girl."

"You've got me there," I laughed. "But my God, I can't see how any man who loves you could leave you in the middle of the night without making love to you."

"It wasn't in the middle of the night. It was just after dinner. He said he had an important engagement. He gave me a thousand pesetas and told me to stay in my room and not let anyone else in. I thought of course he meant that he would be coming back. But when he didn't return, I was glad. I hope he has found another girl."

Just after dinner. In Spain that meant any time from eleven to midnight. So far, perfect score.

I looked at my watch. It was almost noon. What a hell of an hour to be leaving a bordello! I stood up, walked over, and buried my face in the back of her neck.

"I must go, honey. I'll try to get back tonight or tomorrow night. Anyway, I'll send you word before I come. In the meantime, don't tell your boy friend that I've been here. I want it to be a secret between you and me until I can get you away from here. O.K.?"

She promised. I asked her if there wasn't a back entrance I could sneak out. I wanted to know if there was some way Despojo could get in and out without being seen. She got up and took my arm.

"I'll show you, but you mustn't tell the señora."

I gave her a *mil* note and asked her to pay for the wine we'd had the night before and to keep the change. She tucked it in a pocket.

"I'd feel happier," I said, pausing at the door, "if I knew for sure that it was only Tuesdays your boy friend calls."

She squeezed my arm and laughed.

"Well, he was here *last* Tuesday. I remember, because every Wednesday I go home for the day. And as I didn't have to dance the night before, I got up and took the early *camión*."

She led me into the hall and down a narrow stairway. We saw no one. At the street level she drew back a bolt and I stepped out into a sun-splattered alleyway. I kissed her and whispered, "Every night but Tuesday, then."

Out in the Borne I picked up a cruising taxi and started touring the bars looking for Tomás. I finally ran him down in the Patio. He was sitting in the corner having his lunch. He looked up as I walked across. I pulled out a chair and sat down.

"She must have been quite a girl," he observed with a laugh.

"Hell, I've been looking for you all morning."

"It's not the hour, it's the contented, slightly worn-out expression in your face. Want a brandy eggnog?'

"Don't be vulgar. You got it all wrong, and when I tell you the story you'll understand that slight look of satisfaction I'm carrying around. In the first place, you can call off your bloodhounds. We know the man. Now all we have to do is get him."

I related the information I had picked up. Tomás let me finish without interruption. Slowly he put down his fork and shoved his plate to one side.

"It looks like he's the son-of-a-bitch you're after," he said finally. "There's only a couple of points I'm not clear on. The first one is, how did Despojo know that Francisco was going to get out of a taxi in that particular spot at that particular hour?"

"You ever been up to Rosita's room?"

"Not yet."

"Well, her balcony looks right down the Borne. After lunch we can walk along and I'll point it out to you. Anyway, he and the girl are sitting out there having a drink. He's no doubt had his orders from Aguzado to get rid of Francisco, somehow, sometime. He's probably turning over in his mind the safest method when he glances down and sees his man get out of the taxi. And he can't help but notice how drunk Francisco is.

"Telling Rosita he's got an engagement, he ducks down the back stairway. But he's smart enough to fix himself an alibi first. He tells the girl to stay in her room and wait for him. Then if he does come back he'll find her alone. And if he doesn't, she's the only one who'll know that he didn't spend the night with her. And he figures that in a pinch she'll go to bat for him.

"Out in the street he follows Francisco, gets him opposite some alleyway, and taps him on the head. He picks up a car, rolls him in, and drives him down to the beach. The rest we've already figured out."

Tomás took out a cigar, poked a hole in the end with a tooth-pick, and carefully lit it.

"Looks like you done a good night's work."

"Well, I didn't get much sleep, if that's what you mean. Right now I'm going back to the hotel and make it up. In the meantime you get to thinking how we're going to take care of that bastard so *he'll* go out knowing who did it but nobody else. See you later."

I woke up just in time to catch the cook before he went off duty for the night and ordered some food sent up to the room. There were no messages for me, so I collected a few English news-papers from Roberto and got back into bed. My brain felt like the mainspring of a watch after it had been wound too tightly. I decided to spend the night where I was and let it run down a bit.

At noon the next day Tomás came to see me. I was sitting in the patio of the Victoria, my feet on the rail, sampling Eduardo's idea of a Daiquiri. I offered Tomás one. He sniffed it, wrinkled his nose, and ordered Cinzano.

"O.K.," I said. "Let's have it. I know you're bursting with something."

"You're not going to like it," he said. "Our bird has flown the coop, taken a powder, or whatever the expression is now."

My feet hit the tiles with a thud.

"You mean—"

"Yes. Señor Despojo left for Barcelona two nights ago on the ferry."

"Son-of-a-bitch!"

"Exactly."

"Is he on the run?"

"As far as I can make out, no. He's gone over to the mainland on business. In fact, I don't think he even knows you're on the island."

"That's something, anyway. He'll leave a wide-open trail. But it's going to make it difficult."

"Too difficult, *amigo*. Despojo comes from Barcelona. I doubt if you know your way past the Barrera China."

I stared out over the bay. From the very first I had had only a hazy idea of what I would do to Francisco's killer once I had found him. I had concentrated solely on identifying him. But I had felt that when and if I knew who the man was, it would not be a case of simply pulling a gun and paying off a debt. It wouldn't help my standing in Juanita's eyes to return to Tangier and tell her I had shot the man who killed her father. Besides, I could see little satisfaction in sneaking up on a man one dark night and pumping him full of lead. Particularly a man like Despojo. It was too good for him. And the more I learned of him, the more I relished the thought of having him to myself for a few hours. I wanted him to *know* why he was getting it; to suffer. In the islands it might have been arranged; I had friends to help me. It would have been easy to slip out of sight afterward. It would have been possible to have some witnesses around—something more than just my word to take back to Juanita.

But in Barcelona, no. As Tomás had so rightly said, I'd lose myself one street up from the water front.

I swung my chair around. "How can I meet Aguzado?"

"Why? You going to ask him where his henchman is?"

"Don't be a damn fool. No, I'm going to ask him if he can use another ship."

Tomás let out a low whistle. "You'd work for that rat?"

"I have to work for somebody up here. Now that Francisco has been closed down, there's nobody left but the competition until Ricardo Lewis can make some other arrangements. I got an expensive ship and crew to take care of. I can't just lay her up and go into mourning. Besides, his money is as good as anyone else's, and right now probably a hell of a lot safer."

Tomás stared at me for so long I began to feel uncomfortable. Finally he turned away and called across to Eduardo to bring out two more drinks.

"Well." He leaned toward me. "I'll arrange for you and Carlos Aguzado to meet. But on one condition."

"So?"

"And that is that you'll tell me here and now the real reason you want to go to work for him."

I laughed. "O.K., Tomás, you can stop thinking what a heel I am. But it's certainly true that I want someone up here to handle my cargos. And right now I'd sooner take Aguzado's money than anyone else's. But the main reason is that I see no way of getting my hands on Despojo. I might sit around Palma for a month before he comes back. And sooner or later someone is going to start wondering why I'm hanging around. And you know as well as I do that the grapevine between here and Tangier is a pretty hot wire. And it's not going to be long before everybody on the coast knows that I'm looking for the man who killed Francisco Gonzales. So I think it would be much smarter for me to meet Aguzado and tell him that as soon as I heard about Francisco's death I came up to find another outfit to do business with. After all, he knows damn well that I've been working with Francisco. And he also knows that I'm not the type to retire from the coast because one contact died. So either he gives me a job or he doesn't. He may be suspicious and put his own man on board for the first few trips. Let him. But sooner or later Señor Despojo and I are bound to meet up."

I was rather amused when Aguzado shook hands with me the next day in the Club Mallorca. His cold gray eyes reflected no sign of either interest or surprise when Tomás told him who I was. He was a short, heavily set individual and his clothes looked as though he had slept in them. After the introduction I waited for him to say something. But he just stood there, took a cigar out of his breast pocket, bit off the end, and spat it on the floor. Finally Tomás suggested that we go over and sit down.

I decided that any subtle approach to this bastard would be a waste of time, so with my first words I asked him if he would give me a job running contraband.

"Why?" Still those dead fish eyes staring at me.

"Got to work for a living. You know that I used to haul for Francisco Gonzales. When I heard of his death I came up to find another outfit to tie in with."

"What kind of a ship you got?"

"Look, Aguzado." I was damned if I'd give him the compliment of the "Señor." "You know more about my ship and my crew than I do. Sometimes I think you know more about *me* than I do. Let's not beat about the bush."

The beginnings of a wintry smile altered slightly the set of his blue-gray jaw.

"*Muy bien, Capitán.* You go see Bartolomé Losa in Tangier and he'll fix you up with a cargo."

On my way to my feet I said thanks and good-by.

Out in the street Tomás caught up to me.

"My God," he wheezed. "That's one way of asking for a job. It's a wonder he didn't throw you out."

"Let's go have a drink and wash the taste of that bastard out of my mouth."

There was one more piece of unfinished business to be wrapped up before leaving Palma, so shortly after dinner that night I found my way back to Señora Dolores' establishment. When Dolores met me in the hallway I asked if Rosita was busy. She paused just long enough to give herself away and explained that the girl was resting now, but later she had to dance. I said O.K., what would it cost to postpone the dancing to another night? She said a thousand pesetas. I said hell, I should be able to sleep with you for that much. But when her smile began to tighten up I peeled off a *mil* note and handed it to her. The last money, I said to myself, she'll ever collect for that babe's body.

When I opened Rosita's door I found the room in darkness. I felt along the wall for a switch, found none, and walked over to the pale square of the window. I lifted the curtain and in the glow coming up from the street saw her lying on the bed. I let the curtain drop, walked over, and sat down beside her. She stirred drowsily and turned over on her back. I ran my fingers through the long black hair, loosened now, covering the pillow. I bent down and brushed her lips with mine. As I lifted my head, her arm slipped around my neck and pulled my face down to her breast.

Softly rubbing her chin in my hair, she said, "Ah, *americano,* you have come back to me."

"How did you know it was me?"

"I was dreaming of you. You were holding me in your arms."

"You've got a wonderful line, kid."

"I don't understand."

"I don't, either. But let's not try to sort it out now. Let's just take it from here."

I could feel her breast awakening under my cheek. The smell of her flesh, faint perfume, faint sleep, faint woman, started my blood pounding. She took my face between her hands and pulled my lips to hers. Her small slender body was writhing, twisting beside me, ankle rubbing against ankle.

I got up, found the door, and shot home the bolt. When I reached the bed again I was undressed. She pulled me down beside her. Now she was all pure flaming passion. Her mouth met mine, and her kiss was like a dart of scalding lightning. She arched her back, and when I kissed her firm breast I was afraid of crushing her as she pressed me to her. I explored the small body, the dancer's muscles, the hard torso, the quivering lithe legs. She was all motion, and the small sounds she made were of no language or of every language.

A shaft of moonlight reaching across my face awakened me. I lay there staring out into the brightness, not knowing what hour it was or what night. Nor did I care. I seemed to be suspended outside my other life. Vaguely I wanted a cigarette; I wanted to get up and close the curtains, which she must have opened at some time. I turned and looked at her there in the moonlight, so calm, so relaxed now in sleep. Softly I put my arm under her head. Without awakening she turned her back to me and slid down until her body fitted into my body. I pulled the cover over us to keep out the moon madness and went to sleep.

Via the alleyway we both left the establishment of Señora Dolores the next morning. I put Rosita in a taxi and sent her home, and she promised to remain there until either Tomás or I found her a job dancing. I told her that until then, Tomás would pay her five hundred pesetas a week to live on. Just how Despojo was going to fit into the scheme of things occupied me considerably as I caught the morning plane to Madrid.

CHAPTER NINE

A RRIVING in Tangier late in the afternoon, I went directly
out to the ship. The only news that Paco had was that we
were nearly out of fresh water, so I told him to go ahead and use
what he required; we'd go alongside the following day and fill our
tanks. I felt travel-weary and completely deflated. I suggested to
Paco that it was about time he went ashore. I would be remaining
on the ship that night. I had no desire to face Juanita.

He stared at me.

"You not feeling well?"

"Just tired. Not enough sleep."

"*Qué va!* Those Mallorcan señoritas."

I was halfway through breakfast next morning when Ricardo
came alongside. He said he'd heard that I had returned the night
before. I poured him a cup of coffee and described my activities in
Palma. When I informed him that we had pretty well established
the fact that Despojo was the man responsible for Francisco's
death, he voiced some rather pungent remarks in regard to the
man's ancestry. I explained that he had left the island before I
had my evidence, and that so far as I knew, he was not yet aware
that anyone was checking up on him; I saved the bombshell until
the last.

"Oh, yes," I concluded rather casually. "I saw Aguzado. I'm
going to work for him."

"Why, you son-of-a-bitch! After all these years we've been
together."

"Yeah. But look at it from my standpoint. You've lost your man in Mallorca and it's going to take some time to get another organization going up there. In the mean-time, what am I supposed to do? Sit out here and let the bottom rot?"

"I see your point. But hell, man, I'll get you cargos—to France, Italy, or the Spanish mainland."

"You know as well as I do, *amigo,* that I gave up making trips to anywhere but the Balearics a couple of years ago. I know the islands. I know the people I deal with there, and I'm still in business. How many ships have been lost running to the south of France? How many loads have been brought back because some damn fool Frenchman got drunk and forgot his rendezvous? And what about those two ships that got shot up in the Bay of Naples last month? You can double the ante and I still won't play. It's not worth it."

"I know, I know," he said. "But hell, to work for Aguzado! Think of Francisco, think of . . Oh, hell, what's the use?"

He got up. Complete disgust was written on his face.

"Well, I'll see you around," he said.

I followed him up to the deck and leaned against the rail. He climbed down into his launch and told the boatman to start the engine. He looked up at me.

"You didn't tie up with that bastard so you could get next to Despojo, did you?"

The hopefulness in his voice was so obvious I couldn't help smiling. He shoved his hand through the rail and squeezed my ankle.

"*Vámonos,*" he said to the boatman.

Later that morning I went ashore, walked up to the Grand Socco, and bought an armful of tuberoses. I crossed back into the casbah and climbed up to Juanita's alley. I found the door closed. I tried the handle. It was locked. I rapped the panels with my knuckles and waited. I was impatient, yet pleased that Sherrif had taken my instructions seriously and kept the place locked up.

Again I knocked, this time so loudly I could hear the sound rolling up the passageway behind the door.

I assumed that even if Juanita and Sherrif were out, one of the three or four servants hanging about the place would answer. Again I banged the door, but the only attention I drew was that of a couple of women gossiping in the next doorway. They stopped their chatter and stared at me. Finally one of them, waving her finger in front of me, said:

"*No, no están.*"

I asked her if everybody had gone out. She said yes. I asked her what time.

"Three days ago."

"What? You mean they've left? Where did they go?"

She shrugged her shoulders. She had given all the information she knew; she lost interest in me. I shoved the flowers into her surprised arms and practically ran down the street.

Ricardo was sitting in his office getting his fingers caught in a portable typewriter. He looked up and smiled.

"You changed your mind?"

I cut him short and asked where Juanita was. He shrugged his shoulders and said he didn't know. If she wasn't home, she must be out in the town somewhere.

"You don't understand. She left three days ago with her servants and Sherrif."

He swung around and faced me. "The first I've heard of it. I haven't seen her since you left. Where do you think she's gone?"

"Hell, I'm asking you."

"She didn't go back to Mallorca? There must be a lot of things to settle up there after her father's death."

"That must be it. In fact, they asked me in Palma to tell her that she had to go up there. Francisco's affairs are in a hell of a mess. He left everything to her and they're afraid to do anything without her say-so."

"Maybe she passed you on the way down."

"That's an idea. Any way we can check?"

"Well, there are only two ways she can get over to Spain, by plane or by boat. To travel either way you have to give your name. I'll see."

While he was telephoning I got up and took down the bottle of whisky from the bookshelf and the dirty glasses. I poured out a couple of drinks. I knew what Ricardo was going to say long before he had finished his last call and looked up. She hadn't gone to Mallorca.

"Do you think she's still in Tangier?" My stomach felt full of gravel. I remembered the premonition I had had when I left her; that when she broke down, it would be complete.

"No," Ricardo said. "If she was going to hide out here, she wouldn't have taken the servants. Sherrif, perhaps, but she'd realize she couldn't bury that menage even in the casbah if you really wanted to find her. She got a passport?"

"Yes, Spanish, but it's a good one."

"She's probably gone down the coast to French Morocco, and holed up in Rabat or Fez or somewhere."

"Well, we can find out from the garages if she hired a car. If she went by train, I don't see how we can check."

"How is she fixed for cash?"

"That's what I've been worrying about," I said after a long moment. "I don't know. I used to give her a handful of money every time I returned from a trip. But after paying the bills she can't have saved such a hell of a lot."

"Well, she's got all Francisco's now."

"Sure, but you know as well as I do that you can't send money out of Spain. You can't even *bring* it out legally. She could get one of the skippers to smuggle it out, but that takes time. What's more, you know them all. You'd have heard about it. But in many ways, remember, she's only a kid. She wouldn't think of it. She just made up her mind to get away from me, and I'll bet she won't even consider money until she's nearly broke. I only pray that when she does, she still has enough to get home with."

"I'll get the boys out making inquiries. For God's sake, cheer up. If she was going to jump off the cape she wouldn't have taken the cook along."

I stood up. "Get in touch with me if you hear anything. I'm going up to El Morocco and try to find some of her girl friends."

"You know," he cracked as I left, "it would be easier to find you a new girl friend."

CHAPTER TEN

I CONTINUED to run contraband for Aguzado. We made our contacts off various landfalls in Mallorca and had no trouble. I hated the bastard, but I had to admit that he had good men working for him. Never did I have to wait at a rendezvous and never did I have any difficulty over payments.

But no sign of Despojo. He had disappeared as completely as Juanita.

Then I met Aguzado again.

We had picked up our contact south of Andraitx about ten o'clock one night, but instead of the customary fishing trawler, a small fast motor launch came alongside. As soon as it made fast I asked its skipper where he thought that he was going to store the cargo. He climbed aboard the Chucha, and before I knew what he was up to he had ordered his launch to go on.

"Tonight," he explained, "we will be able to go right into Andraitx."

"The hell you say!" I countered. "Why?"

"You know what night it is?"

Despite the man's bubbling good humor, I was still cold. "January sixth," I said.

"Sí, sí, Capitán. La fiesta de los Reyes Magos."

Suddenly it struck me. Here we were trying to transship a cargo on one of the year's greatest festivals. The day of the Three Kings is more important to the Mallorcan than Christmas and

New Year's combined. Somebody had slipped up somewhere; there wouldn't be a sober fisherman in the islands.

"Tonight Señor Aguzado is having a fiesta at his *finca*. All the *carabineros* are there. We have the *camiones* waiting on the quay. When you are unloaded, we too will go to the fiesta. And for this Señor Aguzado told me to tell you he pays you more."

Paco, who had greeted our visitor enthusiastically, was leaning against the rail behind us. I spoke to him in English.

"What do you think?"

"Well, we either stay out here until tomorrow night or go inside. It's certain no one will come out tonight to unload us."

"But how in hell could they have made such a mistake?"

"Maybe it wasn't a mistake," the mate said.

"You know this fellow?"

"Sure. He's my brother-in-law."

"Why didn't you say so?"

"You didn't ask."

For some reason Paco's taciturnity softened the ice and I burst out laughing. It had probably been decided before we left Tangier that we were to go right into the port.

"O.K.," I told his relative. "We'll play along with you. But any sign of a cutter and we're off like that." I snapped my fingers.

I turned out all lights and headed shoreward. I could just see the weak beacon marking the end of the outer quay of the harbor. Some time later Paco came up and spoke to me.

"I think it's safe enough. The three serviceable cutters are taking part in the water pageant in Palma this evening, and even if they should leave right after the fiesta, they couldn't reach here before three o'clock tomorrow morning. That is, if they can find a sober crew. Aguzado has all the officials of the port out at his *finca*. My brother-in-law, Tito, saw them there just before he left. He says Aguzado's cognac is very strong."

Recalling the fish nets that were usually thereabouts, I kept well clear of the great headland that guards the entrance to the port. I eased back the throttles opposite the end of the outer quay. Tito was standing beside me and told me to swing the ship around and bring her alongside halfway between the beacon and the shore.

I made a wide circle and came alongside with the bows facing seaward. I was taking no chances. I told Paco to climb up on top of the sea wall and keep a good lookout. If he spotted a ship coming in he was to call down and get aboard as quickly as he could.

There seemed no end of helpers on the quay. A dozen or so had swarmed aboard and already one of the three trucks standing on the dock was loaded. I told the rest of the crew to forget the cargo and stand by the lines. Much against my will, I accepted Tito's advice to shut down the engines. He said they made too much noise in the still night. But I remained close to the starting buttons.

Finally the last truck disappeared into the night. "Now we go to the fiesta," said Tito.

"Whoa. Not tonight. When you've paid me we're on our way."

I thought he was going to burst into tears.

"But señor, Señor Aguzado wishes to pay you himself. The money is at the *finca*. Please, he will never forgive me if I don't bring you."

That one stopped me.

"But the ship—"

"It is safe, señor. You have nothing on board."

A tiny thought that had been lingering in the back of my mind ever since I had turned in toward the port began to grow. Was this to be the fateful night I would meet Despojo?

"Muy bien. Let's go."

I paused long enough to explain to Paco what was going on. I told him to stand by the Chucha, that I'd return within an hour or so. If a *carabinero* came along, he was to invite him on board to have a drink and keep him there until I returned. In the event a revenue cutter appeared, he was to slip his lines and take the ship out to sea and back to Tangier. I'd get back as best I could.

Tito led me to the shore and uncovered an ancient car tucked under a tree. We climbed in and headed toward the *pueblo*. We made a two-wheel turn and followed a narrow road back into the hills. We pulled up finally in the patio of an immense farmhouse. I was taken up to the first floor and into what I presumed was the reception room. The air was literally solid with the smoke of cigars, flickering candles, and oil lamps. Somebody shoved a glass and a bottle of cognac into my hands.

There must have been a hundred people jammed into the room. At one end, where the lights were somewhat brighter, a guitarist was banging away and a couple of señoritas were dancing. Every so often one of the locals rushed in and gave his version of a *sevillana*. But the wine soon took care of his wind and he would collapse amid the laughter of the crowd.

I had started to work my way toward a great long table covered with food when a firm hand caught my elbow. I glanced down into the swarthy face of Aguzado.

He led me back to the hall and into another, smaller room. Several men were gathered around the table playing cards. Quickly I searched their faces. Some I recognized as having come out to meet me at various times. Despojo was not among them.

Aguzado took the bottle from under my arm and poured me a drink. "I am pleased that you have come to my house," he said.

"Rather risky, don't you think?"

"*Nada, nada.* All the *carabineros* are in there. Later we will go and have a drink with them. But first, have you the list?"

I dug out the paper containing the list of goods I had landed that night. The prices had all been entered and totaled. He took out his pen and wrote a figure below the total; the bonus, I gathered, for coming right into the port. I didn't see the amount. He walked over and unlocked a cabinet and took out a wad of bank notes. I had to split it into several packets before I could get it all in my various pockets.

"Don't lose it." He winked. "It is very gay tonight."

I assured him that even *his* cognac wasn't that strong.

"You know, there is something that I have been meaning to explain to you." Aguzado spoke slowly, distinctly. I couldn't see his eyes; he was busy writing some figures in a book he had taken from the cabinet. "I didn't kill your friend Gonzales."

"I know."

He glanced up with a hard, quizzical look. "And I didn't order anyone else to kill him."

"What are you trying to do, buy somebody time?" I demanded.

"I just wanted you to know. You've been working well for me and I don't want you to entertain any wrong ideas about me."

"You're breaking my heart. Besides, I thought Gonzales committed suicide."

A flinty grin. "I knew Gonzales very well, and ..."

"Yes. Everybody was a friend of Francisco's. He's still dead."

"I know he has a daughter in Tangier."

"Had."

I looked hard at Aguzado. Was this the time to throw Despojo at him? But his eyes baffled me. They had shifted back to blank coldness. They seemed to say that I could take what he had just told me or leave it. I decided to leave it ... for the time being.

"How's the bottle making out?" I asked.

We returned to the large room and watched the dancing. There was no sign of Despojo. I glanced at my watch and realized that I had been away from the ship for well over an hour. And I began to think that I had better be on my way before the cognac and gaiety deadened my saner senses. I could imagine with what rare enjoyment the whole port would view the long black hull of the Chucha moored to the quay next morning. Sort of like going home in your dinner jacket after breakfast.

Aguzado had disappeared, but I managed to find Tito. I explained that it was time I was going, another hour or so and it would be daylight. He started to protest, but I waved him down and headed for the door. He spoke to several bystanders and followed. We found the courtyard and the car. I got into the front seat, Tito slid behind the wheel, and four or five more piled in the back. Somebody produced a bottle and passed it forward. I took a strong pull and handed it to Tito. He rounded the corner of the stable with a bottle to his lips. I grabbed the wheel and got the car back onto the road. I passed the bottle back.

Without too much damage to the ancient buggy we got back to the quay. Tito swung out toward it, but I had had enough. I turned off the ignition and pulled up on the hand brake. I thought he was going to burst into tears again. I placated him by saying that it was a beautiful night for a walk. The bottle was passed around for the last time, and arm in arm we rolled out to the ship.

As we swung across the Straits and headed for Tangier, I prayed that this time there would be some word from Juanita; a message from Ricardo that he had discovered where she was. But I knew that there would be nothing.

Often during the long night watches I would think of her, wondering where she was and what she was doing. At first I had felt confident that after a few days she would return to me, that she just *couldn't* continue to believe that I had been the cause of her father's death. Surely, I argued with myself, when time had softened the blow she would become more reasonable. But as the days ran into weeks I began to turn sour. I realized that she must have run out of money by now. They had not heard a word in Mallorca; I had kept that end well covered. Of course, she might have found a job. More likely, I thought bitterly as I slammed the helm over, she's found another sucker to pay the bills.

As we ran up to the anchorage, I yelled down to Paco to stand by to let go. To hell with Despojo. I had tried my best. To hell with the whole bloody outfit. Instinctively I closed the throttles and let the ship lose headway. I would go down the coast and look for her myself. And if I didn't find her at the end of two weeks, I'd go back to the States. Fifteen days, not a moment more. I gave Paco the signal and felt the ship quiver as the anchor chain ran out.

Someday, I muttered to myself as I swung down off the bridge, maybe you'll smarten up when it comes to women.

CHAPTER ELEVEN

I REPORTED in to Aguzado's agent, Bartolomé Losa, paid him his share of the money, and said that I was going to relax for a while. I blamed it on the fact they had caught some fishing boats recently, that it appeared as though the *aduana* were making one of its periodic cleanups.

"But all you have to do is keep outside the three-mile limit," he said.

I gave him a weak smile. "Those bastards carry guns, not charts. Three miles, ten miles, it's all the same to them if they can get away with it. I'd rather let things cool down a bit. When I want to go back to work again, I'll let you know."

He asked me if I was going to remain on the Chucha. I said no, that if he wanted me he could ask Ricardo Lewis. I was going down the coast to find some sunshine.

I stopped by Dan's Bar and went in for a quick one. Dan told me Ricardo had been looking all over town for me. I called his office but he wasn't in. I asked whoever answered the telephone to tell him where I was when he returned.

Now that I had made up my mind to leave the sea and try to pick up Juanita's trail, I relaxed. Whether I succeeded or not wasn't so important right now as the fact that the period of doubt and uncertainty as to whether I had been following the right tack was over. I never questioned my ability to convince her how wrong she was once I found her.

Three drinks later Ricardo barged in. He greeted me with the observation that I looked terrible.

"Don't those bastards ever let you sleep?"

"You ever flogged the western Med in January?" I retorted.

"Come over to a table. I got news."

My hand trembled slightly as I picked up my glass and followed him to a corner table. I asked Dan to send over two whiskies. Ricardo leaned toward me.

"We found your girl friend."

"Where?"

"Fez."

"She all right?"

"Sure. But boy, are you poison!"

"What do you mean?"

"Just what I said. She thinks you're the number one rat of the species. In fact, after they made you they threw the mold away. They were afraid to make another."

"Stop running off at the mouth and get down to it. How did you find her?"

"Well, Gabriel, my brother, was down in Fez last week to see about a gold shipment. He's walking down the street one day and spots Juanita. They know each other well; his wife's a good friend of hers. She tries to avoid him by ducking into a shop. He follows her in. When she sees he's caught her, she breaks down. He finally gets her to tell him where she's staying so he can take her there. Gabriel said that it was some cheap pension and he gathered the girl had been having a rough time of it. She'd run out of money and Sherrif was having a hell of a job scrounging enough for them all to eat. She didn't even have the dough to send her women back here. He got hold of Sherrif, gave him some money, and told him to find a decent place and move them in.

"The next day Sherrif comes around to Gabriel's hotel and tells him Juanita wants to see him. She asks him to promise not to tell you where she is. Gabriel acts dumb and asks why. She says that if it hadn't been for you her father would be alive today. He tries to tell her the truth but she isn't having any. To prove her point she reads him a letter that's been forwarded from some relative in Mallorca asking her to send up a few things the next time you made a trip. This relative points out he's a good friend of Aguzado's and will fix it with him to get the things landed. And I can see Gabriel's point when he says he couldn't explain why you started to work right away for the man who is supposed to have murdered her father."

"You got her address?"

He took out a notebook, flipped the pages until he found the right one and handed it to me. I wrote down the street and number.

"If you're thinking of going to see her, you'd better have a talk with Gabriel first."

"No, I'm not going. What's the use? But I can write to her. How much did Gabriel give her?"

"Forget it."

I counted out ten thousand pesetas and handed the bills to him and asked him to see that Juanita received them. I suggested that he let her think that they came from him.

"Geez, I damn near forgot," Ricardo said. "Here, I've got a cable for you."

I tore open the envelope and read:

YOUR LITTLE GIRL FRIEND IS BREAKING HER HEART AND MY POCKETBOOK. ADVISE. TOMÁS.

I slapped my forehead.

"What's the matter, you got more trouble?"

I tossed the cable across to him. He read it and looked up, a query in his eyes. I explained that I'd met a dancer in Palma and had promised to find her a job. Slowly shaking his head, he said, "You can't leave 'em alone, can you?"

"Jack your mind up. This is on the level. She helped me track down Despojo. In fact, she's his girl friend, or was."

"Or was before you came along. O.K., what do you want?"

I asked him if he would contact his Madrid friends and see if someone there could find her a job in a cabaret. I would guarantee satisfaction.

"You should know," he cracked. "But so help me, this is the last dame I take care of for you. You softhearted *contrabandistas* give me more headaches than all the revenue cutters in the Mediterranean."

I picked up a taxi outside the bar and rode back to Losa's office. There would be no stopping now. I'd go to sea every day if they wanted me to. I *had* to find Despojo. But from now on, discretion would go by the board. Time was at a premium.

Losa was about to close shop for the afternoon. I explained that I had changed my mind about laying up. "You got anything on hand?"

He dug through a pile of papers and brought forth a cable. He said that he had received it that morning from Palma via Ceuta. He'd been looking around for a ship to do the job, and if I wanted it and was ready to go to sea again I could have it. The cargo consisted of two hundred cases of cigarettes, fifty sacks of coffee, twenty sacks of sugar, and some white flour. Conditions were the same as before. He would post a bond with Moses Pariente's bank for the value of the ship, plus the amount of my carrying charges. If I got caught I was to say nothing and let them tow me into whatever port they chose. As soon as possible I was to get word to Aguzado's office in Palma. He would take care of the rest. If they confiscated the ship and the cargo, all I had to do was walk away, return to Tangier, collect the bond, and buy another ship.

It was the usual routine and I let Losa ramble through it while I was trying to make up my mind whether I dared ask him anything about Despojo. I decided against it. After changing my mind the way I had, it might cause suspicion.

I knew from experience that there was no use asking him where the rendezvous was. He brought that on board after we had the anchor up. Even then we weren't supposed to open the sealed instructions until we had almost reached the islands, in case we were stopped en route. If we didn't know where we were going, we couldn't be made to tell the revenue agents.

I did remind him, however, to make sure it was well outside territorial waters or I would turn back.

That night they loaded us and I sent word back that I would sail just before dawn. I left Paco in charge of stowing the cargo and spent a couple of hours composing a letter to Juanita. The first one I tore up. When I got to thinking of her nearly starving to death in Fez, the criticism I'd expressed sounded pretty sour. Finally I wrote simply that I didn't blame her for running out on me, that I accepted much of the responsibility for what had happened, and begged her either to return to Tangier or to go to Mallorca. I concluded by explaining that the sole reason that I was working for Aguzado was that it was the only sure way I knew to find the man who had killed her father.

I begged her to burn the letter as soon as she had read it. I sealed it up and asked Harry to go ashore himself and mail it.

The weather had definitely changed and we had a beautiful run up the Spanish coast. Our rendezvous was set for a point five miles south-southeast of Cabo Salinas on the south coast of Mallorca Island.

Just before midnight the second night we picked up the lights of Cabrera Island and Cabo Salinas. I took several bearings until I was sure of our position and altered course for the land. At the slow speed we were running, I calculated we'd be at our contact point just before the appointed hour. But it was too calm; there would be another early-morning fog.

I kept all lights off until three-thirty A.M. Then I slowed up and switched on the white masthead light. I was praying that whoever was going to meet us would be early. The fog was thin, but visibility was not good. Seven miles off the coast I stopped. I decided to wait until just before four o'clock, then open up and run in the last two miles. I was nervous.

The minutes dragged. The men had heaved some of the cargo up on deck, and I rather envied them the physical distraction. The only sound was the chuckle of the exhaust and soft slap as the ship worked in the seaway. Paco came up and stood on the opposite wing of the bridge.

I looked at my watch. Three-forty-five. God, I said to myself, it's not worth it. When I get back from this trip I'm going to retire. Right now most men are sound asleep in their beds. What the hell am I doing out here sitting on a load of dynamite waiting for someone to come along and light the fuse? Even for twice the money it's not worth it. I looked again at my watch. Three-fifty.

"Let's go, Paquito *mío*. We'll run in to five miles. If we don't spot our ship, we'll turn around and go back to Tangier."

Suddenly the whole left horizon flared alight. A long opaque finger of white stretched ahead of us. I spun the wheel to starboard and banged open the throttles. I glanced over my shoulder. The beam was swinging slowly toward us. It picked up our boiling wake, climbed up over our stern, then I could almost feel the heat of it as it found the bridge. It was a very powerful light. In the blinding glare I could only guess when I had it astern. I steadied the wheel and noted the compass heading.

The strength of the ray didn't lessen. I looked down at the rev counters, although I knew from the vibration of the ship that the motors were giving all they had. Glancing backward, I was momentarily blinded. I yelled down to Harry to go and see if he could get more power out of her; maybe he could work some miracle.

He crawled back out of the hatch and said he couldn't squeeze another revolution; we were already doing away over the maximum permissible.

I spun the wheel to port and several cases of cigarettes went over the side as we heeled over in the tight turn. But the cursed blinding glare followed us. Standing there on the open bridge, I felt naked, completely ineffectual. I prayed for a fog bank.

I didn't think it possible, but gradually the light strengthened.

Paco had come up and was standing behind me.

"I think they have us," I called over my shoulder.

"No revenue cutter. Searchlight's too high off the water."

Rapidly now, the ship chasing us came up astern, and swung out and alongside. I could follow her movements only by the shifting shadows.

I told Paco to get the cargo below. He called Harry and Jim and the three of them hurled cases and sacks into the hold.

Out from the light megaphoned a voice.

"Stop or we fire," it commanded in excellent English.

This is it, I said to myself as I slowly closed the throttles. The ease with which he had overtaken us made me realize that he must have had twice our speed.

A moment later the chatter of a machine gun came down from overhead.

CHAPTER TWELVE

THE VOICE came again.

"Leave your cargo alone. I'm sending a boat alongside."

"No use, boys," I called aft.

Paco dropped a sack back onto the deck. The three of them moved forward and stood in the shadow of the bridge. I dropped down and joined them. The physical relief of getting out of the blinding glare was tremendous.

I spoke quietly but rapidly.

"You fellows know the routine. Your papers are in order. You were signed on by me, and you don't know anything about the men I work for."

And thank God you don't, I thought to myself.

"Just sit tight, answer no questions or refer them to me, and everything will be all right."

Paco dug out a cigarette, lit it with a steady hand. He could take care of himself, but I was worried about Harry and Jim.

"Just remember we're not the first ship to be nabbed." I loaded my voice with casualness. "And we won't be the last. The main thing as far as you're concerned is that they can't *do* anything to you."

While I had been talking, I had taken out the envelope with the paper containing the time and place of our rendezvous. I tore it into shreds and one by one let the bits drift off into the night. They'd find no other papers aboard that could connect me or the ship in any way with running contraband.

I turned to Paco and said, "They must have smartened up at last and bought themselves a fast cutter."

A longboat came out of the blackness and made fast alongside. Six men of the Spanish navy poured over the rail and took up stations in various parts of the ship. They had a job managing their rifles, and as one banged his against the housing, I hoped he didn't have a cartridge up the spout. An officer brought up the rear. He came over to where we were standing.

"May I see your papers, Captain?"

"Sure. But first, can't you turn off that damn searchlight? We're almost blinded."

He walked back to the rail and called over to his ship. A moment later blessed darkness folded in. When I could see again, I looked across the water. There, a black shadow in the night, sat a destroyer.

I led the way into the deckhouse, snapped on the light, and proffered a chair. The officer carefuly removed his gloves, dropped them in his hat, and sat down. I took out the ship's registration paper, the manifest, and the crew list, and laid them on the table in front of him.

"Have a drink?"

"Thanks, no." He almost managed a smile.

"Mind?" I lifted a bottle of whiskey.

"Please."

I poured myself a stiff drink, lit a cigarette, and sat down opposite. He had got as far as the crew list.

"You have one Spaniard on board?"

"Yes. Signed on in front of the Spanish consul in Tangier." I pointed a grubby finger at the consul's seal.

Finally he folded the papers up, but kept them under his hand. Well, now is as good a time as any, I thought. Let's get on with it.

"Please tell me, Commander, why you have stopped me on the high seas, opened fire, come aboard, and demanded my papers. In my slender knowledge of marine law, that's an act of war."

"You have been caught," he spoke slowly, beautifully, "running contraband into Spain, by a Spanish government ship."

I pulled toward me the chart of the coast I had been using. On it was a pencil line, our supposed track on the way to Italy. It had been drawn as a precaution several trips previously. The track never came within five miles of the coast of Mallorca. On it I made a small circle with my pencil.

"I think that your navigating officer will agree, Commander, that that is about the position you first saw me, well outside your territorial waters."

"Captain, if you were not about to unload contraband in Mallorca, just what were you doing?"

I pointed to the manifest.

"If you will take the trouble to read, you will see that I am cleared for Genoa with a legitimate cargo."

"Why, then, do we come across you close in to the coast running without proper lights, with contraband stacked on your decks?"

"Perfectly simple. Our generator broke down today. I couldn't charge the batteries and was saving light. If and when I saw another ship, naturally I would put them on. The cargo you found on deck because there was water in the hold. The bilge pump is electrically driven, and before we could rig up the hand pump, some of our cargo got wet. We were in the process of pumping our bilges when you came upon us."

"You are very clever, Captain. There remains one more question. If, as you say, you felt perfectly within your rights, why, when we turned our searchlight upon you, did you attempt to run away?"

"A good question. I will answer you with what I think is the truth. You know as well as I do that these waters are infested with *contrabandistas,* either coming up from Tangier or going out from the land. I have heard that if they can, they sometimes stop small cargo vessels such as this and highjack their cargos. The first I knew of your existence was when you turned on your searchlight. Since you had no navigation lights showing previously, I naturally suspected that your intentions were not, if you will excuse the expression, honorable. I hardly expected to encounter a Spanish man-of-war under such circumstances."

This time, the smile won through.

"No, Captain, I am sure you didn't."

He stood up, tucked the papers in his pocket, and told me he was sorry but that they would have to tow us in to Palma. He asked me if I would accompany him back to his ship.

"Do I ride in with you, or will I be coming back?"

"I think it would be better if you came aboard with us."

I went down, got my passport, and put a couple of packages of cigarettes in my pocket. I folded up the chart of the coast and took it with me. I explained to Paco what was happening, and asked him to keep an eye on the towing warps and see that they didn't damage the ship. I told Jim to stand by and sent Harry to get his seaman's papers.

"Mind if I bring along one of my men?" I asked the officer. "I'd like someone to be with me as a witness."

He voiced no protest, so we climbed down into the boat and were rowed across to the destroyer Ascending a monkey ladder, I pulled myself up to the steel deck, paused, and, in appreciation of the politeness I had been tendered so far, saluted the quarterdeck.

We were led forward and up one companionway. Our guide stopped and knocked on a door. We entered a small cabin. A man sitting behind a desk looked up. I noticed that his sleeve bore a half stripe more than the boarding officer's and presumed him to be the senior officer on the ship.

He spoke in rapid Spanish. Our friend made his report, finally taking out his papers and laying them on the desk.

"Name of your ship?" he barked at me.

I told him.

"Your ship and cargo are seized in the name of the Spanish government. We take you in to Palma."

He matched the other's politeness with rudeness. But I had a feeling that in my position it would not be politic to retaliate. It was a long way to Palma Harbor.

"Just a moment, sir." I spooned on the sugar. "Would you have your navigation officer show me our present position?"

I avoided the scowl that darkened his face and unfolded my chart.

"You are impudent. Certainly not."

I looked around the cabin. Besides the skipper, there were the boarding officer and a seaman standing guard inside the door. I could almost see his ears flap as he followed the conversation. I began to fold up the chart.

"Under the circumstances, I find myself in a position where I can only protest. However," I glanced around, "besides yourself there are two members of the Spanish navy present. I am sure that when the time comes to argue this case in the naval courts, they will feel honor bound to bear witness that you have refused to reveal your position. It reassures me that you have captured me outside Spanish territorial waters."

I thought he'd burst a blood vessel on that one. Pounding his desk with the flat of his palm, he bellowed, "We are going to take you fellows wherever we find you. We are going to run you off the seas."

He looked over at his junior officer.

"Commander, take this man up to the chart room and give him a lesson in navigation."

I was glad to get out of his presence without losing my temper. On the way along the deck, I explained briefly to Harry what had taken place. His ability to speak Spanish was poor; to understand, worse.

We entered a cabin back of the lower bridge. In the dim light I made out two or three officers sitting around. Our guide explained to one of them who we were and why we had come up. Someone switched up the lights, and we were inspected with smiling interest. One of the men pulled a chart toward him, picked up his dividers, and measured a distance along a pencil line running south-southeast from Cabo Salinas. At a point I guessed to be about five miles offshore a cross line had been previously drawn.

Our rendezvous. It had not been ill luck that caught us this night; someone had sold us out.

The navigating officer—at least, that's what I assumed he was—finally nicked the chart with the point of his dividers. He took a pencil and drew a small circle around it. I got out my chart and spread it alongside his. I borrowed his pencil and made a circle in the same spot.

"*Estamos aquí ahora?*" I looked up.

"*Sí, señor.*"

I picked up the dividers, opened them to fit between Cabo Salinas and the circle. I compared them against the minutes printed on the edge of the chart. It measured seven sea miles. With rather exaggerated slowness, I wrote opposite the circle. "Seven miles off-shore." I folded the chart and slipped it back into my pocket. Pointing to the naval chart, I showed Harry where we were. I told him to have a good look and not forget; one of these days he might be required to swear to it.

On deck I asked the Commander if there was anything more. He said no. I could feel the slow heavy movement of the ship as we got under way. He took us below decks and showed us into a tiny cabin. I tossed Harry for the lower berth and won. Going out to the head, I found an armed sentry in the passageway. He showed me the way and waited till I returned to the cabin.

We arrived in Palma just before noon. With unexpected consideration, they came in rather slowly so as not to strain the tow; I presumed that they now considered the Chucha their personal property and were going to take care of her.

Entering the inner basin, the destroyer dropped her anchor and maneuvered into the quay. The warp was shortened, and as I looked down from the deck, the Chucha was brought up and made fast along the off side. Already the curious were beginning to gather on the dock. I kept out of their sight

"What do we do now?" Harry, at my elbow, asked.

"Well, several things. The customs will come aboard, and depending on how tough they want to be, they can rough us up a bit and try to make us sign a paper to the effect that we were taken inside territorial waters. If we were Spaniards, that's what they'd probably do."

"The navy let them get away with that?"

"Once we're brought in, I presume the navy washes its hands of us."

"But can't we protest to the consul?"

"Sure. But you can bet your buttons they won't let us get in touch with him till they've decided what they're going to do. Besides, consuls aren't too happy about situations like this. You can't count on them to come through when you need them."

A sailor came along and said the skipper wanted to see us.

"You better leave this to me," I told Harry. "Go back to the ship and stay with Paco and Jim."

I found the cabin jammed with plain-clothed individuals whom I presumed to be customs and police. The skipper of the destroyer was the only naval officer present. One tough-looking type asked to see my passport. I handed it to him. Then the questions started. They tried to break down my story that I was on my way to Italy and that I was outside territorial waters. They said they knew who I was, knew the ship, and were aware of the fact that I was working for Aguzado. They told me how many trips I had made recently, and surprisingly enough, they weren't far wrong.

My answers droned on like a broken phonograph record. I repeated that I was en route to Italy and had been seized on the high seas by a man-of-war. The navy had corroborated my position; now it was a case for the courts to settle.

Finally they got tired of that angle and one of them said that if they wished, they could make me tell the truth. I pretended I didn't understand that one, and asked him to explain. He walked over and folded a large fist under my nose.

"*Usted sabe muy bien,*" he said.

"I don't think the navy would stand by and let you do that," I said as nonchalantly as I could.

The officer spoke up for the first time.

"The navy has been instructed to adopt any methods to stamp out smuggling into Spain."

No help from that quarter.

One of the men who had taken little part in the interrogation finally asked me to step outside and wait. I drew the fresh air down into my lungs. My God, I thought, it shouldn't be a crime to bring good tobacco into this country.

Even from the rail, I could overhear the heated argument going on. I found the palms of my hands wet. For the first time I began to think that it wasn't going to be as easy as before. Maybe I should do something about getting a message over to the consul.

In the end they appeared to have reached some sort of agreement. One of them came out and walked over to me. I crossed my fingers. As far as I could make out, his had been the only sobering voice in the cabin. I gathered that perhaps he was more than a friend of Aguzado's.

He informed me that the customs were confiscating the ship and the cargo and that I would be fined the usual three times the value.

"What about the crew?" I asked.

"They won't be held. Neither will you. You can go ashore when you please."

"And my passport?"

"That's a matter for the police "

I watched the rest of the party file out. When I spotted the man who had taken my passport, I moved across and asked him for it. He told me that he would keep it until after the court settled on the fine He drew out a pad and wrote me a *salvoconducto*. He told me to tell the members of my crew to check in with the port police and have their papers stamped.

I climbed down into the Chucha, and gathered the men in the cabin. There was a naval guard near the door, so I closed it and spoke quietly in English. I explained what had happened and said I considered we'd been lucky; we were going to receive only the usual treatment. Paco laughed when I related how much they knew about us.

"That's not news. Everybody in the islands knows who runs contraband. And now it's beginning to look as if they know not only who but when and exactly where."

"You can say that again."

I instructed Paco to stand by the ship, and check off the cargo as it was landed and get a signature for it. I counted out five thousand pesetas each for the other two, and told them to make their way quietly back to Tangier and wait for me there. I packed up my clothes, sent Paco down the quay for a taxi, and went ashore. I had a last look at my little ship and wondered when I'd see her again.

CHAPTER THIRTEEN

T HAT EVENING before dinner, Tomás and a man I had never met before came to see me in the Hotel Victoria. Roberto, after some rather colorful comments on my stupidity for letting myself be caught, had produced a beautiful sitting room and bedroom overlooking the bay. From the balcony I could just make out the Chucha alongside the quay, sacks and cases piling up on the deck as they unloaded her. I had shut that unhappy scene and the past twenty-odd hours from my mind, and slept most of the afternoon.

Tomás introduced the stranger as one Fernández, Aguzado's lawyer. I shook hands with him and explained that I had intended to get in touch with Aguzado in the morning.

He said, "It is going to be a delightful case. They are not sure of their ground, having picked you up outside territorial waters. We will fight it through to the courts in The Hague."

"In the meantime, what do I do?"

"Don't worry. The case will come before the tribunal in three or four days. Either we shall be fined, or the ship and cargo will be seized, or they will return everything. If we are fined, the fine will be paid immediately, and you will be completely free. We will then protest the decision in a higher court and so on. If they return the ship and cargo, I don't think that we will claim damages—although, mind you, we could. You will simply take your ship and depart."

Later over dinner at the Patio, I remarked to Tomás that Aguzado certainly took care of his men.

"They all do. If they didn't, they wouldn't get a foreign skipper to work for them."

"To hell with it. Let's get drunk. Where's our girl friend?"

"Which one?"

"That beautiful dancer, Rosita."

"Geez, didn't you know? She left for Madrid some time ago. Told me you'd fixed her up with a job at the Casa Alegría, a damn good night club in Madrid. If she can hold down the job, she'll be doing all right."

"She'll keep it," I said. "Let me know how she gets along. By the way, I had an interesting conversation with your friend Aguzado not so long ago."

"So?"

"He up and told me he didn't kill Gonzales, and what's more, he didn't give the order to have him eliminated. I'm still trying to figure out why he felt it necessary to explain it to me."

Tomás caught the eye of the waiter and ordered cheese and fruit.

"It fits in with what I've been hearing around the port," he said, finally. "Aguzado and Despojo aren't too fond of each other at the moment, it seems, so it makes sense. Despojo still works for the outfit over on the mainland, but I'm beginning to suspect that Aguzado was pretty upset over the killing. He's a hard character; about as hard as they come. But he's not stupid, and after all, *killing* Gonzales *was* unnecessary. The rumor now is that Despojo and Gonzales met that night just as we figured out, somewhere around Señora Dolores' establishment. But just where the shooting took place no one seems to know. It seems they had a fight, Despojo pulled a gun, and it went off. Of course, Aguzado is going to cover up for him.

After all, what Despojo doesn't know about their *negocios* isn't worth knowing."

"But why does he go to so much trouble clearing himself with me?"

"I got an idea Aguzado realizes what's running around in the back of your mind. After all, everybody knows you spent a lot of time with Francisco's daughter down in Tangier. Maybe he doesn't want you to stick a knife into him some dark night. Then again, maybe he's giving you the green light; he might have reached the conclusion that Despojo has outlived his usefulness."

"I never thought of that angle."

"Well, you better not act on it till you do. After all, I'm only giving you my opinion."

After another bottle of wine we reached the coffee stage and I asked Tomás what was new in the town in the way of excitement. He said there were a couple of good dancers at the Casa Blanca, so we got a taxi and went to have a look at them.

The Casa Blanca, as usual, was full of people and smoke. But Tomás managed to scrounge a table near the postage-stamp-sized dance floor. A guitarist gave us an *alegrías*.

Halfway through the number Juanita walked in.

My first reaction was pure admiration for the manner in which she had spent at least some of the money I had sent to Fez. For she was dressed well enough to cause comment in any night club; in this tired *bistro* she was terrific. And as I noticed the heads turning as she threaded her way across the room, I realized that I wasn't the only one who thought so. She was wearing a black dinner dress severely but beautifully cut. Over her shoulders hung a blue fox cape. In her hair, drawn back in a tight low bun, snuggled a crimson rose. The dress, split from her throat to a wide silver belt, gave a tantalizing glimpse of each curving breast. She was wearing no jewelry and, with the exception of the scarlet lips, no make-up. She must have had on very high heels, for she seemed taller and slimmer than I remembered her.

There were two men following her; one young, about her own age, the other much older. The older man looked frightened. I didn't recognize either of them.

"Somebody you know?" Tomás had been following my eyes.

"Yes. You do too, but I imagine it's some time since you've seen her. Juanita Gonzales."

"My God! The last time I saw her she was a scrawny kid in pigtails."

Slowly I finished my drink and stood up. "I don't quite know what's going to happen," I told Tomás, "but if I don't come back within a reasonable time you'd better come over and pick up the pieces."

It wasn't until I was facing her across the table that she looked up, her eyes catching mine.

"Hello, Juanita," I said softly. "What are you doing here?"

For a long time she stared at me. I could see the tears nearing the surface.

"I came to do what I thought you were going to do." Her voice was a good deal harder than her eyes.

"May I sit down?"

She shrugged her shoulders. I pulled over a chair, sat down, and said, "I don't know your friends."

She introduced the older man as a good friend of her father's, the other as his son.

"How long have you been in Mallorca?" I asked.

"Since yesterday." Her voice was almost back to normal, but those tears were still close. I had to be careful of what I said. She'd hate me even more if she broke down in a place like this.

"Have you heard about me?"

"I received your letter."

"I got picked up yesterday. I've lost my ship."

Instinctively she reached over and seized my wrist.

"What did they do to you? Were you hurt?"

I smiled and patted her hand. It's going to be all right, it's going to be all right, I kept saying to myself.

"How do I look? No, darling, no one was hurt, and there are a lot more ships where that one came from."

Self-consciously she withdrew her hand. She glanced around the table. "Isn't anyone going to buy me a drink?" she demanded.

"I didn't know that this was one of your old haunts," I observed while the older man was busy trying to catch a waiter's eye. "What are you celebrating?"

"We're not celebrating. We came here to meet a man called Pepe who was one of the last persons to see my father alive."

"You mean the Pepe who used to work at the Bodega?"

"Yes," the young fellow broke in. Instinctively I disliked him. He was too attractive and could spot me too many years. "He works here now. He said that if we came tonight he would introduce us to someone who would help us. I didn't want Juanita to come, but she insisted."

I turned to the father. "Sorry," I said. "I didn't catch your name."

"Velásquez. Antonio Velásquez."

"Well, Don Antonio, would you give me five minutes at the bar? There are one or two things I'd like to discuss with you. I don't think they're fit for young ears."

I tried a disarming smile. Juanita wasn't fooled.

"Please, if you have anything to say, say it here."

Velásquez took her hand. "I think that the señor is right. Why don't you and Diego dance?"

She pouted, and it was all I could do to keep myself from leaning across the table and kissing those lips. I stood up and walked over to a less noisy section of the bar.

"What'll it be?" I asked the older man.

"Cognac, Soberano."

"Make it two," I told the barman. "One with soda."

I turned my back to the bar and looked at my companion.

"You know who I am?" I asked.

"Yes, Juanita has told us about you."

"What's she up to?"

"Well, she arrived in Palma yesterday and said that she knows her father was killed and she wants to find out who did it. I've tried to talk her out of it. I told her no one knows for certain that her father *was* killed, and that even if he was, she'll only get into trouble by getting mixed up in it."

"You know who did it?"

"No."

"Well, I do. I know all about it; why, when, where, and by whom. I'm just playing it the safe way. But I'm playing it. And I don't think you or she are going to do yourselves any good by messing around with some of these wharf rats you'll meet in a place like this."

His look of relief was so spontaneous I could hardly suppress a smile.

"I'm so glad," he said. "You see, I knew little about that side of Francisco's life. I live very quietly. In fact," he glanced around the room, "this is the first time I've ever been in a place like this."

"I gathered that when I saw you come in. Shall we go back and try to cheer up Juanita? And by the way, if you're unhappy here, why don't you leave? I'll look after her."

"Oh, do you think I could? You don't think she'd consider it rude if I left so early?"

"Don't let it worry you. I'll straighten it out. But what about Diego?"

For the first time he smiled. "Oh, he'll have to drive me home."

"You look pretty well satisfied with yourself," Juanita threw at me as we returned to the table.

"You know me too well, darling."

"Juanita *mía*," Velásquez broke in, "Señor Hart has a great deal to tell you. Please, you must listen to him and do what he says."

"Well, I'll listen."

"And now we must go. Come tomorrow and see me. I think you will be happier then."

When we were alone, I said, "Look, darling, this isn't quite the place I had in mind when I dreamed of the moment I'd find you again. But I don't suppose you'd go anywhere else with me right now, so here it is."

I took hold of her hand in both of mine.

"Your father was shot by a man called Despojo. They had a fight over running contraband into Andraitx. Despojo works for Aguzado. There was no tangible evidence that I could find and no witnesses, so I couldn't just turn him over to the police, even if I'd wanted to. As I wrote you, I decided to settle the matter myself, and the only way I thought I could do that was to start working for the same outfit. I figured I was bound to meet him someday at sea. Well, so far I haven't. He went over to Barcelona after the shooting and has managed to avoid me ever since. Sure, I could get a gun and go call him out. But what good would that do? They still have laws in this country. I wouldn't get away with it. But if that's what you want, I'll do it.

"Another thing I want you to know: It wasn't through any information they got out of me that your father got killed. It was one of those stupidly simple things that happen sometimes. One of his fishermen let him down. That's all."

Slowly she lowered her head, shaking it from side to side. I felt a tear splash on the back of my hand. I reached up and lifted her chin.

"Look, honey, if you like we can beat this around tomorrow. But I told you most of it in my letter; it's just something you've got to get used to. Get used to, then forget."

"Give me a cigarette."

As I held my lighter for her I said, "Let's cheer up. What about a bottle of champagne?"

"You'd better order two. I'm going to get very, very high."

"Well, that's one way to forget," I said with a short laugh. "But before you pass out, will you tell me one thing?"

"What?"

"Did you miss me?"

"Terribly. But up until you walked over here tonight I was never going to see you again. Now I wonder how I was able to stay away from you as long as I did."

"That's what I love about this Spanish temperament. It's either a blizzard or hot sunshine."

"I don't understand."

"Darling, I don't either, but I love it just the same. Wait till I order that champagne. Better still, let's go over and see Tomás. It's a shame to make him suffer with curiosity any longer. He tells me he used to know you when you were a sniveling little brat cadging pennies dancing in the streets."

She wrinkled her nose at me. But the smile defeated the tears.

A couple of hours and a couple of bottles later, Tomás had decided that Juanita was the most beautiful thing he'd ever seen, Juanita had decided that this was the most wonderful night of her life, and I'd decided that we were all getting very drunk.

From time to time the dancers we had originally come to see appeared, and to the accompaniment of the guitar went through the whole gamut from flamencos to folk dances. And they were excellent. One was particularly attractive, a small, finely proportioned girl with an exquisite body. She wore a *castellano* peasant costume, the bright colors of which heightened her milky complexion and flashing black eyes.

I caught Tomás' eye and nodded toward the girl.

"I see what you mean."

Although I had spoken in an undertone, Juanita had a pretty good idea of what I was referring to. She had been watching me as much as the show. She shrugged her shoulders, annoyance wrinkling her beautiful brow.

"I can dance much better than that."

I kissed the tip of her ear.

"Darling, they start where you left off," I said.

"Then why do you stare at her?"

"But you're not dancing."

She started to get up.,

"Hey, where are you going?"

"I'm going to dance."

I grabbed her arm and pressed her back into the chair. "Good God, you'll start a riot. Here, have a drink." I pushed over her glass. She picked it up and downed the contents. I thought for a frightened moment that she was going to hurl the glass at the girl. I glanced over at Tomás and winked. He gave me a wily smile.

"I'll tell you what we'll do," he said. "I'll get María and we'll all go out to my house and have a competition."

"María being?"

"The girl." He nodded toward the floor.

"You know her?"

This time the smile was really superior.

"And your señora, she'll break your bloody head," I put in.

"She's gone to Manacor to spend a few days with her mother."

"What are we waiting for?"

We found a taxi and waited for Tomás and María outside. They finally turned up together with the guitarist. The girl still wore her costume. They piled in and Tomás introduced us. It seemed he knew the dancer rather well. He led us into the house and up a flight of wide stairs to a den on the second floor. Juanita had temporarily buried the hatchet and the two girls were laughing and giggling as they talked to each other. Tomás took me along the hall and showed me a bathroom and bedroom, saying I might as well stay the night after the fiesta was over.

By the time I returned to the den the guitarist was picking out a tune and María was swaying to the rhythm. Tomás opened a cabinet, brought out several bottles, and asked me what I'd have. I accepted a strong brandy and filled the glass with soda water. I walked over to Maria and asked her if she knew a *seguidilla,* a popular Andalusian dance. The musician found the tune and she whirled away.

After watching her for a few minutes, Juanita got up and whispered to Tomás. He led her out of the room. On the way past the piano she switched a large Spanish shawl off its top. Tomás returned and sat down beside me.

Maria had no sooner stopped dancing than I heard the crack, crack, crack of hands beating time behind me. The guitarist must have known his cue, for he quickened his beat to the rapid tempo of a *jarabe gitano.* Juanita strode past, her hands on her hips, her shoulders slouched forward. As she passed me, she gave a disdainful snap of her fingers.

The alcoholic haze dispersed as I watched her. She had wound the shawl around her waist so that it just touched the floor. One end was brought up over her shoulder and covered her right side. Her left breast was bare. So far as I could see, the shawl was all that she had on. She held the crimson rose between her teeth.

For the next few minutes we were treated to an intoxicating, sensuous interpretation of the ancient dance. I had watched frenzied *gitanos* perform it in the fire-lit woods near Seville. But where they were crude, she was graceful; where they offered, she suggested. The play of her hands and arms, the exciting backward sweep of her body and head, the sensuous rhythmic motion of her hips and torso made even Rosita's considerable ability pale in comparison.

Suddenly she stopped. So suddenly one could hear above the pounding of one's blood the last chords cascading down the hallway. The girl stood in the center of the room. Slowly she took the rose from between her teeth, cupped it with her two hands, and kissed it. She flung it away from her, turned, and walked through the doorway. I stooped down, picked up the flower and followed her.

Still quivering with the passionate intensity of the dance, she had thrown herself across the bed. I sat beside her and took her in my arms. A warm smile made her eyes shine. I tried to kiss her. She held back her head.

"Am I better than that other girl?"

"I've never seen anything so superb, so perfect, so exciting …"

"Be careful," she laughed gaily, "or you will run out of Spanish words."

I slipped the shawl off her shoulder and buried my face between her warm breasts. I could feel her muscles still flowing, still answering the call of the wild music. Running her hands down her body, she shoved away the shawl that covered her. Her hands continued to move over her stomach as though she were trying to smother the fire that was burning within her.

Suddenly she opened her eyes wide and stared at me. "When I dance for you I go mad. I am like a *gitana*. I have no shame."

"If you love me there is no shame."

"*Madre de Dios,* how I love you! How I have ached for you!"

I crushed her to me, bruising my lips against her teeth as slowly she opened her mouth and breathed her fire into my body.

CHAPTER FOURTEEN

S OMETIME after daylight I woke up and lay there half thinking, half dreaming. I thought that I had known something
about the art of making love, but that night I had had the book
thrown at me. Slowly the dreams, the memories faded and reality
came seeping in with the sunlight. I began to work out a mental
balance sheet. I glanced over at the relaxed face buried in the
pillow beside me and made a big entry at the top of the credit
page: She's come back to me. But out there in the awakening city
were little men who had a great deal to do with my immediate
future. Would Aguzado really put up the large amount of money
to clear me? Or would he think this might be a good time to bury
the case of Francisco Gonzales once and for all and abandon me
to the wolves?

And if he did, just how tough would the wolves be? I had
enough money in Tangier to pay off the fine; enough to get
another ship. But it would take nearly every cent I had. Five hard
years of cents.

But the outstanding debit item was Despojo. I hadn't even
started to pay off the interest on the debt I owed Francisco; that
I owed Juanita.

She must have sensed that I was awake. I could feel the soft
caress of her hair as she turned and stared at me. In the first light
of the day her eyes were like two black opals shot with fire. She
slipped her hand behind my back and pulled me toward her.

"Oh, darling, it's been so long and I have been so miserable," she whispered.

"It was your idea. I've missed you too. More than I ever thought I would. But why did you run away? Why didn't you give me a chance to explain?"

She buried her head in my shoulder. I could feel her body shake as she sobbed. "Oh, I know," she said finally. "It's difficult for you to understand. You see, I blamed myself as much as you. If you had only stopped sooner it might not have happened. And if I had been taking care of my father, I know it wouldn't have happened. I was running away from myself as much as from you."

"I imagined that at the time. But I still don't know why you stayed away so long."

"I heard you had started to work for Aguzado. And Sherrif told me he was the man behind my father's death. What was I to think? That the only thing that mattered to you was making more money. You know you do talk that way. I loved my father and I loved you. I thought I had lost both of you. I almost went out of my mind in Fez. I would go to bed with a little thought. I couldn't sleep. The little thought would grow and grow until it became a waking nightmare. I would get up and walk the streets. Sherrif was sure that I was going crazy."

For a long time we held each other in silence. Finally I said, "Well, that chapter is finished. You're here and I'm here. But you'd better start building up a little faith in me, don't you think?" I swung around and sat up. "By the way, what have you done with Sherrif?"

"I left him in Fez. He finally got another job, but he told me to send for him when I wanted him."

I got up, found a bottle of mineral water, and filled two glasses. I handed one to Juanita. "How is your head? You really pinned one on last night."

"Terrible. How is yours?"

"Hanging way over, but my heart is happy. Incidentally, I didn't realize you were such a magnificent dancer. No, I'm serious. You really are. How would it be if I retire and *you* start paying all the bills? I'll be your manager."

At last the gay laughter I remembered so well. "How do you think I made a living after I left home?" she demanded.

"Well, I have ideas."

She threw a pillow at me. "You are a bastard, you know. I don't know why I ever fell in love with you."

"You use that kind of language in New England and they'll run you out of town."

"Oh, Brian, darling!" Suddenly she was serious. "What are we going to do?"

I sat down on the edge of the bed. "Look, my sweet. I'm afraid right now it's not a question of what *we're* going to do. The question is, what are a lot of other people going to do? At the moment I'm right smack behind the eight ball. Or to put it more plainly for you, *estoy en dificultades.* And until Aguzado and the *aduana* and the navy decide what they're going to do with me, discussing our future is rather a waste of time. For the next little while let's make it every day for itself. O.K. with you?"

I looked at my watch. It was nearly nine o'clock. I wondered where Tomás had got to and whether his wife was still in Manacor. And I thought that some coffee, strong, would be an excellent prelude to a large breakfast. I went into the bathroom, turned on the water, and called to Juanita that we'd better get dressed and be on our way.

She was staying at the Alcina, so I walked over with her. She explained that she hadn't been able to face the house when she returned to Mallorca, but that she supposed there was no use putting it off any longer. I suggested that she get busy and get all her affairs in shape, because there was no telling when I might want her to leave the island. I told her I'd meet her for dinner that evening, and crossed back to the Victoria. And I really upset the cook when I insisted that when I said five boiled eggs I meant five boiled eggs.

Paco came to see me at the hotel. He said that the customs had unloaded the ship and stored everything in their warehouse. He gave me an itemized list bearing the seal of the *jefe de aduana*. I had no original to compare it with, but gathered it was fairly exact. He also told me that they had removed the injectors from the engines and taken them ashore.

I asked him what he wanted to do now, and he replied that if I didn't need him for a few days he'd like to go and visit his family. I gave him some money and told him to go ahead. I told him to come and see me when he returned to Palma, and to come on to Tangier if I had gone.

Tomás burst in as Paco was leaving. He had just learned that the tribunal was to hear my case the day following.

"When do they tell *me?*" I inquired.

"What's eating you? You really worried about getting caught?"

"No. If Aguzado doesn't pay up, it'll be unpleasant, but I'll simply sneak off the island. No, I'm still looking for Despojo."

"So that's it. Well, as far as I've been able to find out, he's never returned to Mallorca. I heard the other day that he's running the Barcelona end of the business now."

"Barcelona, eh? Aguzado do much over there?"

"Most of the contraband he lands in the islands ends up there," Tomás explained. "He also has a few ships carrying direct."

"I thought the fellows didn't like running to the mainland; too risky."

"They don't, but he owns several cargo schooners that operate between Cádiz, Almeria, Barcelona, and a few other places. On the way around from the Atlantic, a small boat meets them in the Straits of Gibraltar and passes over the contraband. When the schooner berths in Barcelona or wherever, she hasn't touched a foreign port, so there's no reason to search for contraband."

"Too easy. Why don't they all do that and put us out of business?" I asked him.

"Simply because every Spanish ship entering port is subject to a routine customs checkup, no matter where she's from. Naturally, if she's from a foreign country she gets a good going over. If she's bound in from another Spanish port, it's cursory. But they can only hide so many cases or sacks among the cargo. To stock up like you do would be too obvious."

"Anyway, you can find out for sure what Despojo's doing in Barcelona?"

"I'll try," Tomás agreed.

The tribunal sat in semiprivate; whether because the public was excluded or because people just didn't know about it, I wasn't sure. I was rather pleased, however, that half the port wasn't packed behind me. One of the three judges was a friend of mine, and he tipped me a wink as I sat down beside Fernández, the lawyer.

There was nothing to it. A clerk read out the charge and ran through the list of goods found on board, concluding with an itemized valuation. When he reached the cigarettes, the price he quoted was so low that I nudged the lawyer and whispered, "Better get that fellow to buy for us. He can beat your man in Tangier."

"We have friends," he replied with a smile.

In true Mallorcan fashion, everything had been arranged beforehand. One of the judges read out the amount of the fine from a slip of paper, and Fernández handed the clerk a check for the exact sum already certified. I hadn't been asked to open my mouth.

The lawyer and I walked across the plaza and sat down outside a café.

"When are you leaving?" he asked.

"Soon as I can. What about the police? Will they make any trouble about returning my passport?"

He opened his brief case, extracted my passport and an envelope.

"I picked it up this morning. And I also booked you a passage on this afternoon's plane to Madrid. You stay there overnight and catch the plane next day for Tangier. Here are the tickets."

"You fellows certainly take care of your men. How much do I owe you for the tickets?"

"Nothing, nothing."

"Tell me one thing, Fernández. I thought we were going to fight this case."

"We are, my friend. We pleaded not guilty. You'll probably never know it, but you might well become a *cause célèbre*."

"So long as I don't know it, I don't much care what happens."

I picked up a taxi and drove out to the Alcina. Juanita was waiting for me in the lobby, and the look of relief that flashed into her eyes when I told her that everything had worked out all right brought a catch to my throat. I explained that I was returning to Tangier that afternoon, that under the circumstances I had better get off the island before someone changed his mind.

We had a terrific battle during lunch. It started when I suggested that Juanita stay in Mallorca for the time being and straighten up her father's affairs. I informed her that I had asked Tomás to give her any advice she needed, and told her to be sure to call on him when necessary. I explained that I'd be away from Tangier anyway for some time, getting another ship, but that I'd send for her as soon as I got back.

When I mentioned another ship I thought she'd hit the ceiling. She had been sure, she cried, that when I got out of this mess I'd stop. I tried to explain to her that the very fact that I was free, that the fine had been paid, the loss of the Chucha made good, made it impossible for me to stop right away. If Aguzado had thought that I was going to blow now, he'd never have paid; he'd have let me rot in jail first.

"Well, pay him back," she retorted.

"Don't be silly. It would take half, if not more, of all the money I've made."

"But he has made a lot out of you. He *has* to pay your fine."

"Sure. He figures I'm a damn good investment. That's why he coughed up. But if I don't keep on producing he's not going to like it. And I don't have to remind you what happens to people he doesn't like. Sorry, I shouldn't have said that. But you're being unreasonable."

I reached across the table and tried to take her hand. She snatched it away.

"It's just like I told you in Tangier," she said, her eyes blazing. *"Está en tu sangre.* You will never stop."

"You're wrong. Three, four, let's say five trips more, and Aguzado will be well out of the red as far as I'm concerned. I promise you I'll quit then. And within five trips I'll have taken care of Señor Despojo too, or know the reason why."

"Despojo!" She fairly spat his name at me. "He's just an excuse, like everything else. I don't believe you want to find him."

I stared at her incredulously. I waited, hoping, praying that she would take it back. But her eyes had sharpened to angry black pin points.

Slowly I shoved my chair back and stood up. With both hands on the table I leaned toward her.

"And that, my sweet," I said quietly, distinctly, "is the last crack you will ever make to me. From here on in I'm sailing alone. I'll find Despojo and I'll send you his heart. You can keep it in place of mine. *Se ha acabado.*"

Without looking back I walked out of the restaurant. I picked up a taxi and drove out to the airport.

CHAPTER FIFTEEN

W HEN I arrived in Tangier I remembered the lawyer's words and I certainly felt like the cause of something. The ribbing I had to take for being caught was, to say the least, extensive.

"What are you going to do now?" Ricardo asked me later that day. "Get another ship?"

"I'm certainly not investing in an M.L. like my last one. How fast do those Spanish destroyers go?"

"About thirty knots, I suppose. They're pretty antique. Why? You going to buy a cruiser?"

"I've got ideas."

I went up to see Bartolomé Losa. He was very much interested to hear my news. He admitted that he had received instructions from Mallorca to stop all shipments for the time being. He said that two other ships had been captured by the navy; one off Almeria, the other off Alicante.

"Suppose," I said, "I find a ship that will go faster than their destroyers. Would you pay me more per trip?"

"If it goes on like this, I'm sure we would. After all, we have to get the goods through somehow."

"O.K., get out your pencil and figure out how much more you'll pay running from here to Barcelona."

"Why Barcelona? I thought you'd only work to the islands."

"I'd be a damn fool to go back there for a while. If they pick me up again, I doubt if they'd land me alive."

From Losa's office I walked up to the cable company and sent a long message to a friend of mine in England. Two days later I had my reply, on the strength of which I caught the commuter's plane to Gibraltar, transferred to a B.E.A. plane, and landed in London that night.

Michael met me at the airway terminal and took me around to his flat. "You're in one hell of a hurry," he said.

"I am. Tell me what you found out about these ex-German E boats."

He dug around his desk until he uncovered some papers. "I located one down at Shoreham that can be bought for around four thousand pounds. So far as I know, she still has the armor plate around the deckhouse. I know her original engines are still in her. That's why the bloke wants to sell. No one can afford to expend that much fuel oil tootling around the coasts."

"Fuel oil? I thought they had gasoline engines."

"Diesel. Three whopping great engines, twenty-four cylinders each."

"That'll be something to see."

"It is, provided you have the cash to buy the fuel."

"What's their top speed?"

Michael turned out another sheet of paper and handed it to me. It described in detail the German E boat.

"Forty knots!" I whistled.

"When they were built and in calm water," my friend rejoined. "I doubt if they'll touch that now."

I doubted it too, but I still thought it would outrun the Spanish destroyers, so I went down to Shoreham the next day and bought the thing.

While the ship was being readied for sea I spent some of the time getting in touch with an armaments officer I had once been friendly with in the RAF. I finally tracked him to an Essex pub in which he had bought an interest by marrying the owner's daughter.

This encounter led to a fast trip with him by car to the RAF station at Boscombe Downs. I waited at the hotel while he went on to the station to see some old friends. That night we returned to London, and in the back of the car were several large cans he'd brought back from the station.

The following day he took me out to Farnham, where we visited a war-assets disposal section. We found a pile of drums, about the size of forty-gallon oil drums. I bought four of them for a song, and told the salesman I'd telephone him shipping instructions in a day or two. My friend unscrewed a large plug from each drum, and brought them with him.

Before leaving London that night, he showed me the plugs, or detonators, he'd brought, and gave me careful instructions on how to wire them up.

"I'll write down everything I've told you and mail it on to you. It's perfectly simple, but if you don't do it exactly as it's laid down, it won't work. But for God's sake," he begged as he said good-by, "if anyone catches you with this stuff, don't mention me."

The weather favored us and we had a quiet run across the Bay of Biscay and down the Portuguese coast. Off the Tagus we found we had plenty of fuel oil left, so we carried straight on south. We arrived in Tangier just after dawn, and I dropped the anchor in our usual spot off *quatrocientos*.

When we had shut down, I called the crew into the deck cabin. I told them that under no circumstances were they to mention the speed of the ship or the size of the engines ashore. I said that if anyone was curious, we carried two Gray Diesels, and our top speed was around fifteen knots. I told Harry the first thing he had to do was install a good lock on the engine-room hatch and to paint the bottom side of the glass deck lights with white paint. There would be workmen aboard constructing a hold in the after part of the ship, and while they were there, he was to cover his engines with canvas. Even when he was working in the engine room that hatch was to be kept locked.

On the passage down from England we had unscrewed the wooden boards bearing the old name Gypsy on each side of the bridge, broken them up, and tossed them overboard. We had replaced them with boards on which was painted the new name, Erinys. Paco had doctored the paint so that it didn't look too fresh.

I went ashore and arranged with a shipwright to construct the hold and gave him my plans. I said that he would have to do the work while the ship was at anchor out in the harbor, that I wouldn't bring her alongside. He said that he could manage it, but that it would take a little longer. He promised to have every-thing completed within a week.

Next I called on Losa. I told him that I had brought in a new ship and that I'd be ready to go to work in a week. I asked him what he was offering.

"I've been in touch with Señor Aguzado," he replied, "and told him that you promised to get a ship that would guarantee delivery. He figures you don't know what you're talking about, but he's willing to give you a try."

"And?" I rubbed my thumb and forefinger together.

"He wouldn't say definitely. He left it up to me. What's your idea?"

"Double."

"That's a lot of money."

"I know. How many shipments you lost this past month?"

"Three."

"That's a lot of money, too."

"Don't mention it," he said. "I've reached the point where I can't sleep at night. And suppose we pay you double the price, and *you* get caught? We just can't afford it."

"O.K., make it double or nothing. For every cargo I get through, you pay me double. If I don't get through, you pay nothing."

"And the value of the ship if you're caught?"

"You can skip that, too. I'll carry the risk."

"I think we can do business. Let me know when you're ready."

After the hold and hatches were finished and the last workman had gone ashore, I told the crew to bring up the four drums we'd brought from England. I showed them where I wanted them fixed aft, two on either side. Harry cut out cradles, bolted them to the deck, and lashed the drums to them.

"What are you going to carry in these?" he asked, pulling down the last lashing. "Fuel oil?"

"Yeah. A special kind."

He laughed and said, "Geez, someday you're going to open up and tell us something."

I was serious. "What you fellows don't know in this game, they can't beat out of you. Don't forget it."

I told Harry and Jim that they could have the rest of the afternoon and night off; I'd be staying on board. After they had gone and Paco had brought back the dinghy, I got out several of the tins my ex-RAF friend had scrounged at Boscombe Downs. Following the instructions carefully, I emptied the contents into the drums. Next I measured out a quantity of liquid and poured it in. I loosened the screw holding a large cap fixed to the end of each drum, but didn't remove it.

I screwed the detonators into the filling holes, and ran the wires down through a hole we had punched in the deck and forward through the ship to the bridge. Here I connected each to a separate push button, then back to the batteries. Just before the batteries I installed a master switch. When the job was finished I left the switch open and carefully explained everything to Paco. I told him exactly what he was to do and when.

CHAPTER SIXTEEN

W HEN WE cleared Tangier on our first trip, I felt the enthusiasm of a child with a new toy. Leaving the Straits, I set course to keep us equidistant from the Spanish and African shores. When we were a good twenty miles off the Spanish coast, I altered course east and northward, but maintained the twenty-mile sea room all the way to Barcelona.

I experimented with the engines. On one she would cruise at eight knots with a fairly low consumption of fuel oil. Using the two outer engines, she would drive along at fifteen to eighteen knots, but the fuel consumption doubled. Full out on all engines she got up to thirty-eight knots and held it nicely.

But at that speed the consumption was terrific. One could almost see the needles dropping in the tank gauges. With full tanks I reckoned we could maintain full speed for just under four hours. After satisfying myself as to what the ship would do with a full load, I shut down and rolled forward on one engine; we had plenty of time to make our rendezvous, and my one idea with this packet was to conserve fuel oil.

The trip went off without incident and I think we were all slightly disappointed that we hadn't had the opportunity to show our heels.

We made two more runs up the coast with no interference. I had nothing to keep me in Tangier, and I hounded Losa until he gave me cargos. I became the white-haired boy around his office. They'd lost another ship to a destroyer off Valencia.

She'd been captured fifteen miles off the coast. Various skippers had tied up their ships in Tangier and gone ashore; others were working what we termed the "Straits trade." They would load up in Tangier, go out and sit in the middle of the Straits of Gibraltar until a Spanish or Italian cargo vessel came along, and sell it contraband. It was a safe business; it was always done by daylight, and if anything that looked like a warship appeared on the horizon, they simply pulled into Tangier. But there was little money in it.

I felt that I was getting very close to Despojo. I knew that the men meeting me around Barcelona were working directly under him, and I was sure that any suspicions he might have entertained that I was after him were being allayed simply by the fact that I was carrying on normally, as though he didn't exist. I realized that there was a great deal of speculation about my new ship, and the fact that I had so much confidence in her that I not only continued to work, but accepted cargos for what was always considered the most dangerous area of the coast. He would be out, if only to see the Erinys.

The first few days after I left Juanita, I went through hell. Only the fact that I was constantly busy getting the ship into shape had kept me from going back to Mallorca. But gradually as time passed I became pretty bitter, and I found the feeling easier to live with. A sentence in a letter I had received from Tomás helped me to achieve this state; unaware that we were washed up, he kidded me that Juanita was being seen around the town with young Diego Velásquez.

My old haunts in Tangier welcomed me back with open arms. But it wasn't long before their consolation proved a poor substitute. I found myself spending most of my time in port with Ricardo and a bottle.

It was getting on toward the end of March, and the weather was making up for the equinox. Losa asked me if I could carry a deck cargo.

"What's the trouble? Haven't you any other ships?"

"Right now I can't find another skipper. They're afraid of either the weather or the Spanish navy, or they're down in Marrakech basking in the sunshine with their girl friends. You're about the only man who seems to like work these days."

"If that's the case, it's about time you raised the ante."

"You're doing all right."

"But for the deck cargo—"

"*Caramba,* you play close to the chest!"

"O.K. But anything I take on deck will get wet."

"It won't hurt this shipment. It's automobile tires."

"When do we go?"

We plunged up the coast with a strong so'wester on our tail, and breaking my usual practice, I cut Cabo de Palos rather close in to get away from the tremendous seas as we turned northward. As luck would have it, the wind came around, and crossing the Gulf of Valencia we got it on the port bow with hurricane force. Fortunately we weren't far off land, so the seas didn't rise too high. We were throttled back to less than seven knots; any faster and I was afraid the little ship would break her back as she pounded into the waves.

When we were somewhere off the mouth of the Ebro, the sun dropped behind a black curtain of cloud. The barometer had steadied at 29.4. The wind came up stronger with the night and the wire rigging was giving off a high continuous scream. The worse the weather, the more I preferred the open bridge. I could duck the spray as it was whipped across, and no wet glass obstructed my vision. Paco was squatting beside me in the lee of the dodger.

"You think anyone will come out to meet us tonight?" I asked him.

"*No sé*. But even if they do, we are going to have much work getting the cargo across in this sea."

"You have something there. We're supposed to meet them six miles out. Six miles in this wind, even when it's off the land, means a pretty big sea. I don't want to smash up the ship."

It was the one constant worry we had during the winter months; that we would make a trip and meet our contact, only to find we couldn't transship the cargo because of the sea. For to try to bring even ships as small as ours alongside one another in a heavy sea would result in enormous damage.

"Well, we've come this far. But if they don't come out tonight we'll return to Tangier. This weather looks as though it's going to last for a few days."

Asking the mate to take the wheel, I dropped down to the deck and went aft. I checked the deckload; so far we hadn't lost anything. Moving back to my four drums, I removed the canvas covers Paco had made for them, folded them up, and stowed them away. I unscrewed the caps covering the holes in the ends of the drums, took them forward, and placed them in the deck cabin. I climbed down into the engine room and closed the master switch connecting the push buttons to the batteries. It had become routine practice. Each time before reaching a rendezvous I had carried out the same drill.

Nearing our contact point we found a confused breaking sea. It was hopeless even to think of trying to make fast alongside another ship; the first wave and our sides would be crushed in like eggshells. I turned out all the lights but the masthead and just kept the ship dodging into the waves. I felt pretty safe. No one in his right senses would be thinking of running contraband on such a night; certainly revenue cutters would be lying snug in their berths.

I waited half an hour and was just about to give up when we spotted a light ahead. From the tremendous arc it was making, it was a small ship, and undoubtedly our fishing boat. And from the way the light was obscured from time to time, she was making heavy weather of it. I flashed the signal. It returned the right answer. I told Paco not to open the hatches. The way we were rolling our scuppers under, it would have been dangerous even to take the covers off.

Over the noise of the storm we could make out the thud-thud-thud of the other ship's engine. Swinging astern, she turned around us and came up on our starboard side. A strong voice asked me if I would return the following night. I picked up the megaphone and said no, the weather would be the same and I wasn't hanging around outside for twenty-four hours. The voice came back asking me if I would follow him in to the coast and get under the lee of the land. When I demanded to know where, he said that the best place was off Sitges, that all the Barcelona boats were fishing there tonight.

I had a look at the chart and decided that it was worth a try. If I didn't like it, I could always sheer off southward. I told the fishing boat to go ahead and leave a light on so I could follow. I let him get two or three hundred yards ahead, then plunged after him.

Calling the crew up, I explained what we were doing and told them to stand by in case we had to make a run for it. I warned them that if we did find water calm enough to get the cargo off, they'd have to work as they had never worked before, because we'd be in very close to land.

We followed our fisherman shoreward until I began to think he was going to take us right up on the beach. We were slightly to the north of Sitges, but one could easily distinguish the town's lights. We passed several trawlers fishing and gave them wide berths. But the seas flattened out as we got into the shadow of the high cliffs.

It wasn't until we could actually see the shore as a deeper black against the murky horizon that the other ship stopped and waited. I estimated that we were less than half a mile off the land. We crept alongside, and almost before our lines were made fast, the men started heaving the tires across.

I greeted the skipper as he jumped across into the Erinys.

"I thought you were going to take us right into port."

"Muy bien aquí. Es un lago."

"It may be a lake, but if there are any *carabineros* up on those cliffs they can pot us with their rifles."

"No, no. You must come right in under their noses or stay out. It is halfway that is dangerous."

I wasted no time in getting the accounts settled. The more I looked at the land, the less I liked it. I told the men to get a move on. I went forward as far away from the mutter of the engines as possible and listened. Seaward I could make out the lights of the fishing fleet, shoreward nothing. A projecting cliff cut us off from the lights of the nearby town. We appeared to be lying just off a wide shallow bay.

For some time I imagined that I could hear the peculiar mechanical wheezing of a big ship's engines. But when I tried to figure out from which direction it was coming, it faded elusively into the noises of the night. I returned aft, let go the stern line, and tossed it over to the fisherman.

"We'll keep together on one rope only," I said to Paco. "I think I hear a ship. How much longer will you be?"

"About five minutes." I could almost feel the sweat pouring off him.

I returned to the bows. This time there was no doubt about it. Off to the south came the whoomp, whoomp, whoomp of a ship's engines, and it was no motorboat and it showed no lights.

I stooped down, undid the bowline from the bitts, and chucked it over to the fishing trawler. Running back to the bridge, I shouted across that a ship was approaching. I opened all three engines and took off straight from the side of the fisherman, leaving a good bit of our paintwork behind.

Whatever vessel was approaching, those in her were maintaining a good lookout. For no sooner had the thunder of our engines broken across the night than a searchlight was switched on. It swung first to seaward and gave us precious seconds as it slowly moved across the water. It caught the fishing boat just getting under way, paused, then swept relentlessly on toward us. Once it had picked up our wake, it lifted and held us in its glare.

I reached down and pressed one of the push buttons. I heard a loud crack from close astern. Shielding my eyes with my hand, I looked back. From one of the drums poured a thick white cloud of smoke. I could almost feel the rays of the searchlight dim as the smoke screen streamed out behind us, cutting its strength. Finally it was just a white blob.

Paco was jumping up and down beside me, clapping his hands and yelling, "Son-of-a-bitch! Son-of-a-bitch!"

I turned to smile at him and ducked. A stream of heavy tracers whooshed by and buried themselves in the horizon. They were certainly twenty millimeters.

I spun the wheel to starboard and fired another detonator. A second stream of smoke mingled with the first. I kept going to starboard until I could see the pursuing light sharply. The ship chasing us was coming up fast on the seaward side of the smoke screen, and she hadn't lost any ground. I swung back to port, straightened her out, and let her roar. Just before the third drum emptied, I again nosed out to starboard and looked back. The destroyer, for it could be nothing else, was still there; farther back now, but still within range and just outside the long white wall of smoke.

I swung back to port and closed the throttles. The deceleration almost threw the mate off the bridge. The little ship made a tight turn as she settled back into the sea. I kept her going slowly ahead and turning until I had doubled back to our smoke screen. When we passed through the first wisps of the acrid fumes I straightened out and let her roll slowly ahead toward our pursuer, making sure I kept to the opposite side of the smoke.

From time to time we could see the reflection of the searchlight on the smoke. I told Paco to start praying. If that skipper ever decided to cross through the screen he would either cut us in two or come so close he would swamp us. But with only one drum left I had to take the risk. If we were still within range of his guns when we'd run out of smoke, he'd certainly sink us. I knew that I could outdistance him in a straight race, but I wasn't willing to gamble on whether I'd have the time to outdistance his guns as well.

The destroyer swept past us not fifty yards off with the noise of a tidal wave. I kept my engines just ticking over; I didn't want their sound to give us away. But when she was abreast, I opened up and turned hard toward her, telling the men to hang on. A few seconds later her enormous bow wave hit us and we shipped water right up to the wheelhouse. I swung back to the south and gave her all she had.

For the next half hour we hugged the coast. I realized that as soon as the destroyer reached the end of the smoke screen she'd guess that we'd doubled back and come racing after us. In the comparative calm waters close in I certainly had the edge in speed. But outside in the seaway I wouldn't be able to make half the speed a destroyer could with her steel hull.

When we had the lights of Tarragona on the starboard bow I swung out to sea. Astern we could see nothing. But I had a strong feeling that somewhere in that blackness a powerful ship was bearing down on us. I maintained full throttle until Harry came up from below and told me we'd have to ease up, the hull wouldn't stand much more pounding. I knocked the center engine out of gear, but kept it ticking over. Fortunately the seas were making up astern and she rode fairly easily at twenty knots.

Dawn found us plunging through tremendous seas well out in the Gulf of Valencia. We were running on one engine and Harry told me he was worried about the fuel supply. We had emptied four of the six tanks during the night, and with the ship rolling so much it was difficult to gauge accurately just how much remained in the tank we were presently using.

I made a rough calculation and decided that provided we didn't have to use more than one engine at a time, a full tank should see us back to Tangier.

What really worried me, though, was the thought that every warship on the south coast would be out searching for us after last night's performance. I could see the destroyers steaming out from the naval base at Cartagena. They would know that I had to turn the corner at Cabo de Palos to get to Tangier, and they'd be waiting for us there.

I turned the wheel over to the mate and went down into the cabin. I checked the speed and distance indicator with the time and made a rough calculation of our present position. I got out the chart of the western Mediterranean, marked our position, and drew a straight line down to Algiers. I ascertained the true course, altered it to magnetic, and passed it up to Paco.

Telling Harry to relax, I explained that we were going into Algiers for a few days and have a rest.

"It's not so much the oil I'm worried about," I explained. "But the Spanish navy isn't going to sit back and take what we gave them last night. When they saw that smoke screen we laid, they probably thought we were some Red outfit delivering a special atomic bomb with Franco's name written on it. So we'll try to outsmart them. Instead of returning to Tangier, we'll head east and south. And I'd love to watch them roughing up the seas between Cartagena and Gibraltar."

"Well, one thing I learned last night," he said, "and that is what those damn drums were for. I didn't know whether we were carrying poison gas, depth charges, or what."

I smiled.

"I learned that trick over the beaches of Normandy. Those drums are aircraft smoke containers."

Before we had picked up the African coast I asked Paco how much of the cargo had been left on board. He said that they had got everything off except eight sacks of sugar. It was a good thing he'd left the sugar till the last; it was the least valuable. When he took over the wheel I told him to keep his eye open for a fishing vessel, and if he saw one to go alongside and give them the sugar. I wasn't going to risk trouble with the French customs in Algiers over a bit of sugar.

As we got farther south the seas mounted, and I was beginning to look forward to reaching shelter. Nearing the port I told the mate to dump the sugar over the side; it was so rough that even if we saw a fishing boat we'd never be able to get close enough to make a present of it now.

After rounding the outer quay I called the crew up to the bridge and gave them their instructions. I told them that so far as the authorities were concerned, we were on passage from

Gibraltar to Malta, and that we'd put into Algiers because of the weather. Some time previously I had had Ricardo Lewis make me up a false certificate of registry carrying the name Erinys.

We motored through to the inner basin and made fast alongside. The police, customs, and port doctor were aboard soon after we had our lines ashore. I produced the ship's papers and poured them a drink while they were taking down the details. The customs had a good look around, but when they found the hold empty they lost interest. They knew, and I know that they knew, that we were *contrabandistas,* but as long as we had entered the port empty they had no proof and accepted any reasonable story I wanted to tell. It made it much easier for them, and they showed their appreciation by telling me of one or two good *bistros* ashore where I might find amusement.

I asked Paco, who could get along on less sleep than anyone I ever knew, to keep an eye on things for the rest of the day and turned in.

I awakened after dark feeling like death warmed over. The strain of the past few days had been terrific. I had been lucky to get away with it. How long, I asked myself, was this luck going to last? From where I sat, the whole future stretching out before me looked pretty somber. I certainly didn't feel a victim of circumstances, but I think that the cards were so stacked against me that unless I started to deal from the bottom of the pack I'd never win.

I took hold of my bootstraps with the knowledge that I had more money than I had ever had before; enough to go home, give up this dangerous way of life, and build something that I could be proud of. And I didn't forget to remember those lean days when I thought that to be able to snap my fingers at financial responsibility was the most important thing in life.

Well, I had reached that stage, only to find it *still* wasn't the goal. What was it, then? Juanita? But that was finished, dead and buried. There can't be love without faith, and if she had had one ounce of faith in me she would never have put me through the wringer the way she had these past months. And right now she was probably teaching that young bastard Velásquez some of the finer points of making love.

Despojo? But was he so important? Hadn't he just become an obsession?

My feet hit the deck with a thud as I jumped down from the bunk. I yelled for Paco to bring me some hot water.

"You want to go ashore?" I asked him.

"No. I've been here before."

"O.K. You stay aboard. I'm going ashore and I won't be back till tomorrow, if then."

"You going to get drunk?"

"I'm going to get so drunk you'll probably have to take the ship back to Tangier yourself."

"Why don't you get yourself a woman instead? You won't have such a hangover tomorrow."

"Paquito, you are a very smart man," I said as I patted his shoulder. "If you could cook I'd marry you."

Sadly he shook his head. *"Capitán mío,* why don't you stop? Go back to the States—go back home for a while."

"And why the hell should I stop?" I demanded.

"These last weeks you are not the same. You are too hard. For me I don't worry, I can always take care of myself. Señor, I would give my life for you, but I am afraid that when the time comes my life will not save you."

I poured the water into the washbasin. When I looked up at him again his eyes were misty. Abruptly he turned to leave the cabin. I walked over and put my arm around him. "O.K., Paquito, we'll make just one more trip. I seem to remember promising someone that I'd only make five in the Erinys. And we'll both go to America and I'll make you *capitán* of the best goddamned fishing boat on the east coast."

He gave me a warm smile. "*Bueno.* Now you go and get drunk."

CHAPTER SEVENTEEN

W HEN I STOPPED by Losa's office upon my return to Tangier I found the place in an uproar. Obviously they had heard we had arrived in the port, and besides Losa there was practically every member of his entourage waiting to welcome me.

"*Muy bien, muy bien,*" he kept saying, his arm around my shoulder as he led me into his office. "The whole Spanish navy is after you. And what do you do? You snap your fingers at them; you thumb your nose. *Olé!* Ah, *amigo mío,* you are the toast of the coast. If I were a younger man, I would wish to go with you and laugh at those stupid admirals."

I had to give them a play-by-play description of the last trip. I explained why I had decided to go to Algiers and wait for a few days.

"Ah, but that was the touch of the maestro," broke in Losa. "We heard that from the naval base at Cartagena six destroyers have been patroling the coast waiting for you."

"But tell me, did the fishing boat get away?"

"Of course. The destroyer was too busy trying to catch you. By the time he returned, our fishing vessel had disappeared."

"I'm glad to hear it. But someone is out eight sacks of sugar. We broke away before we could finish unloading."

He waved his hand. "Don't think about it."

On the way back to the ship I called at Ricardo's office, and here I had to go through my story once again; apparently everyone on the coast was talking about it. Smugglers' Row had been pretty upset when the navy had taken a hand, and the knowledge that we had outsmarted them spread quickly along the water front.

Finally I informed Ricardo that I had decided to give up the game after the next trip, and asked him to look around for a buyer for my ship.

Long before I had any intention of getting up next morning, Paco came into my cabin and said that Losa was on board and wanted to speak with me. I wrapped a heavy dressing gown around me, told Paco to make some coffee, and went up on deck.

"Please, I am sorry to disturb you so early," Losa said.

"Forget it. It must be important or you wouldn't be here. What's on your mind?"

"How soon will you be able to make another trip to Barcelona?"

"Why?"

"I have a special job. A certain Catalan wishes us to bring down a large sum of Spanish currency. It seems he requires foreign money for some *negocio* and he needs it in a hurry. He is willing to pay us well if we can deposit the money here for him within eight days."

"How well?"

"On the way up you can take the usual cargo and receive the customary amount. For bringing back the currency we will pay you a bonus of fifty thousand pesetas."

"That's about a thousand dollars in my money. But what about the hullabaloo we just stirred up? Don't you think it's a bit risky making another trip so soon?"

"No, no, now is the time. The Spanish authorities will have heard by now that you have returned safely here. They will call off the search. They certainly won't think you so stupid as to return so soon."

"But as soon as I clear from Tangier, some of these little rats along the water front will be up to the Spanish consul with the information that I've sailed and demanding their blood money."

"True, and I have thought of that. I will spread the word about the port that you are afraid to return to the Mediterranean; that you are running a cargo up the Atlantic coast to Cádiz."

"I still don't like it. And for only a few thousand dollars I like it even less. Haven't you any other skippers who'll take the job on?"

Losa smiled. "I have several. But this is a very large sum of money and you are the only one, my friend, who I am sure will get it down here safely."

"Thanks for the compliment. But if it's that important, you'd better double the pin money you're offering."

"That I cannot do. I will have to telephone Señor Despojo in Barcelona and see if he will agree."

The cup I had raised halfway to my lips paused in mid-air. When I heard that name it was all I could do to set the cup back in the saucer. Slowly, carefully I reached in my pocket for a package of cigarettes. I took one and handed Losa the pack. I got up and looked for a match.

"Despojo handling this job?"

"Yes. He will bring the money out to you."

"Will he be coming down to Tangier with me, too?"

"No."

"Why not?" I was coldly calm now. "With that kind of dough on board I might take it into my head to keep going."

He leaned back in his seat and exhaled a long plume of smoke.

"I don't think you would be so foolish. The world is not big enough for you to hide in, my friend."

I laughed and sat down.

"O.K., I'll think about it. Incidentally, does Despojo know I'm the man who's supposed to be coming up?"

"No, he simply told me to send our best skipper."

"Well, since he's a friend of mine I'll help him out. Don't bother to telephone him. When I see him I'll chisel the extra money out of him myself."

As soon as we were clear of the Straits of Gibraltar, I edged over toward the African coast and headed east. I had laid out a course that would take us almost halfway to Sardinia before we turned north. Then we would make a wide circle east of the Balearic Islands and approach the land off Barcelona from the east. It meant an extra four hundred or five hundred miles, but we had plenty of fuel oil, and if we speeded up a bit it wouldn't take much longer. I had loaded several extra drums of oil on the deck.

The second night out I was standing on the bridge waiting to give Paco a new course before turning in.

"*Capitán mío,* there is something I do not like about this trip."

"Why? You feeling seasick?"

"No, I'm serious. I don't understand why Don Bartolomé insisted that we must be the ones to go and bring down this money. Many ships smuggle money out of Spain. It is not difficult."

"But this is a great deal of money, Paco."

"No, señor, I do not think so. If it was a great amount of money they would not risk it all in a ship like this. They would pay a little more and transfer it overland from Tetuán to Tangier. Or they would split it up; so much on this ship, so much on that one."

"But you heard Losa say that his customer had to have this money in Tangier pronto."

"Yes, but everybody knows that is it impossible to dump a large amount on the Tangier exchange at one time. It would break the market."

"For a sailor, you're a damn fine financier, Paquito," I laughed.

But in the soft glow of the binnacle lamp I could see no softening of the grim line of his jaw. I became serious.

"O.K., Paco. But you may be wrong. Perhaps some big Catalan manufacturer suddenly finds he needs a lot of dollars to buy cotton in Cairo. If he can close the deal today he gets a better price. Or maybe he's heard of a shipload of rubber somewhere in the States. If he can pay cash for it, he can have it. I can think of a hundred reasons why he'd risk losing a peseta or two by flooding the Tangier exchange to get some quick dollars."

"There's another thing," Paco broke in. "You know that we only carry coffee this trip."

"So what? I heard there's a shortage and they're paying a hundred and fifty pesetas a kilo in the shops."

For some time he remained silent. I stared off into the night, letting the anticipation of meeting Despojo push Paco's fears out of my mind.

"You know, *Capitán*," he said, giving the wheel a half turn, "for many years I have handled sacks of coffee. Always they are the same; sixty kilos. When you come to lift one you sort of prepare your muscles for the strain. If it is more than sixty kilos, your muscles cry out like a little child and ask you why you didn't warn them. So you must apologize, tell them that the strain is going to be greater, and take another hold."

Paco's observations brought me back to the present.

"You think someone is trying to pull a fast one and shipping overweight sacks while they pay us for the standard size?"

"*No sé.*" He shrugged his shoulders. "But I think that many of those sacks weigh more than sixty kilos."

"Tomorrow morning I'll have a look. And if they're over-weight, someone is going to be very unhappy."

Running north the next day we had beautiful weather. Not even a swell disturbed the oily surface, and I told the man at the wheel to keep an eye out for sleeping turtles. They were quite easy to catch with the special gaff I'd made, and one thing the mate could cook was an excellent turtle stew.

After breakfast I had Paco remove the afterhatch cover. I climbed down into the hold and rolled a couple of sacks of coffee over. So far as I could tell, they might have weighed 160 kilos when I attempted to pick one up. Paco laughed and dropped down beside me. Expertly he caught hold of two corners and lifted one a few inches. He dropped it and picked up another. The third one he hoisted two or three times.

"Seventy, maybe seventy-five kilos," he said, shaking his head. I tried it. But it seemed no different from the others; just damn heavy. We laid it alongside the first sack. It appeared no larger. We stood them both up and shook the beans down until we had about the same amount of space in the top of each sack. I ran my hand down the outside. Nothing but coffee beans.

"You think they've put something in with the coffee?" I asked him.

"It's an old trick," he replied.

I told him to get a piece of canvas, spread it on the deck, and dump out the heavier sack. We'd soon see.

When he had cut the string a mound of dirty gray coffee beans spilled out. I ran my hands through them and found nothing. He turned up the sack and let the last few kilos pour out. Two objects came with them, slid down the side of the pile, and hit the deck with dull thuds.

I picked one up. It was a heavy, solid article wrapped in cloth. I took out my knife and cut the threads. I unwrapped a .45

automatic. I laid it on the deck and untied the second. It was a similar weapon. Using the cloth, I wiped off the protective grease and searched for the manufacturer's name. There was none, not even a serial number. I extracted the magazine. On it were stamped two words in Russian.

"Those double-crossing bastards!" I said slowly, as I tossed the guns into the sea. "Somebody is going to get hurt for this."

I had the men work in shifts throughout the rest of the day, emptying each one of the hundred sacks. In the first heat of anger I was tempted to simply dump the lot, coffee and all, over the side. But then I realized that if I turned up to meet Despojo with no cargo, it would look too suspicious.

In all we found 160 guns and 3,000 rounds of ammunition. The ammunition was packed in plain cardboard boxes, but on the cap of each shell were stamped three letters of the Russian alphabet and the number .45. I kept one gun and a box of shells and threw the rest into the seas.

And by nightfall the crew and I had so much coffee dust in our nostrils we felt we'd never be able to drink it again.

Paco was much happier that evening. I congratulated him on his alertness and told him that from now on he'd better stay right beside me; without him to take care of me I'd probably get into trouble crossing the street.

"What are you going to do now?" he asked.

"Play it straight. They'll probably give us a package of old newspapers and say it's the money. All they wanted were those guns, and they knew damn well we're the only ship that would be sure to get them through. It was worth an extra thousand dollars. God, how stupid can you get?"

"How were you to know?"

"I should have made some inquiries in Tangier. I should take the trouble to inspect the cargo once in a while."

"But loading at night makes it difficult."

"Yeah, and they know we always load at night."

Sometime later I said, "Somehow I can't connect Aguzado with this. All the years I've been working the islands there were two things that Aguzado wouldn't touch, any more than Gonzales or any of the other smugglers: guns and dope."

"I have been thinking the same thing," Paco agreed. "Even before and during the Civil War they never ran guns, and there was big money in it in those days."

"Who's behind it, then?"

"*No sé.*"

Just before night took possession of the sky I called the crew up to the bridge. We had altered course for the last time and were making our run-in to the coast north of Barcelona. I explained to the men what they were only too well aware of: that someone had attempted to run a load of arms into Spain. I pointed out that this went on from time to time on a small scale. There was always a market in and around Barcelona among the die-hards who would never accept the fact that the Civil War was finished. But it was a mug's game for the gun-runners. One might get away with one shipment, probably two. But once the authorities knew you were running arms— and they had means of finding out—you were in for it if and when you were caught. And it wasn't a case of a fine; you'd spend the rest of your life in jail if you were lucky enough to get there, and you could bet your own government wouldn't lift a finger to help you.

Ordinarily, I went on, I would have dumped the cargo over the side and returned to Tangier. But at the end of this trip I hoped to see one Pablo Despojo, the man who had murdered our friend in Palma, Francisco Gonzales. I described briefly how I had gone to Mallorca and tracked him down, and how we had taken on the Barcelona run because I was sure that one day we would meet.

"Well," I concluded, "I'm hoping that tonight will be the night. He's supposed to rendezvous with the fishing boat to turn over a wad of currency. But I'm inclined to think the money angle is only a front. I'm hoping, though, that he'll still be there to ensure the transfer and disposal of what he assumes are still inside those sacks of coffee.

"I don't know whether Despojo realizes that I'm after him. But we won't take chances. Before we come along-side, Paco will assume command. I'll be below in the cabin, out of sight. We can only hope that Despojo doesn't recognize Paco when he comes aboard. After all," I turned to the mate, "it's a good many years since he's seen you, isn't it?"

Paco nodded.

"O.K., Despojo comes aboard in the usual manner. Paco tells him I've just gone below and shows him the way. From then on I'll take care of Mr. Son-of-a-bitch Despojo.

"Paco returns to the bridge and keeps watch. Any sign of trouble from below or outside and he yells across to the fisherman that there's a patrol vessel coming. Harry, you take the bowlines and let them go. Jim, you let go the stern and we're off. If and when I hear the engines open up, I'll come up and take over. In the meantime, if there's no trouble you two fellows get cracking and get that coffee transferred. Ask some of the men in the fishing boat to help you. I want them to nurse those sacks ashore carefully, and it'll give me great pleasure to think of them when they spill the contents out on the floor of some dive in Barcelona and find only beans."

"But won't the skipper of the fishing boat wonder why Despojo doesn't return to his vessel?" Harry put in.

"That's something we'll have to take care of when it comes up. I should be back on deck long before you have the coffee transferred, and I'll deal with the other skipper."

It was a beautiful night as we neared the coast. I was able to get good fixes from the lights at Barcelona and Tossa. Our rendezvous had been set well north of the port this time, just off the flatlands separating the city from the Costa Brava. The fishing fleet was out in strength, and it looked like a string of iridescent pearls as their powerful lamps stretched out ahead. A slight offshore breeze carried out the tangy scent of pine fires.

Fifteen miles off the land I slowed down and double-checked our position and time. The contact point was seven miles south-southeast of Tossa lighthouse, which, as the coast fell away southwest, would give us about the same distance from shore. Time of contact had been set for eleven P.M. Just after ten-thirty I told the men to start stacking the cargo on deck. Opening up to fifteen knots, I ran up the line north-northeast to the lighthouse.

In the quiet night the noise from our engines seemed unusually loud. I could only hope that from the shore it was blending well with the exhausts of the score or more fishing trawlers around us.

The mate came forward and reported that the cargo had been stacked. "*Capitán*," he said, staring off into the night, "what happens if Señor Despojo doesn't come aboard?"

"I've been thinking of that, Paco. I hope he will, but if he doesn't, I'll go over to the fishing boat and see *him*."

"But that will be dangerous. He will recognize you. He will not be alone."

I gave a short laugh. "I'm afraid that's a chance I'll have to take."

"Let me go to the fishing boat, *Capitán*. During the *movimiento* I learned to kill. One more to me is nothing. A bottle

of *anisete* and it is forgotten. But you *americanos* are different. You will kill Señor Despojo, but afterward you will question yourself if you had the right. You will begin to think and
think... ."

"No, Paquito *mío*. I'm going to take care of Despojo and I
promise you it won't keep me awake nights."

"Give me your hand, señor."

I grasped the hard-calloused palm of the mate. He let go and
rubbed his thumb across his fingers.

"You see," he said. "Already it is wet. Your body is not as hard
as your words."

"What the hell do you expect?" I retorted rather shortly. "I've
been waiting a long time for this moment. Sure I'm sweating.
I'm sweating for fear something will go wrong to spoil our little
picnic; that Despojo won't come out, that they won't keep the
rendezvous. No, my friend. You do as you're told. This is strictly
my affair." Mine and Juanita's, I said to myself.

I could feel him stiffen beside me.

"Muy bien, Capitán."

I put my arm around his shoulders. "Sorry, Paquito. But this
is one time you can't help me. How about getting me a drink?"

CHAPTER EIGHTEEN

A LAST-MINUTE cross bearing of the powerful light at Barcelona put us about a mile away from the rendezvous. I switched on the masthead light and scanned the horizon. Almost immediately a small white light started to flash off to port. I slowed the engines and swung over toward it, tapping out the call letter on the light button. The correct answer came back. When the Erinys was heading out toward the open sea, I steadied her and let her drift.

"They're certainly anxious tonight," I said to Paco. "It looks as though they've been waiting since sundown for us. Now don't forget what I've told you."

The fishing boat, a big trawler, came up astern. A strong flashlight played over our superstructure for a moment and went out. Not only anxious, but curious, I thought.

"O.K., Paquito, she's all yours." I ducked down into the cabin. I shifted my shoulder holster slightly forward and loosened the butt of the .38. I took a pair of brass knuckles from my pocket and slipped them over my fingers.

The fishing boat came alongside with a heavy bump. Standing below the companionway, I could hear people talking, then the thud and patter of feet as several men leaped aboard. I turned on a small lamp and found the palms of my hands wet. I held one out before me. It was steady.

"Capitán," Paco called softly down. "Señor Despojo says that it is necessary for you to go over there. He is afraid that if a patrol ship comes along we will go away so quickly he won't be able to return to his own ship."

I thought that one over. And I'd figured that everything was going to be so easy. I slipped my hand out of the brass knuckles and dropped them back into my pocket. Halfway up the ladder I paused and whispered to Paco.

"Where is he?"

"He's standing up behind the wheelhouse in the fishing boat with one or two other men."

"Think he's suspicious?"

"He knows who we are. He mentioned your name."

"O.K., I'll go over. Keep your eye on me, and if I give the word open up quickly, understand?"

"*Sí, sí, Capitán.* But why not kill him from here? It will be very easy. I will provoke him, and if you still insist on the pleasure of action, *you* shoot."

"No, Paco. I want to talk to him first. I've waited a long time for this moment. It won't satisfy me simply to shoot him blindly in the dark."

"Be careful, señor."

"Don't worry. He won't try any rough stuff. He wants those guns he thinks we're bringing him."

I walked back along the afterdeck and found the men hard at it shifting the coffee. Again it amazed me how easily those tough little fishermen handled the heavy sacks. I watched them for a few minutes until I reckoned half the cargo had been transferred. I climbed the rail and dropped down into the well of the fishing boat.

A figure broke away from the shadow of the wheelhouse.

"Captain Hart?"

The last time I had heard that voice was just before I lost consciousness a long time ago. But I would never forget it.

It was Despojo.

"Yes. Sorry you won't come over and have a drink."

"Some other time, yes. But tonight I am rather worried. Here. The sooner you take this and hide it, the happier I will feel."

He handed me a bulging brief case.

"How many sacks of coffee did you bring?"

I handed him a list. He switched on a small flashlight and looked at it. In the glow of the lamp I caught sight of a short figure standing close beside him. As he too glanced at the paper I noticed his face. I couldn't suppress a small smile as I recognized him. His nose looked as though a train had backed into it. He kept his hands buried in the pockets of his topcoat, and I imagined from the glint in his eyes as they turned up and caught mine that one of those hands at least was warming the butt of a gun. I could smell the hatred surrounding me.

Despojo snapped off the light and drew a thick package of notes from an inside pocket. I stuffed them away.

"You wish to count them?" he asked.

"No. No time. If it's not right I'll charge it against you next trip."

"Captain, I am glad that you are working for us. And I hope that you have forgotten a little unfortunate incident that happened some time ago."

"Forget it. I'm in this game to make money—I don't care whose. Aguzado pays well and his men don't keep me waiting. So long as he and his men stay on the level with me, I'll haul his cargos."

All the time I was speaking, my mind was racing so rapidly I thought sure they must feel the tension. I glanced around the fishing boat. Besides the three of us, another man was standing by the wheelhouse keeping a lookout. I presumed him to be the skipper. Several shadowy figures were stacking the sacks along the rail and in the hold. Four or five more must have been on the Erinys helping my men. We were so outnumbered that to attempt to get Despojo across by force would have been futile. And I knew too well that the little man beside him was only waiting for the slightest excuse to start blasting. It was maddening to be able to reach out and touch the man I had been seeking for so long, and have to just stand there making conversation.

I found myself even hoping that a patrol boat would come along and discover us; anything to disrupt this stalemate. In the excitement I might have a chance. Surely Despojo would prefer to come and escape with us rather than risk capture in the slow fishing trawler. After all, he didn't know we'd lifted the deadly cargo.

But I could see Paco's silhouette on the bridge. His calmness as he leaned against the dodger bespoke no danger.

Harry's voice broke across my thoughts. He informed me that the last sack was coming over. I told him to let go the lines.

"Well, Captain Hart, let's hope this is the first of many successful trips," Despojo said. He reached into his breast pocket and drew forth two cigars. He handed me one.

My mind clicked like the shutting of a door. That cigar would cost Despojo his life.

I failed to see his hand as I bade him good-by and climbed back into the motorboat. He followed me to the rail and said something about taking good care of the brief case.

"One moment," I said. "Losa sent you up a box of cigars. I'll get them."

I dropped down into the cabin and snatched up a half-empty cigar box. On the way back to the rail I called to Paco in English and told him to get going and to press one of the smoke buttons. Two feet of water separated the ships. I leaned over and held the box in front of Despojo. His hand stretched across. I let the box drop into the sea and caught his wrist. With my other hand I took him up under the armpit and pulled. The low rail of the fishing boat caught him below the knees and he fell forward. He must have seen the water swirling below him, for instinctively he grabbed me with his other hand and held on. I jerked him across the rail and we both fell backward to the deck as the ship surged forward.

Almost at the same instant a gun roared from the other ship. Something hit me on the left shoulder like a sledge-hammer. I slackened my hold on Despojo. He scrambled to his feet. As he dove for the rail I caught his ankle with my good arm and threw him heavily. The firing was continuous now, but dropping rapidly astern. Despojo lashed out with his free foot and caught me in the face. When I could see again he'd disappeared.

"Head straight out to sea," I yelled to Paco. "And keep her rolling as fast as she'll go. And keep down. I don't know whether Despojo has gone over the side or not."

A sharp report from aft brought relief surging over me. He was still on board, and he was mine, all mine. If he'd jumped over the side they might have spotted him while they were still close to us and picked him up. Or he might have just drowned. I lay flat on the deck behind the housing.

"What's the matter, Despojo, can't you swim?" I called out. "Or are you just a *cobarde*?"

The quick shots hammered back at me. He knew he wouldn't have a chance if he jumped overboard now. They'd never find him in that black night.

Well, that was four shots he'd fired. That left him two if he had a revolver, or four if he had one of his own automatics. My betting was on the revolver; Despojo was too smart to tote a Russian-made automatic about Spain. And I didn't think he'd be carrying spare ammunition.

"I'm going to kill you, Despojo," I called out slowly, distinctly. "But I'm in no hurry. It won't be light for five hours and I want to see your face once more. I want to see how a *cobarde* dies."

This time he didn't fire.

"Paco, tell the crew to go below and stay there. I want no interference."

There was no answer.

"Paco, you hear me? I want no interference."

"*Sí, Capitán.* I have put my gun away."

"Good."

"He is in the stern behind the oil drums."

"Good."

I lit a cigarette. It tasted like old rope. I flicked it into the night and ran my hand inside my shirt. I could still move my fingers, but the arm was becoming numb. I couldn't locate a bullet hole; the whole area was too inflamed. As I rolled over I found the deck wet beneath me. God, why did this have to happen now? Suppose I passed out? The executioner could not keep the appointment because he fainted on the way. A drink. That's what I needed; a long, strong pull of brandy. I toyed with the idea of asking one of the men to roll a bottle out of the companionway. And how would that sound to Despojo? *El americano* had lost his nerve. He was afraid. He had to get his courage out of a bottle.

And then I thought of Francisco Gonzales. I thought of his eyes that last moment of living, bloodshot with wine, trustingly trying to focus as Despojo blasted the light out of them. I could hear Francisco whisper as he stumbled to his knees, whisper as his life, his reason ebbed away, "*Amigo, amigo, por qué ... ?*"

"You know why I'm going to kill you, Despojo?"

Only the heavy throb of the motors broke the silence.

"You remember Francisco Gonzales?"

"It was an accident, señor." The voice was almost inaudible. "We had a fight."

"It was no accident, Despojo. Francisco never carried a gun."

"I had orders, señor." The voice, defiant, was stronger now.

"You're lying, Despojo. Just the way you lied about this cargo. We found the guns. How many other times have I brought you guns, Despojo?"

"But it was not my doing."

"You know what they'd do to me if they caught me, Despojo? They'd hand me over to the *policía de seguridad,* wouldn't they? And I'd pray they'd shoot me quickly. Is that what you had in mind, Despojo? Was it to be the next trip you turned us in, or the one following?"

Another long period of silence. Using my good arm, I pulled myself along the the corner of the housing. There was no question of waiting till dawn now. I'd be lucky if I lasted another fifteen minutes. If I could only find out which side of the stern he was on, I could go down the opposite side, using the housing as shelter. I took off my cap and shoved it forward beyond the combing. A gun roared. I inspected the cap but found no hole. But to have seen it he must be on the starboard side.

Five times he's fired. Has he one bullet left or three? I crawled back to port and around the corner. It was hard going, pulling myself along with one arm and keeping below the eighteen-inch housing. Halfway to the stern I could see the loom of the wake between the smoke drums. If he crossed over now, I'd get him. If he had crossed before he'd have seen me. I crawled to the corner and stopped. Less than six feet separated us. Pressing against the deck I said, "You're too fat, Despojo. I can see you."

A blast of gunfire chipped the woodwork over my head. Were there four or five shots? It didn't matter. I knew now that he had spare ammunition.

"You're frightened, Despojo. You're wasting bullets."

A wave of faintness swam over me. My whole arm had stiffened until the pain was almost unbearable with each move. I bit down on my lower lip until I tasted a spurt of salty blood. Oh, God, oh, God, please give me five more minutes. Call Paco, man. Tell him to get the Tommy gun and blast the stern before it's too late. If you pass out now, Despojo will take you and the rest of the ship. Juanita, I'm trying so hard, so very, very hard to avenge your father's death. Will you understand if I give up now and let someone else finish the job?

I laid my revolver on the deck and dried my hand on my pants leg. Gradually the sweat on my face, evaporating in the cool night air, revived me.

"You've lived too well, Despojo. I can still see you. I can see your fat backside."

Again he fired. Only once. Was that the metallic click of a hammer falling on an empty cartridge?

For a long period there was silence. I was afraid to speak, afraid the weakness would show in my voice.

"Señor, let us make a deal. There is no reason why we should kill each other." His voice, so close, startled me.

"What's the trouble, Despojo—run out of bullets or courage?"

"No, señor. I have plenty of both. But we are intelligent men and I have a great deal to offer you."

"You have only one thing to offer me, Despojo, and it's not worth very much. That's your life."

"Please, señor." His voice was breaking, whining now. "Let us go to Tangier. You will not regret it."

"You've done very well, haven't you, Despojo?"

"Well enough, señor." A note of hopefulness replaced the whine.

"You've done better than I have, haven't you? I've lost the best friend I ever had. I've lost the girl I loved."

"Señor, I can explain."

I inched slowly toward the corner.

"How much do you think you should pay me, Despojo? How much are you worth to yourself?"

"We can discuss that, señor."

"And don't forget there's Gonzales. How much was his life worth?"

"You set the price."

Now my forehead caught the draft swirling around the end of the housing. God, I was weak. Pressing down close to the deck I glanced around the corner. I could see the end of the oil drums. Behind the last one I saw a black shadow. I brought my gun forward and aimed low down.

"Are you ready to die, Despojo?"

"Please, señor! Look, I have thrown away my gun. I am on my knees! *Madre de Dios*, spare me!"

A hand and arm appeared above the drum. As he fired I squeezed the trigger. The black shadow increased. I squeezed the trigger again. And again and again and again.... .

Five seconds or five minutes later I came to. I could see the dark body that was Despojo jammed behind the oil drum. I crawled forward until, reaching out, I could touch his face. I pressed down on the uncovered eyeball. There was no reaction. I kicked his gun over the side and walked forward.

In the companionway I found Paco with the Tommy gun.

"I was coming to get you, *Capitán*. Is it finished?"

"Yes. Have one of the boys wire an anchor to his feet and dump him over the side. You'd better give me a hand with this arm."

He had to cut away the jacket and the shirt. Running from my elbow underneath to the armpit the flesh lay open as though someone had run a can opener up under the arm.

"You are fortunate, *Capitán*. Another inch and that slug would have buried itself in your chest."

"Well, she's all yours, Paco. Take us to Gibraltar."

CHAPTER NINETEEN

L ATE THE next afternoon I awakened. I was still groggy but the pain had receded considerably.

I got out the brief case and papers we had found on Despojo. There was nothing but a few cards of identity and several letters of no interest. The heavy brief case was locked. I twisted off the snap with a pair of pliers and looked inside. It was full of old magazines. I showed them to Paco. He wrinkled his nose and slowly shook his head.

"They sure played us for a bunch of suckers," I said. The mate handed me a heavy automatic. It looked very similar to the kind we had discovered in the coffee. He said he had found it in the pocket of Despojo's topcoat. I removed the magazine. There were the same two words in Russian. Slowly I fired off the clip into the sea. After the last shot I flung the gun overboard.

It was late in the morning when we were abreast of Gibraltar. I rounded the Rock, motored up past the naval dockyard, and stopped off the coal dock. The port medico was right on the job and was alongside almost before we had lost headway. He proved to be an old friend, and as he wrote out a landing clearance for the ship, I asked him to telephone the police when he returned ashore and get them to come and give me the usual passes for going ashore as soon as they could.

We continued on around the inner basins and dropped the hook just off the airport. I told the men to get the dinghy over the side and Paco to stand by to take me ashore.

As soon as the police had boarded us, checked our papers, and issued landing passes, Paco rowed me over to the Water Port. I picked up a cruising taxi and drove to Martinez' office in the old town. Martínez was a fairly respectable ship's chandler, and once I had it out with him over short weight and bad meat, we got along quite well.

I cut short his voluble greeting and led the way into his office. "May I use your phone?"

"Anything in my house is yours."

"Thanks. You can start with a bottle of whisky, some soda, and a glass. Close the door and don't let anyone in. I got some very important business to transact."

He gave me a conspiratorial smile. There was nothing Martínez loved more than to be close to the *contrabandistas* of the coast. But not too dangerously close.

I picked up the phone and put in a personal call to Tomás in Palma. I asked the operator to explain to the Spanish operators that it was *urgente*. My experience had taught me that when one used the word *urgente* in Spain, it was like sounding an alarm clock. They woke up a little sooner and got to work.

By the time I had finished my first drink the Gibraltar operator called back and said that it would take two hours to get through. I went out and explained to Martínez that I expected an important call within a couple of hours, and asked him to be sure to have someone standing by in case it came sooner. I said I was going down to the yacht club but would return in plenty of time.

In the club I found Dick just opening the bar and had a drink with him. I left before the noon-hour rush started. I wasn't too sure how notorious I'd become on the Rock, and I didn't want to embarrass anyone.

I had just succeeded in talking Martínez into allowing me a case of whisky instead of the usual ration of six bottles per ship when my call came through. Speaking in English, I asked Tomás to go and see Aguzado and find out if he knew anything about a load of guns I had been given for delivery to Despojo in Barcelona. I told him I'd leave it to him how best to go about it, but that I wanted the truth, and wanted it that night if humanly possible. I gave him Martínez' number and asked him to call me at eight o'clock.

And I was very grateful for Tomás' knowledge of American slang. For it was a dangerous conversation over any European telephone, dynamite over the Spanish. But instead of guns, I said "rods;" Aguzado I called "the big shot;" the late Despojo was "the lug I'm after."

It was almost eleven o'clock when Tomás finally got through to me. Martínez, who had been sitting around matching drink for drink, had folded up an hour previously and gone home to pass out.

"Sorry I'm late." It was Tomás' voice, more distinct now without the interference of the day traffic. "I've had one hell of a job getting in touch with your boss. He said I was a damn fool to even ask him such a question. He's never touched the stuff and never will. What's more, he told me to tell you that if you have anything to do with that racket while you're working for him, he'll personally carve out your guts. He's plenty worried, and he's sending a man down your way to see you. He says for you to keep your mouth shut."

"You think he's telling the truth?"

"Sure of it. What d'you take us for up here? Damn fools? By the way, you're sure you know what you're talking about?"

"I'm not blind. I had 'em right in my little hands."

"What have you done, kept them?"

"Fed them to the fish."

"Good thing. You see your boy friend?"

"Yeah. And for the last time."

"He had it coming."

I told Tomás that I'd write him the whole story and hung up.

Paco had fallen asleep waiting for me in the dinghy. I woke him up and we rowed back to the ship. I asked him to rouse the men, get the dinghy aboard, and take the ship over to Tangier. I was going to turn in.

The sudden silence of the engines awakened me. I heard the anchor chain running out and glanced out a porthole. It was still dark, so I went back to sleep.

Paco came down later in the morning with some coffee. I got up and dressed. I wanted to be ashore before Losa had an opportunity to come out to the ship. I asked Paco to put on his shore clothes and come with me into Tangier.

We found a taxi on the quay and drove to Losa's office. I had given Paco my .38 and suggested that he keep it handy. I could feel the hard lump of the Russian automatic in my side pocket.

A clerk greeted us in the outer office and asked us to sit down while he saw if Losa was busy. I winked at Paco, told him to make sure I wasn't disturbed, and followed on the clerk's heels. As he opened the door of the back office I could see Losa sitting behind a desk. The boy, when he noticed me right behind him, stopped, looked dumb for a moment, then went out and closed the door.

Losa stared at me, his face the color of the yellow blotting paper in front of him.

"So you've heard?" I said, walking toward him. "Makes it easier."

His hand dove toward a side drawer, but before he could reach it I slapped him across the face with the .45. The blow knocked him off the chair. He lay on the floor whimpering, his hands covering his face. I pulled him up to his knees and hit him

with the gun again. This time he started to yell for mercy. I told
him to shut up or I'd kill him.

I picked him up and shoved him back into his chair. I opened
the drawer, took out one of those tiny French bedroom automatics, and dropped it in my pocket.

"You know where Despojo is?" I asked him.

He brought his head up enough to look at me.

"He's holding down an anchor about twenty miles off
Valencia. And if I ever so much as set eyes on you again, you'll be
joining him. That is, unless Aguzado gets to you first."

The shock of the pain was replaced by a look of fear when I
mentioned Aguzado's name. I could think only of a rat cornered
in some cellar, its beady eyes searching for a way of escape.

"Here." I tossed the .45 onto his desk. "Tell them they can use
this for your grave marker."

I found Paco nonchalantly leaning against the door-jamb.
"Everything all right?" I asked him.

He looked back over his shoulder at me and grinned.
There was deathly silence throughout the office. Several of
the clerks and stenographers looked up, then quickly away.
Unhurriedly we crossed the room, regained the street, and
climbed into the taxi.

I got out in front of the Minza and told Paco to return to the
ship. I checked into the hotel, asked the manager for a room and
bath, and told him I didn't want to be disturbed; in fact, as far
as anyone else was concerned, I wasn't even staying at the hotel.

He picked up the registration slip I had just signed and tore it
up. He told me with a wink that I could sign another one when I
had decided that I was staying there.

I took the key of the room and walked up. A half hour in the
bath soaked a lot of the pain out of my arm. I pulled down the
shades and went to bed. I dropped off to sleep with the thought

that if Losa *was* going to do anything about it, he'd wait for darkness.

It was well after eight o'clock that night when I found my way down to Ricardo Lewis' store. He was busy filling out an order for some ship. When he saw me he turned the work over to one of the men, took my arm, and lead me into his office. I winced as he pressed my bad arm. When I saw his look of concern, I hastened to assure him that it was nothing; I said I'd just been vaccinated.

"Against what?" he asked.

"Against running contraband. I'm through."

"I've heard that before, but tell me about it."

"It's a short short story. Despojo is dead, I've made my pile, and I'm going home. And besides, things are getting too hot. They planted a load of guns in my last shipment."

"God, you do get around! But explain yourself, boy, explain yourself. What do you mean, Despojo's dead? You finally caught up with him?"

I got up, reached down the bottle of whisky, and poured the dregs into two glasses. Looking down at the empty bottle in my hand, I said, "You must be feeling the pinch."

Ricardo yelled through to the store for another bottle.

I gave him a blow-by-blow description of the last trip. He listened without interruption until I described how Despojo had died. Then his mixture of Spanish and English four-letter words was something to hear. When I had finished he asked me what I had said to Losa that morning.

"Slapped him around a bit with one of his guns. I don't suppose he'll be able to eat for a while. What do you think he's going to do about it?"

"Ordinarily he'd have some of his little men wait for you one dark night and beat the hell out of you, or if he thought he could get away with it, shoot you. But I'm thinking that right now, Losa doesn't even remember your name. Once he realized that Aguzado knew about the gun-running, the only thing he'd think about would be saving his own skin. As for Despojo, that bastard Aguzado will probably want to pin a medal on you for getting rid of him."

"Well, I wish someone would explain to me why men like Losa and Despojo, who have been doing all right, would risk everything by getting mixed up in the gun- running game."

"A sign of the times, a sign of the times," Ricardo said. "Russia is becoming mighty powerful. Today she controls the East. Who knows, maybe tomorrow she'll take over the West. And when she starts walking through Europe, there's only one country with an army big enough and loyal enough, and a frontier tough enough, to make her pause. I use the word pause purposely. Because Spain will never stop the bear; you can't stop Stalin tanks with peashooters. And that's about all Franco has.

"But the Russians like to play both ends against the middle. And they're afraid that by the time their armies reach the Pyrenees, America will have got around to outfitting the Spaniards with modern arms and equipment. It's certainly no secret that there are a lot of Spanish Reds, both inside and outside Spain. France is full of them, so is Mexico. As for Spain itself, you can't wipe out the memories of the Civil War in one generation; memories of Almeria, Barcelona, and Valencia. Why, even today there are Spaniards who cross to the opposite side when they see a Falangist coming down the road. They're afraid they won't be able to control their actions if he gets close to them. Maybe they're still Communists, maybe not. But they've seen their wives attacked, their breasts hacked off, a bayonet shoved up their middles by the representatives of the men in power today.

"Give those men guns, tell them it's open season on fascists, and whether they're Reds or not, they won't stop till they run out of bullets or life. True, the secret police, the *guardia civil,* and the army will act quickly, but it will take a lot of them to police the whole country; good loyal men who should be up front defending the frontier.

"So Russia is willing to pay plenty to dump arms into the country. And what amuses me is that she's paying for them in good Spanish gold. I remember those last days in Barcelona during the Civil War. I was there getting my wife's family out. Russian freighters were queueing up for the last serviceable dock to load gold bullion brought down by the Spanish Reds from the banks in Madrid. Those cargos disappeared into the. Black Sea and haven't been heard of since.

"And there are always men like Despojo and Losa who, for a price, will sell out their own mothers. They're the dangerous ones. In neither one camp nor the other. You can't put your finger on them. By working on the side for the Russians they take out double indemnity. If the Reds overrun Spain, they return as heroes. If they don't, they still have enough money to retire and live in Spain happily ever after. You'd be surprised how many like them there are. If I were Franco, I'd round up every Spaniard studying the Russian language at the Berlitz schools and put them all up against a wall. Or else subsidize you, you bastard, to go around knocking them off."

"I've just been thinking—I wonder if they slipped any guns through on my previous runs to Barcelona," I said.

"Might have. How many trips have you made in the souped-up speedboat you've got now?"

"Let's see ... four, five including the last one."

"Well, if they have, it'll be known up there by now."

"So soon?"

"Sure, and they've probably rounded up half the guns you took in, as well. That's the beauty of a secret police; you never know who's with you and who's against you."

"Maybe it wasn't a coincidence that that destroyer was patrolling around Sitges. You remember, the one I smoked out."

Ricardo picked up the telephone. "Well, let's see how hot you are. Maybe you'd *better* retire."

"Who are you going to phone? Franco?"

"No, somebody better than that. I've got a friend over in the Spanish consulate, if I can find him at this hour."

Apparently the friend was there. Ricardo gave him my name and the name of the ship, and asked if there had been any reports other than the routine notifications sent out from time to time. We knew that the Spanish government issued a list every so often containing the names of all ships and their masters running contraband. This list was circulated to every port in Spain and to most of the Spanish consulates in the western Mediter-ranean. I had been on it for years.

I tried to make out from Ricardo's expression whether the news was good or bad. But he had spent too many years thinking behind that blank look. Finally he thanked his friend and hung up.

"Well, it could be worse," he said.

"Meaning?"

"They might have caught you."

"O.K., open up. What did he say?"

"He said they'd been informed by Madrid that you're working for the Reds; that you're running guns; that the Reds had supplied you with that smoke-laying gear and that high-speed boat. How else, they ask, could you have got hold of such equipment?"

For a long moment I thought that one over. As Ricardo had said, it could have been worse, but not much. "You know," I said finally, "I'm so goddamned smart, I've outsmarted myself. If I *did* tell them where I got that smoke and my boat, they'd never believe me. And apparently I've buried the trail so well, I doubt now if I could ever prove anything."

"You want the rest now, or have you had enough for this sitting?"

I reached over for the bottle. "Shoot."

"They have orders to pick you up somehow and get you over to the mainland. Or across the border into Spanish Morocco. Apparently they want to talk to you. Also—and this even surprised me—it seems your friend Losa is one of the big Reds in Tangier. I thought I knew them all. You know, they have a pretty powerful outfit here. And you were such a nice guy."

"Stop it, you're breaking my heart. Talk about circumstantial evidence! Good Lord, what a stupid bastard I am!"

"What are you going to do?"

"Take the first plane or ship out of here. I'm going back to the States. If I thought there was any point in it, I'd hang around and clear myself. But what's the use? What have I got to win? Nothing."

"You going alone?"

"What do you mean, am I going alone? You want to come with me?"

Ricardo leaned back and pulled open the top drawer of his desk. "Under the circumstances," he said, "you'd better have a look at these. I promised I'd never mention them to you, but I think it's high time I broke that promise."

He found four letters and tossed them across to me. They were addressed to him, and when I saw the hand-writing my heart seemed to shift from its moorings and start up my throat. It was Juanita's writing.

Slowly, carefully I read the letters. They were short, badly composed, jerky. But I could feel the tears behind each sentence, the hope that gradually gave way to despair. In the first letter—I had sorted them out in sequence of dates—she explained simply that she had been very stupid in handling me and that I had left her. She was frantic with fear that I would meet the same fate as her father if I went on, and thought that if she forced the issue my love for her would make me stop. She began to realize after I had gone, she continued, that perhaps she was wrong and begged Ricardo to keep an eye on me.

Her subsequent letters were pitiful pleas for information about me and requests for Ricardo's opinion as to whether he thought that I would ever forgive her. In her last letter she said she couldn't stand it any longer, that whether I went on running contraband or not didn't matter so long as she was with me. As soon as she could settle her affairs and close the house she was coming to Tangier to see me.

In each letter she begged him not to tell me that she was writing, or to reveal the fact that she was returning.

For a long time I sat there staring at the writing, the words gradually blurring together as though a telescope was being pulled out of focus. Finally I looked across at Ricardo. "But why didn't you tell me—give me a hint or something?"

"I tried to several times, but whenever I brought her name up you started to sound off, so I let it go. As long as she still made you mad I didn't worry too much. I figured you still loved her. If you'd shown no interest I would have done something about it. I even asked Johnny Summers his advice. After all, he's known you a lot longer than I have. But he told me to let it alone, that you were carrying around some pretty phony ideas about women and that I'd be wasting my time trying to interfere."

I picked up the phone and asked the operator to get me Palma, Mallorca. I said I wanted to speak to Juanita Gonzales and gave Francisco's old address. If there was no reply, I asked her to get me Tomás Cazoleta, and gave her his telephone number. In a few minutes she rang back and said there would be a two- or three-hour delay on the call.

"Let's go and have dinner," I suggested. "I have a few things to do tonight."

"Can I help you?" Ricardo asked.

"Not at the moment, thanks. Now that you've shown me these letters, I guess I'll stay long enough to try to clear the air around here. I'm going to round up Losa and take him over to the Spanish consul. I'll make him cough up the truth somehow."

CHAPTER TWENTY

I T WAS A very somber meal. Ricardo appreciated my silence and said little. Outside the restaurant we picked up a taxi and returned to his store. There was still an hour or so to go before the phone call, but I didn't want to miss it in case it was early. The driver pulled up outside the store and Ricardo got out. I paid off the cab, stepped out, and started across the sidewalk. The driver called over and asked me if I wanted him to wait. I paused, turned to answer. A gun barked across the street. I heard the bullet ping as it ricocheted off the wall behind me. I dropped to my hands and knees and crawled up behind the taxi. I could hear running feet; some going, some coming. Ricardo came out with a big .45 in his fist. I yelled at him to keep out of the light and he jumped back.

By this time several passers-by had collected, wanting to know what it was all about. I stood up, brushing the dust off my pants. I told the driver to wait for me. He made some terse comment in Arabic and roared off up the street. I noticed a cop approaching. I took Ricardo's arm and shoved him ahead of me into the store.

"Looks like they're playing for keeps," I said.

Ricardo locked the door, then telephoned two of his men and told them to get over to his store in a hurry. "You're going to need company," he explained.

"Is that their idea of getting me over into Spain?" I demanded.

"Those weren't the boys from the consulate. They're not that obvious. I think you'll find it was some of Losa's henchmen."

"I thought you said Losa would be on the run."

"That was before I knew he was tied up with the Reds."

The telephone rang. It was Tomás. I asked him if Juanita was still in Palma. He said no, she had left that morning. He said she had intended coming to Tangier in a day or so anyway, but when he had told her the night before about Despojo and the gun-running, she had grabbed the first plane.

"What time does that late plane get in from Madrid?" I asked Ricardo.

"About seven."

I looked at my watch. It was almost midnight.

"If you arrived in Tangier and wanted to find me," I asked, "who would you contact first?"

"Me."

"So would I. So would Juanita."

"Was she supposed to be on that plane?"

"Yes."

"Probably missed it in Madrid. You know these women."

"Yes. But you don't know Juanita. When that girl makes up her mind, she doesn't miss planes. Is there any way we can find out if she was on it when it landed?"

"The office in town closed hours ago. I'll see if there's anyone at the airport."

He tried several numbers but there was no answer. Finally he got one of the maintenance crew out in the hangar. It took some time and two tickets to the next Sunday's bullfight to get the man to agree to go into the office and check the passenger list for the last incoming plane. Juanita's name was not on it.

"Relax," Ricardo said. "Maybe she wanted to do some shopping in Madrid. After all, she doesn't know the jam you're in.

She'll turn up tomorrow. Besides, you've got enough to worry about tonight. Where are you going to sleep?"

"Hotel. It's the safest place. I had Paco bring the ship alongside today."

"You'd better get a big room. I'm sending Pantella and Manuel along to take care of you."

"I hope they don't snore. By the way, where's Summers?"

"He got in a couple of days ago. He's been doing all right running up to the south of France lately."

I knew that he had sold his old Seafire and had purchased a Fairmile, one of those 115-foot escort boats they built during the war. They were excellent sea boats but carried too much cargo for this game. Few smugglers cared to risk so much in one ship. But they were fairly cheap to buy and could certainly stay out in any kind of weather.

"See if you can get hold of him. We might need a quick passage somewhere."

"What's wrong with your own ship?" Ricardo asked.

"Too risky. Besides, I'm selling her to you. Didn't you know?"

"With her reputation?"

"Hell, three months after I've gone the heat will be off."

"She'll have to be cheap."

"For you, a bargain."

Ricardo had his car brought down and we all drove up to the Minza. He entered the hotel first, looked around, and came back and told us the coast was clear. I ducked into the lobby, said good night to him, and walked up to my room. Manuel went in first and turned on the lights. I suggested that they toss for the extra bed, but Pantella, who was as tall as I was and about twenty pounds heavier, laughed and said Manuel could have it; he could never sleep lying down anyway. He dragged a heavy chair over in front of the door.

He removed his coat and boots and sat down in it, easing his shoulder holster across his chest.

I was on the phone early the next morning checking with Iberia. They informed me that the first plane in from Madrid landed about noon. Next I called Ricardo, but he hadn't turned up yet. I asked Pantella and Manuel what they wanted for breakfast and ordered it sent up to the room.

It was about eleven o'clock when Ricardo walked in. He had Johnny Summers with him.

"I hear you're in a bit of trouble," Johnny said. "Anything I can do?"

"Get me out of Tangier, perhaps. I don't quite know yet. What are your plans?"

"Wholly dependent on you."

"But this might be dangerous."

"You scare me."

Ricardo told his two henchmen they could relax for a couple of hours. The room was too crowded. I called room service and told them to send up a bottle of whisky, ice, and soda.

The telephone rang. It was for Ricardo. He listened for a few moments, then turned to me and said that Madrid was calling. I moved over and sat on the bed beside him. Even through the distortion of the receiver I recognized Juanita's voice. I took the phone.

"Hello, darling. Are you all right?" I asked.

"Oh, Brian, Brian, are *you* all right? What has happened?"

"Nothing much. When you are coming down here?"

"But that's the trouble, darling," she said. "They wouldn't let me leave the airport yesterday. They took my exit permit away. They said there was something wrong with it. But it's not true. Tomás got it for me in Palma. I *know* it's all right."

"Look, darling, don't say anything more. God knows who's tapping this phone. Just answer my questions yes or no. Did they take your passport?"

"No."

"Have you any money?"

"Yes, quite a lot."

"Fine. Now, where are you staying?"

"At the Almeida."

"Is anyone following you or bothering you?"

"No, not that I know of."

"What did they say when they stopped you at the airport?"

"There were two or three men. They came up to me when I was going out to board the plane and asked to see my papers. One of them said my permit wasn't right; that it hadn't been properly signed. He said they would have to check with Palma. It would take about a week. I had to tell them where I was going to stay in Madrid and they said they'd get in touch with me. Oh, darling, what will I do?"

"Just sit tight till you hear from me. It will be within the next day or so. In the meantime, have yourself some fun. Go to the Casa Alegría and see an old girl friend of mine, Rosita Ruano. She's dancing there."

"Oh, darling, how can you joke?"

"But I tell you there's nothing to worry about. Take care of yourself and don't forget that I adore you."

"Nothing to worry about, the guy says," Ricardo commented as I put down the phone.

I walked over and poured myself a stiff drink. I said, "Well, that saves us a trip to the airport."

I related to Ricardo and Johnny what Juanita had told me. I added that it was my guess that they were keeping her in the country as a suspect. Certainly there could be nothing wrong with her papers. Exit permits were simply routine, and once a Spaniard had a valid passport he could get one from any police station.

"Suspect or hostage," Ricardo put in.

"What do you mean, hostage? Do they think I'd go back to get her?"

"I guess they're forgetting that you're one of those cold-blooded Nordics."

"It's not that. If I can't bust Juanita out of Spain without letting them put the finger on me, I'll start selling peanuts."

"It's a good thing they didn't pick up her passport," Johnny put in. "Without it, even if she does get out of the country she'd have trouble getting into another."

"I was thinking the same thing. That's why I asked her. O.K., you fellows, get down to it and figure something out."

I walked over and stared out of the window. The late spring sun was rolling up from the desert and the heat outside was terrific. I lowered the awning to cut the glare.

Finally Johnny suggested that we run up the coast in his ship to some quiet spot around Cabo de Gata. We could arrange with Juanita to get down to Almeria by train, hire a car, and drive out to the rendezvous. We would pick her off the beach in a small boat.

"Not bad, not bad," I said.

"But not too good," Ricardo broke in. "In the first place, your Fairmile does what—twelve, thirteen knots?"

"With a tail wind."

"Supposing you're intercepted coming out?"

"We go empty. Let them search the ship."

"But we're not sure they won't tail Juanita when she leaves Madrid. They find out where she's going and have a ship waiting. They find Brian on board.... Too risky."

"We'll take the Erinys, then," Johnny continued. "She can outrun anything they have. Mix up some more of that smoke." He looked over at me and smiled.

"Better, but still not good. The moment the Erinys leaves Tangier, they'll either lock Juanita up or escort her wherever she goes with so many plain-clothes men that you'd never get within sight of her."

"They can't do that to her," I put in. "She hasn't done anything. What will they charge her with? Having an affair with a *contrabandista?*"

"She's in Franco's Spain, my friend," Ricardo replied, "not the United States. If they want to, they'll put her in jail because she's a brunette and not a blonde and throw the key away. Hell, you know that.

"In my opinion," he went on after a pause, "the best thing is for you to take a plane down to Casablanca or somewhere, get yourself on an American ship, and go to the States. And once you're safely aboard, spread it around who you are and where you're going. Then with you out of the way, things will quiet down, and we'll pick up your girl friend and send her over to you. Don't forget *you* can't even walk around Tangier without getting pot shots taken at you. So you're not much use when it comes to getting someone else out of a spot."

"Two things are wrong with that reasoning," I pointed out. "First, the Reds are after me because they think I know too much, or because I beat up Losa. If it's only Losa, I might get away with it. After all, he'll get over it. But if it's because they think I know too much—and God knows why they should think that—going to Casablanca will be right down their alley. They're as well organized down there as they are here, if not better. And I haven't any friends like you to protect me there. The second thing that's wrong with your idea is that I won't leave this part of the world without Juanita."

"Well, that settles that. I was going to suggest you go to Lisbon instead of Casablanca. Salazar hasn't let the Commies in there, as far as I know."

"No, Johnny's suggestion is getting close," I went on. "In the first place, it's got to be a ship. It's the only way I can sneak out of Tangier without everybody knowing it, and it's about the only way we can get Juanita out of Spain without an exit permit. But we have to forget the Mediterranean. We're too well known in those waters, and they're too well patrolled. Better make it the Atlantic. Somewhere around Cádiz or the mouth of the Guadalquivir. In fact, the closer to the Portuguese coast, the better. Then when we've picked her up we continue on to Lisbon, catch us a Pan American plane, and start drinking bourbon. But somebody has to go to Madrid and bring Juanita to the coast. Someone we can trust to lose the police if they *are* trailing her. After all, it shouldn't be difficult. I'll set up a dummy around here so that anyone interested will think I'm in Tangier."

For a long time we were silent. Finally Johnny said that he couldn't see anything wrong with the idea, but that it might be difficult to find the right man to go to Madrid.

"That's not difficult," Ricardo said.

"Why?"

"I'll go."

"The hell you will," I protested. "You've stuck your neck out for me often enough."

"Once more won't break it. Besides, what's the risk? I'm a free agent. There's no one to stop *me* from going to Madrid anytime I take a notion to. As I told you once before, I've kept my credit good in these parts. They know I'm not one of these Communist bastards."

"Sure, but everybody knows you're a friend of mine."

"So what? They also know that you stopped working for me and went over to Aguzado. Forget it. Pour me another drink. I'm on my way."

He picked up the telephone, called his office, and told one of his men to go around to Iberia and get him a seat on the late plane for Madrid that day. And then he told him to take his passport and go to the Spanish consulate and get him a visa for Spain.

"Thanks, Ricardo," I said when he had put down the phone. "If you can't do it, it can't be done."

"Well, we've got about four hours to iron out the details. You got any charts here?"

"I'll go down to the ship and get mine," Johnny offered.

"No, I have a better idea," I put in. I looked out into the hall. Manuel was standing by the door. I asked him to take a taxi, go down to my ship, get hold of Paco, and tell him to bring up the charts and the sailing directions for the Atlantic coast of Spain. I suggested that he bring him in the back entrance of the hotel. I had a hazy recollection that Paco had at one time sailed out of Cádiz; he might know that part of the coast.

I called room service and told them to send up some lunch.

"I'd certainly like to get out and get some exercise," I said, looking around the room.

"It's good for you. Maybe you'll put on some weight," Ricardo retorted.

"What about visas?" Johnny asked. "Juanita need one to get into the States?"

"That's a thought. But she can get it in Lisbon. Just the same, I'll check."

I telephoned a friend of mine at the U.S. Legation and asked him if it was difficult for a Spaniard to get a visa to enter the States. He said sometimes yes, sometimes no.

"That's an intelligent answer," I said.

"It depends on who it is."

"It's my girl friend."

"In that case, it's possible."

"How long will it take?"

"About three weeks."

"*Three weeks?*" I shouted into the phone.

"Well, since you're in a jam, we'll give you one in an hour. Bring the girl, her passport, and some photographs."

"What do you mean, since I'm in a jam?"

"Look, I don't know what in the hell you've been up to, but the Spanish consul was around to see my boss this morning and told him that you and Joe Stalin were practically sleeping together. He wanted us to pick up your passport and send you home. Just why, I don't know, but my boss said that if you were sleeping with Joe, then he, my boss, was Joe's chambermaid. Pretty good for the old bastard, don't you think? We'll probably get a blast from the State Department one of these days, but what the hell, life is too dull around here anyway. Bring the girl around. And don't forget the photographs and passport."

"But neither the girl nor her passport is here. She'll be in Lisbon."

"My God, here I am willing to break every rule in the book and you tell me she's in Portugal! I can't do anything for her up there. You'll have to see our people in Lisbon."

"And wait three weeks?"

"I'll give you a letter to a guy there. It might help and it might not."

"Thanks. Send it to me care of the Minza. And thank your boss."

"Who, me? Listen, I haven't even spoken to you. Good luck."

"I'm getting quite a reputation," I told Ricardo and Johnny. "They've been around shooting their mouths off at the legation. I still think I should round up Losa and make him tell the truth."

"Look, we've got enough things to discuss without adding any hair-brained scheme to the agenda. In the first place, you'd need an army division to smoke him out in Tangier. And if you did make him talk, he'd simply say afterward that you had forced him to. Besides, can you see Losa admitting to the Spanish authorities that he's a big-time Communist?"

Paco's arrival concluded any further argument. He said that he had brought the Erinys into the inner basin and that everything had been closed up. The men were standing by on board.

I tossed the charts across to Johnny and briefly informed Paco what had been going on. The fact that we had been unwittingly running guns annoyed him, principally, I gathered, because we had been so stupid not to have known. But the charge that I was a Communist agent didn't register. The Civil War had taught him a lesson. Since that vicious experience he had developed a political philosophy that I could only compare with a complete vacuum. I had never heard him open his mouth when the conversation got around to politics, as it inevitably did in that part of the world. I had the impression that Paco had sealed off certain cells of his brain. At odd times during the years I had known him, his intelligent and considered reactions to various situations surprised me. But when I tried to probe his mind, to find out along what paths his intelligence had been developed, I came up against a wall of concrete. Paco's whole life was now the sea. And as long as she provided him with his means of existence, he asked nothing more of any man.

I explained to him what we had in mind; that we were going up the Atlantic coast to try to rescue Juanita. I asked him how well he knew those waters, and if he could think of a quiet beach where we could get a small boat ashore without being seen.

He walked over and glanced at the chart Johnny was holding. With a grubby finger he pointed to a section of the coast between the Río Tinto and the Guadalquivir, that great river that runs up to Seville. He said that he knew the shore fairly well, that at one time he had fished out of Cádiz. It looked like an ideal situation, but when we checked inland, there were no railroads or highways within miles.

"What about the Bay of Cádiz?" I asked him. "There are good communications with Madrid."

"The channel into the bay is too narrow. We'd be seen," he said. "Besides, Cádiz is a large naval port; too many patrol boats stationed there."

"Well, we've got to find a spot not too far from a railroad or a highway, and away from the big ports."

"We might try Bonanza, at the mouth of the Guadalquivir," Johnny put in. "We could go in there just before high water, and they'd think we were waiting for low tide to start up the river. The place is usually full of small boats."

"What sort of rail connections?" I asked.

"Good," Ricardo said. "I've been there several times on my way up to Seville for *Semana Santa*. That's where you pick up the river pilot. You can get a train from Seville to there."

"That looks like it. What do you think, Paco?" I asked hopefully.

He shook his head. "To get to Bonanza, you've got to cross the bar at the mouth of the river. If a storm comes up you wouldn't get out."

"Hadn't thought of that," Johnny said. "He's right, you know."

"But not far from Bonanza there is a good place," Paco continued. "Around Punta del Perro. It's only a couple of miles or so from Bonanza and outside the bar. There are a lot of reefs offshore around the point, and I doubt if you'd even see a fisherman."

"You know it well enough to take us in?" I asked.

"Yes."

"Good," Ricardo said. "And what's even better, Juanita and I won't go to Bonanza. We'll get off at Sanlúcar de Barrameda; it's the market town for Bonanza, but if I remember correctly, the customs and the coast guard are stationed in Bonanza. We can pick up a car and drive out to the point, or walk if it's not too far."

For the next hour we knocked the idea back and forth until we felt pretty confident we had considered every possible angle. It was finally decided that Ricardo and Juanita would leave Madrid by train two days later. They were to travel south to Córdoba, the large rail center in the southern part of the Spain where lines branched off to Seville and Cádiz, or to Málaga and the east. It would be a good spot to throw off any would-be pursuers. And it was close enough to our rendezvous area so that if the going was really tough they could make a dash for it by car. We allowed them half a day in Córdoba.

From there, they were to go by train or car to Seville. This gave them another good city in which to lose anyone following them. Again it would depend upon circumstances whether they used the train or a car to get down to Sanlúcar.

We arranged to pick them up between midnight and dawn four days from now. They were to be waiting a half mile south of the lighthouse on Punta del Perro. We would come in with a white masthead light showing. If we were seen from the shore, we'd look like a local fishing vessel. Ricardo was to be sure that he had a good flashlight with him, and when he saw us, he was to make a series of short flashes every five minutes.

If, because of weather, it was too rough to get a small boat ashore, they were to return at the same hour each following night until we were able to go in and get them. If they weren't there the first night, we'd stand out to sea and return the second night. If they still weren't there, we'd leave Paco ashore. He would go into Sanlúcar and telephone the Andalusian Palace in Seville, and see if there were any messages for Bonanza. We decided that this was as good a code name as any. If there were no messages, he would then telephone the Almeida in Madrid. If Ricardo had been unable to contact either place, we would pick up Paco the following night and return to Tangier and wait.

I asked Ricardo to be sure to explain to Juanita that they might have to do a lot of walking, so she'd better travel light. I also suggested that he get some waterproof silk to wrap their passports and papers in, for if there was a surf running they might have to swim out to the dinghy.

It was now less than an hour to plane time. Ricardo said that he had one or two things to do at his office and bade us good-by. He said that if anything turned up in Madrid that necessitated a change in plans, he'd telephone me before we sailed.

Johnny pointed out that we should leave Tangier not later than two P.M. the afternoon before we were to pick them up. This would enable us to reach the mouth of the Guadalquivir before dark. We could close in on Punta del Perro, orient ourselves, and have a good look at the rendezvous area, then stand out to sea and wait until the appointed hour. We told Ricardo that if we didn't hear from him by noon of that day, we'd be on our way. As he was leaving I said that no matter what happened to me, Summers would surely be there to take them off.

"You stay right here," he said, patting me on the back. "And nothing will happen. They aren't going to blow up the Minza. You're not that important. Just be careful when you go aboard."

Somehow I got through the next three days. I cut down my body-guard to one at a time; the hotel room was too small. But even so, after the first day I felt suffocated. With the inactivity my mind conjured up all sorts of fantastic and impossible things that were happening to Juanita and Ricardo. I cursed myself for not asking Ricardo to telephone me from time to time to let me know how they were getting along.

As far as my own physical safety was concerned, I seemed to be the forgotten man. In fact, by the end of the second day I toyed with the idea of going over to Dan's Bar. It was less than a block down the street and I felt pretty confident that nothing would happen. But when I mentioned it to Pantella, he was strongly against it. He swore that someone was maintaining a twenty-four-hour watch on the hotel.

Part of the third day I spent arranging my affairs. I had Jim and Harry come up to the room for lunch. It developed into quite a party. Over the Martinis we discussed their future activities. Jim had decided that he'd return to the States. I told Harry I was selling the ship to Ricardo Lewis, and that he could stay and work for him if he wanted to. He decided that he would. Besides, he said with a laugh, I'd be back myself within six months.

I shook my head. "Not these waters. I've been here too long. My luck is changing, and when that happens you might as well pack it in."

"But you'll never settle down."

"I can try, can't I? Besides, I'm getting that derby complex."

"What do you mean?"

"It's when you find yourself glancing back over your shoulder as you walk down the street to see if there's a little man in a derby following you. Maybe he's the law; maybe he's a guy with a gun in his pocket looking for you. Or maybe he's just a little man in a derby. It's the uncertainty that gets you down. Another five years here and you'll know what I mean. Have fun in the meantime."

We settled our accounts and I telephoned the bank and asked them to make the necessary deposits. I also requested the manager to cable-transfer three thousand dollars to my account with the Banco Lisboa and Acores in Lisbon, and the rest of my money to my bank in New York. I told him I'd send over a letter of confirmation by hand.

I questioned both Harry and Jim carefully to find out if either the Reds or the Spanish authorities were interested in them. Apparently they weren't. In spite of the fact that they had been wandering freely around the town, no one had bothered them. I was the only one they wanted. When the men said good-by and left, I felt for the first time that I was really breaking away from the life I had known so well. It was a good thing that others had made it impossible for me now to keep on with it. I might have changed my mind.

CHAPTER TWENTY-ONE

A N HOUR OR SO before dawn of the fourth morning I left the hotel. Manuel had managed to pocket a key to the lower bar, and he, Pantella, and I slipped out into the alley below the hotel. One of Ricardo's Moors had been curled up in the doorway ever since midnight. He said that there had been a man watching the back of the hotel, but that he had left after they had locked up for the night.

Keeping to the back streets, we dropped down to the water front. We gave the entrance to the main docks a wide berth and walked out the short quay toward the yacht club. Near the club Pantella climbed down into a large rowboat. I followed and Manuel undid the painter. I crouched as low as I could in the stern. Manuel sat up behind me and Pantella took the oars.

Outside the basin Pantella made for one of the several schooners anchored in the roadstead. But when we were abreast of Johnny's Fairmile, he turned sharply and came along her off side. Johnny leaned down and gave me a hand. I ducked below into the cabin. Manuel followed. I asked him if he remembered all his instructions. He smiled and nodded his head. We had arranged for him to return to the hotel by the route we had taken, lock the door, and go up to my room. He was to remain there throughout that day and the next, ordering food for two at the usual hours. Each time a waiter entered, he was to make sure the bathroom door was closed, with the bath or toilet running.

I pressed some money into his palm when I shook hands with him and thanked him for the good care he had taken of me. Pantella was to remain on board until we sailed in case there were any last-minute boarding attempts in the harbor.

Johnny suggested that we turn in and get some sleep; we would probably need it that night. He explained that Paco was already on board and was keeping out of sight. His crew would keep watch and call us in case of trouble.

I asked what arms he carried aboard. He said he had four or five revolvers and two carbines. It was a pity, I thought, that he didn't have a Tommy gun. They made a lot of noise and seldom hit anything.

At twelve-thirty we decided to set sail and run slowly up the coast. We had given Ricardo a half hour over his telephone deadline. One of the men rowed Pantella over to the quay.

I tried to catch a last glimpse of the Erinys as we motored out into the bay, but she was buried in the tangle of shipping behind the dock. With a catch in my throat I looked back at Tangier; the buildings of the casbah piled one upon another, shining white and gold in the hot noonday sun.

On our way up the coast we kept well out to sea. Trafalgar was but a dim outline on the horizon, Cadiz a smudge of smoke in the late-afternoon sun.

An hour before sundown we turned in toward the Guadalquivir, and searched for the high yellow tower of Punta del Perro lighthouse. Paco identified it while we were still six miles off the shore. He said there was no use going in farther, that he could take us in at night by using the light on the cape and the lights marking the channel crossing the bar. Johnny took several bearings, then turned the ship and motored slowly seaward. A slight sea had come up with the afternoon wind, but as night approached it lessened. By midnight it should be calm.

As the evening progressed I became so nervous I couldn't sit still. I had one stiff drink but refused the second. It had tasted like undiluted water, but I knew that if I kept on, the alcohol would slow up my brain. Everything was going too smoothly. There was something about it I didn't like.

Paco came up to the bridge about ten o'clock and told Johnny that it was time to go in. And when I felt the vibration of the ship as he opened up, I relaxed considerably. The interminable period of waiting was over. Now we could act.

For the hundredth time Johnny and I pored over the large-scale chart of the area. A long reef extended almost two miles out to sea from Punta del Perro, and at the end of this reef was a bank that dried off at low water. It was marked with an iron beacon but no light. Paco said he intended to run in to the south of this bank, then continue along the southerly edge of the reef to the shore.

We had picked up the powerful light on the point long before and were working in from south-southwest. It was difficult separating the buoy lights marking the river channel from the lights of the towns and villages around the river mouth, but Paco said he could distinguish them and was perfectly happy.

Just after eleven-thirty, he asked us to keep a good lookout for the iron beacon; even in the darkness we should be able to see it against the lighter horizon. But he was the one who found it. After he had shown me the direction I picked it up through the binoculars. It seemed to be coming right out of the water about half a mile off to port. It was nearing high tide, so all the rocks were covered.

As we neared the shore the light from the lighthouse lifted higher off the horizon. Each time it flashed I thought surely the hull must be visible from the shore. But I knew from experience that the ray of the light was directed well out to sea. Close in to shore we were under it.

We scanned the low sand dunes running to the southward for Ricardo's signal. If he was waiting, he must surely have seen our light. But there was nothing but complete blackness.

About five hundred yards off the beach, Paco asked Johnny to take the engines out of gear; we were in as close as we could safely go.

It was ten minutes to twelve.

We had put the dinghy over the side before starting in, and were towing it astern. Paco brought it up and jumped in. I slipped a .45 into my pocket and followed him. I suggested to Johnny that he turn off his masthead light; Ricardo would start signaling as soon as he arrived whether he could see the light or not. Paco rowed me in toward the beach.

I guided him to a point about half a mile from the lighthouse. We grounded some feet from the shore. I jumped out and whispered to Paco to keep the boat just outside the small surf that was breaking.

I walked straight across the sand to a low broken cliff and stood in its shadow. Looking back, I could make out the dinghy much too clearly, but I couldn't see the Fairmile. There was no sound above the whisper of each wave as it curled up on the sand. Johnny must have shut down his engines. It was a beautiful night.

Keeping as close in as I could to the higher ground, I walked slowly toward the lighthouse. Every few yards I paused and gave a low whistle.

Nothing.

I stopped well short of the lighthouse buildings in case the keeper had a dog. I retraced my steps. I went out to Paco, but he had seen no sign of a light. I went on to the south until a fairly high rocky point broke up the beach. To get around I would have to go up and over. But it was almost a mile from the lighthouse. I decided against it.

Again Paco gave a silent shake of his head as I walked over to him. It was nearly one A.M. I felt as though I had been walking for hours. My feet in my wet socks and shoes were beginning to get sore.

This time I struck straight inland. About two hundred yards from the shore I came to a fairly good road. It appeared to curve off toward the lights of Chipiona and Sanlúcar. And for the first time I began to panic. It couldn't be more than four miles to Sanlúcar, and obviously the road led into the town. So that even if they had had to walk, the going was easy; they wouldn't have miscalculated by an hour. Despite the coolness of the night, my shirt was sticking to my back. I spent another hour walking up and down the road. Away from the sea it was deathly silent, and from time to time I paused and listened for footsteps. Then, afraid I might give way to the impulse to walk into the town to look for them, I returned to the dinghy.

I lit a cigarette and gave Paco one. I asked him for the flashlight he had brought and made a series of long flashes toward where I thought the Fairmile was. This was the signal to inform them that everything was all right, but that they hadn't turned up yet.

By four o'clock a long pale ribbon of light lay along the eastern horizon. Once more I walked back to the road and looked toward the town. Nothing but the small sounds of nature awakening. The premonition I had had since early evening that something was wrong was now so strong that I decided to push our timetable ahead twenty-four hours. I returned to the dinghy and told Paco to go ashore now instead of waiting until the following night. I warned him to get away from the beach while it was still dark, but not to go into the town to telephone before midmorning. I said that we would stand off during the day and return to the same spot the next night at midnight.

Johnny must have been able to see me rowing back. By the time I was alongside the Fairmile he had the engines running. He said, as he helped me up, that I had cut it a bit fine. I glanced back toward the land and realized how right he was. The shoreline was easily discernible in the growing light.

All that day we wallowed in a slight swell twenty miles off the coast. Johnny and I spent most of the time sleeping. Then as the afternoon advanced we began to speculate as to what had happened to Juanita and Ricardo and discuss seriously the next move if they failed to turn up that night. Johnny was confident that they had simply been delayed a few hours and that when Ricardo realized he couldn't make the beach in good time, rather than risk arriving after we had cleared off, he had decided to wait inland.

We turned in toward the shore long before it was necessary, but I think we both felt better motoring in at slow speed than sitting still outside. We used the lead a lot going in. Johnny was not too sure of the river beacons that Paco had used and wasn't taking any chances.

We saw the light flashing when we were still a mile off the beach. Johnny let out a whoop and banged me on the back. "I told you they'd be there," he laughed. "Now will you stop worrying?"

I felt as though someone had removed an iron band from around my chest. I was in the dinghy rowing before the Fairmile had drifted to a stop. From time to time the light blinked, guiding me into the shore. Paco had walked out through the small surf to meet me, and I almost knocked him down with an oar before I noticed him. He grabbed the boat and steadied it. I leaped out and ran up on the sand.

"Where are they?" I called to Paco.

"*Señor,* they are not here. They are not coming."

"What happened, where are they?" I found myself almost yelling at him. "Did you speak to them?"

"They are still in Madrid. But please, *Capitán,* let us go back to the ship and I will tell you. If we make too much noise they will hear us at the lighthouse."

The calm low voice brought me back to my senses. I got back into the dinghy and held the oars while Paco pushed us out into deeper waters. He climbed in and started to row.

"O.K.," I said when we were well off the beach. "What happened?"

"Señor Lewis has had an accident. He is in the hospital. The señorita is all right."

"What do you mean, an accident? Has he been shot?"

"No, no, señor. It was in a car. He and the señorita were driving down here. Just outside of Madrid another car ran into them." He shook his head sadly. "It is very dangerous to drive in Spain, señor. There is little gasoline and the people lack the experience. And the cars, they are old and have no brakes."

"Never mind the local traffic hazards, get on with the story. How bad is he?"

"He has one broken leg. Otherwise he is all right."

"A broken leg! You sure the señorita wasn't injured?"

"Yes, señor. I spoke with her. She has a few bruises, that's all. And the man in the other car was not even hurt," Paco concluded rather regretfully.

By this time we were alongside the Fairmile. I looked up at Johnny and slowly shook my head. "They didn't make it. They've had an accident," I said.

"Will I start up?"

"No, hang on for a minute." I climbed over the rail. "We're safe enough here. Let's think this thing over carefully."

I related briefly what Paco had said. I then called the mate over and asked him to go through his story again and not leave out a word if he could help it. He explained that he had telephoned first to Seville, and then, as there was no message, he called the Almeida in Madrid. Juanita had come to the phone. She said that since Ricardo was sure she was being watched, he had decided the safest way to travel was by car. He borrowed one from someone he knew in Madrid, and after various dodges to throw off anyone shadowing her, they started south. A few miles out of the city a car drove out of a side road and ran into them. It was really not a bad accident, she explained, and she was amazed to find that Ricardo's leg had snapped just above the ankle. She imagined he must have caught his foot between the pedals when they were thrown off the seat. They were picked up by a passing car and taken back to Madrid. Before they arrived at the hospital Ricardo made Juanita get out of the car and take a taxi back to the Almeida. And since, on his advice, she had not checked out, no one was surprised when she walked back in.

"Isn't that a son-of-a-bitch," I muttered. "What lousy luck! Now what do we do? It'll be a month before he can walk."

"Ricardo's all right," Johnny observed. "They've got nothing on him. And once they remove the weights he can go home by plane. It's Juanita. Do you think she can make it alone?"

I shook my head. "I don't know. If Ricardo says they're tailing her, you can be sure they are. I wish to God they'd stuck to the original plan and come down by train. But it isn't easy to get hold of a car in Spain. If he went to all the trouble of finding one, the situation must be pretty bad."

"Suppose I go up and have a crack at it?" Johnny said.

"No," I said after a long pause. "No. You don't speak the language. You'd be all right in Madrid, but in the country you'd be lost if you got into a jam."

"Juanita can translate."

"Sure, but the only way to get her out is to keep her well in the background. You'd have to buy all the tickets, make all the arrangements. No, thanks just the same, but I think it'd be a waste of time."

Paco had remained beside us staring off toward the land. We'd been silent for some time when he turned and said to me, *"Capitán mío,* I will go and get the señorita. At least you cannot say that I don't speak the language. And I have spent many years outwitting the police. I don't think I have lost the art."

I put my hand on his shoulder. "And I think you could do it, too, Paquito."

"Bueno. When—"

"But I'm not going to let you. We're playing with dynamite, Paco, the political police, and you're Spanish. If they caught you they'd string you from the nearest lamppost. Don't forget you're still an *hombre malo* so far as the Falangists are concerned."

I flicked my lighter and looked at my watch. "Well," I said, turning to Johnny, "that leaves only me. You feel like standing off and on around here? Shouldn't take more than two days."

"Don't be a bloody fool," he answered. "You're a poorer risk than Paco."

"I can't see it. I don't cross a frontier, so they don't know I'm in the country. I keep away from hotels and other places where I have to show my passport. I'll bet I could live three months in Spain without being found out. I'm certainly good for two days."

I asked Paco to bring up the dinghy. I went below to change my clothes. Johnny followed me.

"I still think you're mad," he said. "But I don't see how I can stop you if you insist. What do you want me to do?"

"Let's see, I should get to Madrid tomorrow night. I could get a plane from Seville, but that's a bit dangerous. There's bound to be a lot of police hanging around the Madrid airport. Second class in the train is best. I'll leave Madrid the same night, if possible, or first thing in the morning, which should get us back here the next night if we come right through. So midnight the day after tomorrow you be here. If we don't turn up, come in the following night. If there's still no sign, you'd better send flowers. What will you do, hang around outside?"

"It's rather a long time, but I don't think it's a good idea to run back to Tangier. I'll probably go up to Portimão in Portugal. That's not far from here."

"I'm glad you mentioned Tangier. I'd better telephone to myself at the Minza and tell Manuel to hang on for a couple more days. He must be going crazy."

Making sure that I had my passport and a large amount of money, I climbed down into the dinghy and had Paco row me ashore. I asked him to pull right into the beach; I didn't want to get my shoes wet. I climbed up to the road and walked toward the town. A mile or so from the first lights I crossed over into a field, crawled under a hedge, and went to sleep.

CHAPTER TWENTY-TWO

T HE HEAT of the sun awakened me shortly after eight o'clock. I was stiff and hungry. The excitement I'd felt as I had come ashore had gone, and in its place I found, as I strode toward Sanlúcar, a confidence building up within me, a certainty that within not too many hours I'd be coming back down the same road with Juanita beside me.

In the center of the town I sat down outside a café and ordered rolls and coffee. I asked the waiter to bring me a railroad time-table. As I was looking up the trains, two *guardias civiles* strolled past. I nodded good morning to them. They touched their comic-opera headgear and passed on.

I spent a long time perusing the timetable. But no matter how I checked and double-checked the connections, the earliest I could get to Madrid was the following morning. There was a day train up from Seville, but by the time I reached Seville it would have left hours before. I decided to catch the next local anyway and wait in Seville for the night express.

I walked over to the Andalusian Palace in Seville and entered the bar through the side entrance. I had stayed at the hotel on various occasions during previous *Semanas Santas,* and recalled that one of the assistant managers was muy *simpático.* I wanted to find out if he was still there. He might prove useful on the way down. I had a quick look around the bar, noticed no one that I'd ever seen before, and sat down at a back table. I ordered cognac and soda. When the waiter returned I asked if Señor Bosch was still with the hotel. He said yes, but that he wasn't around now, he was on night duty. I finished my drink and left.

I wandered about the streets until I found a café with a closed phone booth. I put in a call to Ricardo Lewis' office in Tangier and one to the Almeida in Madrid. I gave a phony name and the operator said she'd call me back. I ordered lunch.

Tangier came through first. I asked to speak to Mateo, and when I heard his greeting I told him in English not to talk, just to answer my questions. Whether he recognized my voice I don't know, but he remained silent. I asked him if Manuel was still at the hotel. He said yes. I told him to keep him there as long as possible or until he heard from me again. When he said he understood, that he would see to it, I hung up.

I had long since finished lunch when the waiter came and told me that Madrid was on the line. The phone rang three or four times in Juanita's room before she answered. The soft, low hello went right down to my heart. For the first moment I was afraid I'd choke if I tried to speak. When she again said hello, louder this time, I pulled myself together and said in Spanish that it was Francisco calling, Francisco Gonzales. I used her father's name purposely, for if she recognized my voice she'd realize that I didn't want to use my own name. And if she didn't recognize me, it would give me time to warn her. After a sharp gasp she remained silent.

I asked her if she was well, and the happiness in her voice told me that she knew who I was. I asked how the patient was doing, and she said he had sent her a message telling her to keep away for the time being, but that he was getting along fine. I told her to write him a note and send it over by hand explaining that Bonanza himself was taking care of things, and that he would write later. Next I suggested that if she wasn't doing anything the next morning, we might take a drive into the country. She replied that she would love that and would be waiting. I said good-by and hung up quickly.

While I was paying the bill I asked the waiter where the nearest *oficina de telégrafo* was. Despite his directions, I was able to find it. I wrote out a telegram to Rosita Ruano in care of the Café Alegría in Madrid. I asked her to meet the night express from Seville the next morning and signed it *"Tu extranjero de Palma"*—"Your foreigner from Palma." It was not too good but it was the best I could think of at the moment.

I bought a second-class ticket and sat up all night in the coach.

I had just started to look around the Madrid station when a bundle of beautiful pulchritude flung itself into my arms. I looked down into the sparkling, laughing eyes of Rosita. With some embarrassment I kissed her and gently untangled myself. She clung to my arm as I led her out into the hot morning sunshine.

We found a taxi, and I asked where there was a good place for breakfast. She gave the driver directions and snuggled against me.

"Oh, I'm so happy to see you," she purred. "I've been waiting so long to thank you. *Olé*, because of you I am a great success. Tonight you must come and see me. I dance for you alone."

We drew up outside a restaurant and I paid the driver. I followed her in and guided her over to a table against the wall. And I must admit that even at that unkind hour she looked very beautiful.

After we had ordered she took my hand and said, "But tell me, what have you been doing? Did you come only to see me?"

"Relax, darling," I laughed. "I won't interfere with your loving public."

"But I would leave them all for you."

I patted her hand. "I'd never ask that. But you can help me," I went on, becoming serious. "It so happens that a friend of mine is in trouble with the police, and I've come to Madrid—"

"Do you love her very much?"

"Yes. But how do you know it's a girl?"

"The moment I met you this morning I knew it wasn't me you had come to see. *Bueno.* It must be another woman. If you love her very much," she pinched the vein at my wrist, "I give my blood. If you don't, *le escupo a ella.*"

"You're absolutely wonderful." I glanced down at my watch. "I only wish I had the time to try to figure out what goes on inside of that beautiful head of yours."

I told her briefly about Juanita. I asked Rosita to get a taxi, drive to the Almeida, and call for her. I'd give her a note. She was to take Juanita shopping at two or three of the larger stores, always making sure they entered by one entrance and left by another. After half an hour or so they were to go to the beauty parlor on the first floor of the Palacio Hotel. They were to go up in the elevator and to make sure, if possible, that they were the last to enter it. If they weren't, they were to say something about forgetting to buy cigarettes and try again. When they got out of the elevator, Rosita was to go into the beauty shop and Juanita was to continue on down the corridor and go back downstairs by the rear stairway. She was to avoid the lobby and leave the hotel by the side entrance, pick up a taxi, and drive to the Capullito de Rosa, the well-known garden restaurant on the outskirts of Madrid.

I would follow from the hotel in another taxi and make sure she wasn't still being shadowed. If she was, I wouldn't contact her. She was to wander about the gardens until lunchtime, have lunch, and return to the Almeida and wait. I would think up something else and communicate with her later.

I emphasized that Juanita must be at the restaurant not later than ten-thirty, which gave them about an hour and a half. But she was not to leave the hotel before ten o'clock. I suggested that they both forget that they were Spanish for the morning and adhere strictly to the times I named.

Rosita listened carefully, but to make sure there'd be no mistake, I wrote a short note to Juanita repeating the directions.

In using Rosita I was relying a great deal on the characteristics and habits of the average Spaniard. For I felt that when the plain-clothes man detailed to watch Juanita saw two girls start out, he would unconsciously relax. He would certainly shadow them, but by the time he had followed their devious shopping tour, trailed them along crowded streets to the hotel, and, after questioning the elevator boy, found out that they had gone to the beauty shop, he would feel pretty safe in ducking into the café for his morning coffee. It was going to be a hot day. I hoped he'd be wearing tight shoes.

I stayed in the restaurant after Rosita left. I was tempted to phone Ricardo, but restrained myself with the thought that if the police were suspicious of him, one of the first things they'd do would be to put a check on the hospital switchboard. Instead I asked for writing paper and wrote him everything that had happened. When I had finished I suddenly realized that they'd be checking his private mail as well, and tore it up. Poor Ricardo would just have to wait.

About a quarter to ten I took a taxi to the Palacio and had the driver pull up half a block from the side entrance. I made sure that we were facing in the same direction as the taxis on the rank outside the door. It was then five minutes to ten.

Exactly twelve minutes later Juanita walked out of the door, stepped into the first taxi, and drove off. I waited until her car had passed down the street and swung into the Paseo. No one came out of the hotel. I told the driver to take me to the Capullito de Rosa and let him know that it would be worth his while if he hurried.

He did. And I had a better understanding of why Ricardo was in the hospital. Stop signs meant nothing; as for traffic lights, I could only assume the driver was color-blind. I had him stop just short of the entrance to the grounds of the restaurant. A few minutes later Juanita drove up, paid off her taxi, and went in. I sat there for two long minutes, but no other car arrived. Telling the driver to wait for me, I got out and walked toward the gate. Juanita must have been watching. The next moment she was in my arms.

Keeping to the outskirts of the city, we drove over to a suburban station on the main line south. Fifteen minutes later we relaxed in the Algeciras Express.

Most of the time on the long journey we were silent, content simply with the physical contact as we sat close together, our hands interlocked. The crowded compartment made intimate conversation difficult, and I think we both felt we were still too far away from the frontier to risk tempting the gods by discussing our plans for the future. Juanita's condition, both physically and mentally, worried me. I began to think she had not got off as lightly as she claimed in the automobile accident, and she finally admitted that she was a mass of bruises. I could tell from her furtive air, the quick frightened glances when people passed by or paused, that the past few days had affected her.

As we rolled southward across the sun-bleached country, however, she appeared to relax; for a time she was even able to sleep. But as the night approached, and with it the hour for leaving the anonymity of the train at Córdoba, she began to panic. I prayed that I could get her to the coast before she broke down.

Realizing that we'd never make the rendezvous that night, I decided to press on anyway and get as far as Seville before stopping. I decided to take a car across, as the train connection meant a two-hour delay in Córdoba. I hustled Juanita off as soon as the train stopped and we were among the first to pass through the barrier.

That was my first mistake. Two men were waiting just outside the gates with police written all over them. They stared at us, then spoke to each other. It was too late to turn back; the stream of passengers was making for the street. To turn and force our way back through it would have been ridiculously obvious. I cursed myself for my over-confidence, my haste in leaving the station without first looking around.

I led Juanita down the wide street at a rapid pace. We paused at the first corner and I glanced back toward the station. The two men were following. When I saw them stop and turn toward a shop window a hundred yards behind us, I drew my first breath of relief. They were not going to arrest us on sight.

We crossed the street and entered a café. I walked up to the bar and asked the *patrón* how long the Algeciras Express waited at Córdoba. He glanced at the clock behind him and said that we had about ten minutes. I bought some cigarettes. Back in the street again, I looked around and saw the *policía*—there was only one now—sitting at one of the terrace tables. Our eyes met. He glanced away and took out a paper. It was obvious that his partner had gone off to telephone.

I think it was then that Juanita realized we had been spotted. I had said nothing; I didn't want to frighten her further. Moreover, my mind was too busy trying to find a hole in the net that was closing in. I held her arm tightly as we walked back to the station and explained that we were being shadowed and we would have to alter our plans. I reassured her that they weren't going to arrest us, or they would already have done so. I didn't add that I was also sure that when the *policía* reported that Señorita Gonzales was in Córdoba with a tall man who looked like a foreigner, he'd be told to pick us up immediately. I prayed that the line to the capital was very busy.

As a precaution, I had bought tickets right through to the end of the line. I showed these at the barrier and we reboarded the express. When Juanita had found a seat, I returned to the platform. I dug out a cigarette, lit it, and walked slowly toward the rear. Sure enough, our *policía* came steaming along. When he caught sight of me I gave him a smile and a nod. He threw me a look of surprise, turned, and nipped up into the rear coach. In spite of the circumstances, the man's amateur standing as a detective amused me.

Regaining our coach, the third up from the end of the train, I walked along the corridor and beckoned to Juanita to follow. A few moments later whistles sounded along the platform, announcing the departure of the train. As we reached the end of the coach it started to jerk forward. I threw open the door on the off side and gave Juanita a hand down. I jumped after her, pulling the door to behind me. Fortunately the train blanked off the platform lights and we ran across the next tracks in comparative darkness. I practically lifted Juanita up and onto the deserted platform on the other side. As we gained the shelter of a wide pillar, the Algeciras Express slid out into the night.

It had been a pure gamble. If the man had glanced out the off side of the train, he couldn't have helped seeing us. But I counted on his doing the normal thing: watching the platform side to see that we didn't get off at the last minute. I was glad his partner hadn't returned.

We waited a few minutes until the excitement of the train's departure died away and the people who had come to see it off had dispersed. I noted as we passed through the station that the next scheduled stop for the express was in just under an hour. With any luck we had that much head start.

We were more than careful leaving the station this time. I passed up the taxi rank outside and led Juanita across the town until I saw several cabs parked near a large, brightly lit restaurant.

And here I made my second bad mistake. I had to ask three drivers before I found one who'd risk his battered cab and worn tires on the long trip to Seville and back, no matter what I offered. But it wasn't till we left the lights of the city that I realized that any policeman making even a cursory check of the taxi ranks would soon find out that a big foreigner with a Spanish girl had been trying to get a car to take them to Seville. It would have been so easy to choose a town more or less the same distance in another direction, and then, after we had set out, tell the driver the true destination.

I soon dismissed that bit of hindsight and turned my attention to Juanita. She had borne up wonderfully well, reacting quickly and without question to the demands of the past half hour. But once we reached the highway and the city behind was but a bad memory, she crawled into my arms and broke down. Tearfully she cried that we would never get away. The police were all around us, waiting, watching, and as soon as we got near the coast they would pounce. How did they know that we were on that particular train? How did they know we were getting off at Córdoba?

I tried to reason with her and explained that the machine we were trying to outwit was far from stupid. When they had lost her for some hours in Madrid, they naturally assumed that if she was trying to escape she'd make for the south, for Algeciras, Málaga, or some other port near Morocco. They'd watch the trains, the highways, the airports. Córdoba was a big rail center, an obvious place to cover—so obvious, I thought to myself, I should have realized it sooner and left the train at another, smaller station. That damn overconfidence again. Well, there would be no more of that. From here on out I'd play this game as close to the chest as they were doing.

In the first village we passed through I had the driver stop at a café and buy a bottle of cognac. I kept feeding it to Juanita until the tears dried and she fell asleep. And it wasn't long, despite the tired springs of the ancient cab, before I found myself nodding.

It was sometime after midnight when we reached Seville. I had not even considered stopping for the night in any of the small towns we drove through. Arriving at this hour without luggage would cause no end of comment. Besides, I didn't want to let go of the taxi. The driver had been pretty surly and I figured he'd find some excuse for leaving us at the first opportunity.

I could think of only two alternatives: a quiet night at the Andalusian Palace with the assistance of my friend Señor Bosch, or another taxi and a night in the open up some country lane. I told the driver to take us to the hotel. I left Juanita in the car and went into the lobby. I asked the night clerk for Bosch. He appeared after a few minutes and greeted me enthusiastically.

I told him I was in a spot. I explained that I had my girl friend outside in a taxi and that we'd like a room for the night. We were on our way from Madrid to Cádiz to spend a few days, but my car had broken down along the way, and we had come on to Seville in a cab. He was already offering me the hotel before I'd got that far in my story. But I asked him to wait a moment, that

that wasn't all. I admitted in a lower tone of voice that the girl happened to be the wife of a very important official in Madrid and that we didn't want to use our own names to register.

Bosch closed one eye for a long moment and thought that one out. Finally he said with a smile that he could arrange it providing we were out by ten o'clock the next morning. He was on duty until then and would cover up for us. If we stayed beyond ten I'd have to hand my passport in and register.

After he had agreed to take us in, I said, rather off-handedly, that the girl's husband might have set the police on her trail and asked him to let us know in time to get away if any cops should show up. And I could see by the conspiratorial glance he gave me that he would be very disappointed if the police *didn't* give him the opportunity to help us. He went over to the desk clerk and sent him off on some errand. I went out, paid the taxi, and brought Juanita into the hotel. Bosch took us up in the elevator himself and showed us a room. The effort he made to keep from staring at Juanita amused me.

When I turned the key in the lock I felt as though an iron curtain had dropped between us and the perils of the outside world. Wishful thinking, possibly; but for some unaccountable reason I felt sure that that night nothing would harm us.

The bedroom was enormous; it had the typical high ceiling and was filled with heavy, oversized furniture. But the bed, a wide four-poster, was all that interested me. I threw open the shutters and stepped out onto a star-spattered patio. Running after me, Juanita caught my arm and pulled me back. She closed and locked the windows and drew the heavy curtains.

"Keep the night outside," she said.

I took her in my arms. "Don't worry." I smiled down at her. "This night and all that's in it will stay outside. Here we're safe. Are you hungry?"

"No, no. I just want you to hold me."

"You're wonderful." I laughed, shaking my head. "Wonderful!"

"Be careful," she said as I fumbled with the buttons of her dress. "They're the only clothes I have."

"In Lisbon we'll go shopping."

"Lisbon! Oh, Brian, darling, do you think we'll ever get there?"

The dress slithered to the floor. "I thought we locked all that outside," I said.

"Oh, yes," she cried as she pressed me against her. "Tonight it's just you and me."

Despite our brave words, I found myself thinking of the morning and what it would bring. And my thoughts must have communicated themselves to her, for as I pulled her closer to me I could feel a shudder run down through her body.

"This is no good," I said, swinging around and sitting up. "Let's have a drink. We've got to get some rest."

I went over and found the bottle of cognac. I poured out two stiff drinks and gave her one.

I sat down on the edge of the bed. "To Lisbon," I said, holding up my drink.

"To love," she replied, the warmth coming back into her eyes. She sat up, swept the long black hair over her shoulders, and sipped her drink. "You want only to sleep when tomorrow they may come and take you away from me."

"And you want to make love all night and in the morning be able to walk to the coast," I retorted.

She leaned over and pulled my head down into her lap. Softly stroking my hair, she murmured, "And don't you?"

I felt a strange and unrecognizable happiness flowing over me, a lightness of heart and spirit, a conviction that nothing, no one, could ever stop or hurt us. And then I felt great humility as I looked at her; humility that I had been given the love, the passion, the tenderness of this woman to have and to watch over and to protect.

I fell asleep with my head on her breast, the beating of her brave heart encouragingly in my ear. The next thing I heard was a persistent knocking on the door.

CHAPTER TWENTY-THREE

I TURNED THE KEY and opened the door an inch. It was Bosch. He came in quickly and pushed the door to behind him. Juanita, as far as I could see, was still sleeping.

He apologized profusely for disturbing us, for at least not telephoning first to give us a chance to prepare ourselves. I cut him short and asked him what the trouble was. He said he had heard the police making inquiries at the desk. At first he hadn't thought anything about it, as it was customary for the secret police to check the hotels from time to time. But in view of what I had told him, he began to think he'd better find out if it was more than that. And when he heard them giving the clerk an accurate description of Juanita plus a detailed description of me, he thought he'd better warn us. He concluded by saying in an undertone how awful it was, that the poor girl must be married to a beast.

"Anybody else know we're here besides you?" I asked. "Floor maid, desk clerks?"

"No, not yet."

I looked at my watch. It was just after nine o'clock. "Can you get us a car, a good car with a good driver? And when I say good driver, I mean one that won't mind taking a few risks. Tell him I'll make it well worth his while."

Bosch thought for a moment, said that he would try, and hurried out.

I awakened Juanita and told her to get dressed as quickly as she could, that we were on our way. And as I held her for a long moment in my arms I promised her that no one and nothing would ever separate us again. She was very cheerful. I was glad she hadn't overheard Bosch.

We were ready to go when he returned ten minutes later. He said he had arranged for a car and led us down a series of back stairways and out through the rear patio and into a side street. He told us to wait there, the car would soon be along.

He kissed Juanita's hand, wished her great happiness, and excused himself, saying that he'd better be getting back to the hotel. I asked him how much I owed him for the room. He said, holding his hand up, nothing; that when we were safely back in Tangier I could send him a present. As I shook hands with him I gave him a weak smile and decided that this was the last time I'd try to outsmart a Spanish hotelkeeper.

The next twenty minutes was probably the worst period of the whole journey so far. As the time dragged slowly by I began to feel that our friend had let us down, that there would be no car. He had helped us for the night, but that was as far as he was going; now that we were outside the hotel he washed his hands of us. Just when he had seen through the irate-husband story I didn't know. I could only hope that the police hadn't tipped him off—that they weren't aware yet that I was in the country.

I began to feel naked standing in the quiet street. We started walking up and down, but I hated to get too far from the doorway in case the car did show up. After fifteen minutes I gave up and decided to go and find a car myself. And I went through hell trying to decide whether it was better to leave Juanita in the quiet area or take her with me. She began to suspect that something was very wrong, so I told her that the *policía* had traced us to the hotel. I felt that she should know now, that she should be on the alert for whatever happened. She took it calmly.

But Bosch hadn't failed us. As I was looking at my watch for the last time a large and fairly new car drove up and stopped. The driver reached back and opened the door. We climbed in, told the driver to take us to Jerez, and collapsed.

After we reached the open highway I started to talk with the man. I wanted to sound him out and see how much Bosch had told him and find out just how far I could put my trust in him. I asked him what he was going to charge us for the trip to Jerez, and when he mentioned a pretty high figure I protested. He countered with the usual theme, that he had to buy his gasoline in the black market, his tires from the *contrabandistas,* etc.

When I asked him what the hotel man had told him, he muttered something about an *intriga amorosa.* I decided I'd better give him the straight story. It would probably cost me a great deal, but it would be worth it to know whether we could rely on him or not. And I didn't think the story of our *intriga amorosa,* as he termed it, would stand up very long if there was any rough stuff on the coast. If he wasn't happy about it, I'd pay him off in Jerez and look for another car. From his attitude I was pretty sure he wouldn't report us to the authorities.

He asked me where the ship would be waiting, and when I said it would be somewhere near Bonanza, he said O.K., but it would cost me five thousand pesetas. I took out ten *mil* notes and handed him five. I showed him the other five and told him that if he got us through safely, they were his. It might be the easiest money he ever earned in his life. I'd be content if it was.

Outside a small village on the road to Jerez we got out and sat by the side of the road while the driver went in and bought us some food and wine. We had a leisurely lunch. I decided that our best plan was to arrive in Sanlúcar just before midnight and drive right on out to the lighthouse. And as it was only some twenty miles from where we were, we had plenty of time to kill.

When we entered Jerez the driver suggested that it might be a good idea to continue on down the main highway toward Cádiz instead of cutting over to Sanlúcar. Anyone making inquiries behind us would naturally assume then that we were heading for the great seaport. When we reached the coast at Puerto de Santa María, before entering Cádiz, we could swing right and take the coast road up to Sanlúcar.

I agreed and congratulated the fellow on using his head. And this was the third and by far the most serious mistake I made.

The afternoon and evening we spent between Jerez and Santa María, well hidden from the highway. But by late evening the sight of the sea just over the next row of hills had made us so impatient that I decided to get Santa Maria behind us and wait the rest of the time near the rendezvous. We got back into the car and started off once more. Where the highway narrowed to enter the town of Santa Maria two *guardias civiles* stepped out of the dusk and held up their hands. The driver pressed down on the gas, but when I saw the nearer one level his rifle I told him to pull up. They were *guardias civiles,* not the secret police. It could be just a routine coastal road check.

They strolled over to the car. The leader opened the rear door and asked to see our identification papers. I handed over my passport, and while he walked forward to look at it in the glare of the headlight, I whispered to Juanita to hang on to hers, to claim that she didn't have any papers with her. The *guardia* returned, handed me my passport, and looked expectantly at Juanita. I explained that she had nothing with her, that she was my *novia,* and that we were just driving into Cádiz for the evening. The *guardia* was very polite but insisted that she produce something with which to identify herself. Equally polite, equally voluble, I insisted that she was living in Seville, that I would vouch for her, and what was all the trouble about, anyway? The *guardia* opened the front door, climbed in beside the driver, and directed him to go to the *cuartel de la policía*.

On the way to the police station I got out my address book and scribbled a note to the driver telling him to wait with the car somewhere near the station. I tore out the page, folded it, and held it in my hand. As we were getting out in front of the *cuartel* I dropped it in his lap.

The *guardia* ushered us in to his superior, a small, elderly lieutenant. He explained that Juanita had been unable to furnish any identification. The officer was graciousness itself, invited us to sit down, and asked me for my papers. When he saw I was a foreigner, he apologized profusely for troubling us, explaining that he had been requested by the *policía* in Seville to be on the lookout for a young lady and an older man. He was of the utmost confidence, however, that the *señorita* and the señor were not the type to be in trouble with the authorities. But it was unfortunate, he said, that the señorita did not have something to identify herself, because the *policía* had given him the wanted woman's name. If we would excuse him he would telephone to Seville and ask for a description; and he was sure that within ten minutes we would be able to continue our journey.

He waved the *guardia* out and put in a call to Seville. At that moment I was feeling very unhappy.

The call came through almost immediately. The lieutenant asked for a physical description of the girl they wanted, and his eyes never left Juanita's face as they told him. They must have asked then if she was alone, for I heard him say that there was a foreigner with her. A moment later he lowered the receiver and asked me again for my passport. With one hand he fumbled through the pages, finally got it open, lifted up the receiver, and read out my name. Then he said yes, that I was an American. I am afraid my hand was trembling as he handed me back the passport. My two days were up. They knew now that I was in the country. And all hell would soon be breaking loose.

Finally the officer replaced the receiver and in a voice laden with disappointment and sadness told us that we would have to remain until the *policía* arrived from Seville. I asked how long that would be. He shrugged his shoulders and said that if they left right away it shouldn't take them more than an hour and a half or two hours.

I asked him if I could go out and tell my driver that we would be delayed. The lieutenant promptly gave his permission, jumped up, and opened the door for me. I noticed a *guardia* just outside the front entrance and asked him where the car was. He pointed down a side street. I walked around the corner and found it about halfway down the block. I told the driver that we were being held pending the arrival of the police from Seville, and that if we couldn't make a break before they got here he needn't bother waiting for us; the police would be furnishing our transportation then. I warned him to remain where he was and be prepared for a quick getaway. If he didn't see us again, I told him he had still earned his five thousand pesetas.

While I was talking to the man I surveyed the side and rear of the police station. A typical low wall ran along the sidewalk separating what was obviously the patio of the station from the public thoroughfare. When I noticed a gate in the wall I walked over and tried it. It was locked. The top of the wall just reached my shoulder. Returning to the station, I found Juanita and the lieutenant in amicable conversation. They were talking about his family. After listening for a time, I decided the man was *muy simpático* and began to toy with the idea of trying to buy our way out.

It took quite a while to get the conversation around to the point were I was able to suggest that if he saw fit to release us he would not find himself unrewarded. I trotted out the old story about the husband who had been so cruel to Juanita, and how awful it was that in Spain there were no laws a woman could use to protect herself from such brutes. It sounded pretty feeble, but I tossed a lot of big names and smart places into the tale, hoping it would intrigue the small-town Spaniard. It did. He expressed deep sympathy and understanding of Juanita's situation.

But when it came to giving her a break it was a different story. Sadly shaking his head, he pointed out that now the *policía* were on their way; that if they arrived and found the girl gone, he'd lose his hard-earned commission, probably his job. I took out ten *mil* notes, a year's pay to him, folded them lengthwise, and slid them across the desk. I suggested that we could surely think up some method for us to escape without throwing the blame on him. The lieutenant stared at the notes for quite some time. Then slowly, carefully, he pushed them back toward me. I left them on the desk.

We had been there forty-five minutes. I got up, and after walking about the office I asked him where the plumbing was. He led me out into the hall, pointed to a door at the rear, and told me it was off the patio. I found the customary closet containing the toilet built onto the outside wall of the building. Across the patio I could see the black top of the car. There were several chairs scattered about a long table. I presumed that the *guardias* ate there in the hot weather. I moved a chair over against the wall nearest the car and returned to the office.

I waited another fifteen minutes. I prayed that the man would have some reason for leaving us alone for a moment. But he was perfectly content to sit there talking.

Then the telephone rang. As soon as the lieutenant picked up the receiver, I got up, walked over, and handed Juanita a cigarette. While bending down to give her a light, I whispered, "Lavatory, jump the wall, car, wait." She caught it and gave me a smile of acknowledgment.

A few minutes after he had replaced the receiver she asked him if there was a ladies' room. This embarrassed him considerably, and he apologized, explaining that it was only a *cuartel*. She gave him a warm smile of understanding and said she didn't mind, but would he show her where the lavatory was anyway? He got up, led her down the long hall to the same closet. A moment later he was back at his desk. As long as one of us was in sight, he didn't appear to worry.

I gave Juanita five minutes. Then, after looking at my watch several times, I told the lieutenant I was worried about the girl. I said that despite her apparent composure, she was terribly upset. I pointed out that she had been gone a long time, and perhaps we'd better go and see if she had fainted. I don't think he quite knew how to meet this situation, but when I stood up and turned toward the door, he decided he'd better follow.

I knocked on the door of the lavatory and asked Juanita if she was all right. The lieutenant had paused just behind me and to the left. As I spoke, I swung. I don't think he knew what hit him. I picked him up and locked him in the closet. I was glad I'd left the money on his desk. Going over the wall, I heard the driver start up his motor.

During the long wait in the police station I had had plenty of time to think about our next move if and when we ever got a chance to make one. I decided that since the police were coming down from Seville, it would be better if we drove back up that highway, turned off at Jerez, and cut over to Sanlúcar, avoiding the coast till the last minute. I reasoned that they'd naturally assume we had continued on to Cádiz or along the coast road, and would spread the dragnet accordingly. I told the driver to make for Jerez and to step on it.

Just outside Santa María a large car roared past us heading for the town. I felt pretty confident that it was the police. It had been close. I hoped they wouldn't remember passing us.

We raced into Jerez and swung off on the road to Sanlúcar. Halfway to the coast I realized that we were followed. We had met very little traffic, and when I saw headlights behind keeping pace with us in spite of our speed I knew that it could only be the police. I asked the driver if he could go any faster. He shook his head.

I took Juanita's passport and wrapped it together with mine in the piece of oiled silk Paco had remembered to give me, and shoved the package in my pants pocket. I counted out five *mil* notes and, leaning forward, tucked them into the seat beside the driver. I told him that when he reached Sanlúcar he was to turn left on the road to the lighthouse. I'd tell him when to stop.

We hit the town wide open, and I was glad that most of the inhabitants were in bed, or we'd certainly have killed someone. Approaching the lighthouse, I looked back for the last time, and estimated that we had about a mile lead over our pursuers; less than sixty seconds. I began to lose hope.

Soon after we left the lighthouse I caught sight of a small light swinging in wide arcs ahead of us. I shouted to the driver to pull up alongside it. I held the handle of the door with one hand, Juanita with the other. We skidded to a stop. I flung open the door and pulled Juanita after me. The driver roared off down the road. Paco was already running toward the beach. When we reached the sand Juanita paused, kicking off her shoes. By the time I hit the water she was ahead of me. She leaped into the bow of the dinghy. I fell into the stern and shoved the oars into the oarlocks. Paco ran the boat out until he was up to his waist. He climbed in and pulled.

I looked back. The pursuing car had stopped about two hundred yards along the road. A door slammed. Seaward I could hear the sudden thunder of the Fairmile's engines as they started up. I searched the dinghy for another set of oars.

"No, señor," Paco muttered. "I forgot to think of it."

We must have been halfway to the Fairmile when they started shooting.

"They can see our wake," I said to Paco. "Did you bring a gun?"

"Yes, but don't use it. You'll only give them a better target."

I told Juanita to get down into the bottom of the dinghy.

It must have been the third shot that I heard strike the water, whining off into the night. It had been very close. I didn't hear the next one hit, but the one after again was close. They were using a rifle.

"Over the side, *Capitán*," Paco said, his voice low, tense. "It's safer to swim."

"You all right?" I asked.

"Please, get into the water quickly."

Juanita was a sudden flash of phosphorous as she struck the water in a clean dive. I slid over the side.

"O.K., Paco, come on."

"No, *Capitán*. I row the boat over a little way while you swim out. Then I swim to the ship and let them shoot at the boat."

He coughed, dropped one oar, and put his hand up to his mouth. It was then I knew he had been hit. Hanging on to the dinghy, I called across to Juanita and asked her if she was all right. From the faintness of her voice I gathered that she had almost reached the Fairmile.

Paco started rowing again. I climbed in over the stern. Finishing a stroke, he fell backward into the bow. I eased his legs out of the way, took the oars, and pulled toward the ship. The shooting had stopped. I watched the headlights as the police car was turned seaward, but they were deflected too low; we were still in darkness. The next moment I could hear the car racing back toward the lighthouse.

"Take it easy," I said to Johnny as I came alongside. "Paco caught one. Give me the hooks. It's better to leave him in until we get the dinghy on board."

I snapped the falls on fore and aft, and told him to hoist away. We were no sooner clear of the water than I felt the Fairmile surge forward. When we got the dinghy into its cradle one of the crew helped me lift Paco out. We carried him down and laid him on a couch in the cabin. He was dead.

Late in the afternoon, as the sun dipped behind some storm clouds way out in the Atlantic and Portugal's friendly Cape St. Vincent lay on the starboard bow, we buried Paco in the sea he had loved so well. Then we headed up the coast.

Keeping well off the bar, we crossed the mouth of the Tagus River and dropped the hook in the Bay of Cascaes. It was with some trepidation that I rowed ashore with Johnny. Reds and their fellow travelers were no more welcome in Portugal than in Spain. And I wondered if the Portuguese police had been warned.

I walked up through the village until I found a café with a telephone. I called a friend in Lisbon with whom I had once done business. I knew he had good connections. I asked him to find out if the authorities were interested in me. I gave him the telephone number of the café and told him to phone me back as soon as he could.

Next I put in a call to the American Embassy. I got through to the man I was looking for and made an appointment to bring Juanita the next morning. He said that he had heard from Tangier and had been expecting me. I said I hoped he could help me out. He laughed and replied that that was what he had been asked to do.

The third call was to Pan American. They said they had a plane leaving in two days for New York. I booked two seats.

I found Johnny sitting on the sun-splashed terrace. I took off my jacket, sat down, and ordered a Constantino.

"You still a free agent?" he asked.

"So far. I'll know for sure in a few more minutes. If I am, we'll move into the Parc and celebrate."

"What are your plans?"

"Put a lot of distance between me and Europe. Then I'll sort them out."

"What about the Erinys?"

"That's a little job I wish you'd fix up for me. I think Ricardo Lewis wants to buy her. If not, sell her to the highest bidder. Ricardo has all the papers."

"Where will I send the money?"

"Change it into pesetas and get one of the boys to take it up to Paco's wife. They all know her up there."

"That's a hell of a lot of pesetas."

"Paco was a hell of a lot of man."

The waitress told me I was wanted on the phone. My Lisbon friend said that the central police bureau had no report on me. I told him I'd see him the next day, hung up, and ran out to the terrace.

"Come on, boy," I said to Johnny. "Let's go get Juanita. We're moving into the Hotel Parc, and I hope they've got a cellarful of champagne."

I held her hand tightly as the great plane lifted off the runway. Slowly gaining height, we circled over the white city and spar- kling river. Then, turning westward, we left the land behind us. Down, well down to southward, a little ship was plowing through the ground swell. I pointed it out to Juanita.

"Johnny?"

"No, darling. Our past life. Soon it will be over the horizon."

THE END